MW00831674

The Islands Call

Call

by Sandy Frykholm

Paperback: ISBN 978-1-7350376-2-2

E-book: ISBN 978-1-7350376-3-9

Interior design by Julie McDonald Zander

Published by Parenti Publishing
P.O. Box 104, Sequim, WA 98382

Also by this Author

Also by this author, writing as Sandra Lynne Reed

The Drive in '65: An epic road trip, a journey of discovery

A Special Note

Dear readers,

I thank you for buying my books. Writers without readers are a sad lot. One way new books gain attention is for readers to share their reviews of the book on public websites. A brief statement of your opinion and feelings about the book helps that book find its true audience.

I would be greatly honored if you would share your thoughts on my book at the website where you bought it, on social media, and anywhere books are discussed.

You can join my email list for more writing news, and if you do I'll send you a story from my Alaskan childhood. Sign up at www.SandyFrykholm.com. If you find it's not for you, unsubscribe at any time.

With my gratitude,
Sandy Frykholm

Learn more at www.SandyFrykholm.com

Connect on Facebook at
https://www.facebook.com/sandy.frykholm

Contents

You will meet a stranger today
who will change your life.

SARA TRIED TO ENJOY HERSELF, but the party was a little too loud, too crowded, and the wine and cashews were not getting along well in her stomach. But Brittany insisted on staying until she could talk to the fortune teller, some guy wearing a polyester turban and a green satin vest adorned with fake jewels sitting at a card table in a back corner. Britt sat in front of him now, rapt as he gazed into a crystal ball with a weird blue glow.

She cringed inside as Britt pointed her direction and then waved. The fortune teller's dark makeup highlighted his perfect white teeth. Orthodontics, she guessed. He gestured an invitation, held an open palm next to the crystal ball, but Sara shook her head, lifted her near-empty glass, and turned toward the bar. Britt caught up with her as she filled the wine glass with club soda.

"Come on, Sara, it's just for fun, and I think he wants to meet you."

Sara rolled her eyes. "You know I hate that cheesy stuff. Really, I'm beat. So if you want a ride from me…"

"It's only 11:15!"

Sara laughed. "True, but I went to work at 7:30 this morning, and you slept in."

"Let's just get your fortune, then we'll go."

"Can you get a taxi home? I'm not going to last much longer."

"Okay, I'll get a ride, but come and meet…" She glanced at the business card in her palm. "…The Great Cato Jal before you go." Britt tugged her toward the dim corner and Sara gritted her teeth and aimed a polite smile in the direction of the crystal ball.

Just be nice and wrap it up, Sara told herself. She wondered, not for the first time, how she and Britt could be so different and yet be best friends.

The fortune teller indicated the folding chair in front of his table, and Sara took a seat. Britt stood back looking pleased with herself, and Sara shot her a glance that said *You owe me.*

"May I?" He reached for Sara's hand without waiting for a reply, and gently turned it palm up. His hand was warm and comfortable.

"I thought you used the crystal ball," Sara said. She made no effort to hide her cynicism.

"I look wherever truth may be found."

She cringed at his fake Eastern European accent and pulled her hand away, as he began to trace a line on her palm.

"But if you prefer …" He swept his hands over the crystal ball, and a soft light inside it flickered on.

A foot control, Sara thought. He drew his hands away from the ball and stared into it, silent.

"Well?"

"A new career could bring you much happiness."

She narrowed her eyes. Glancing at his business card, she said, "Oh, really? The Great Cato Jal hedges his bets. It could just as well bring misery and regret."

He widened his eyes. "Such wisdom in one so young! You are a natural fortune-teller. Madame Sirena sees all, tells all."

Sara laughed. "'Madame Sirena?' Where do you get that?"

"I think it's the perfect name for you." He continued to lay on the fake accent, but at least he wasn't taking himself too seriously.

"What does it mean—*serene*?"

"This name comes from the siren in Greek legend—*The Odyssey.*"

She shook her head and then a memory surfaced. "Oh, you mean that singing woman? You haven't heard me sing!"

"Yes, a half-woman, half-bird. And her song lures sailors into danger."

Sara eyed him for a moment. "I don't get the connection— I'm not Greek, I don't sing, and I'm not luring anybody anywhere."

He took her hand again. "Madame Sirena is seductive." He leaned forward and kissed the back of her hand, leaving a faint smear of his dark makeup. When he looked up, she expected to see a leer. But he released her.

She leaned back, took a deep breath as the warmth of his touch faded, and looked toward Britt. She was gone. Had she left? She turned and scanned the room but couldn't see her.

"She went down the hall—the bathroom. Do you need her?"

"Actually, we talked about leaving soon." She turned back to him and pushed her chair back. "And thanks for the 'fortune,'" she said with finger quotes, rolling her eyes. As she stood, he pressed a business card into her hand.

"If you want to know more about the future, just call that number."

"The Great Cato Jal. Right." Sara determined to make her escape. She turned the card over and paused. "Oh, is this your real name? Gino Cala…breeze?"

He lost the fake accent. "Calabrese—it almost rhymes with daisy. It's Italian."

"Sorry."

He waved away the apology. "Happens all the time. And yes, it's my real name."

Sara nodded another goodbye, and found Britt in the kitchen, as said goodbye. Britt loved a party more than Sara ever had. As Sara reached into her handbag for her keys, she overheard Gino Calabrese saying his farewells to the host. Checking her watch, she sipped a glass of water with lemon for ten minutes so she wouldn't run into him out on the sidewalk.

It would have worked, had he not been parked two cars behind her, with a flat tire.

He stood up, muttering in Italian, and dropped the jack with a clang in the back of a small pickup truck. She recognized his voice, but not the words. "Gino, is that you?"

He peered up at her. "Hi again."

She didn't want to help change a tire in the chilly, damp midnight air, but compulsion to do the right thing overcame her. "Need any help?"

"Either a spare tire or a ride home."

"Oh, you don't have a spare? Crystal ball didn't warn you, huh?" Sara glanced around at the darkened houses, the foggy nimbus around each streetlight, and the lights from the Space Needle glowing eerily a few blocks away. She'd made the offer, and would have to make good on it. He was still almost a stranger, but she sensed no threat in him. She always carried pepper spray—she clutched it now. "My spare won't fit your truck. How far away is home?"

Gino's dark, wavy hair needed a trim, and most of the makeup had been wiped off. She had to admit that without that ridiculous turban and vest, he was an attractive guy.

"Couple of miles. Fremont area."

Just a ride home, then, and she'd be done with him. "Sure— it's not much out of my way."

"I really appreciate it!" When he opened the door to put away the jack, a powerful aroma escaped the cab. He swore softly.

"Something wrong?" She paused and sniffed. "Do you have a cake in there?"

"The package came yesterday as I was going out, so I put it in the car. From my mom—she made it for my birthday next week. God forbid she should find out I forgot about it."

Sara laughed with him as if they shared a similar family dynamic. "It smells fantastic."

"Almond cake. I better not leave it here." He tucked the package under one arm, and picked up a bowling bag from the sidewalk.

Inside her beat-up Corolla, she tapped the GPS on the dash. "What's your address?" She entered the numbers and street name, even though she knew Fremont well enough to find his place. But the GPS guided her wherever she went, like another voice helping her navigate life, and she didn't feel so totally on her own. She pulled out of the parking space. "Do you have another job or are you a fortune teller full time?"

Gino paused, and his voice tightened. "Both, in a way."

"Ever the man of mystery." She smiled and sensed him watching her, maybe making a decision. Sara inhaled the decadent almond aroma.

"I'm a writer."

"Anything I might have read?" Sara loved reading, especially memoirs about screwed up families. They gave her a sense of normalcy.

"What do you like to read?"

"Mostly nonfiction. What do you write?"

Gino shifted in the seat as they waited for a light. "A newspaper column."

"Wow—maybe I've read it."

"Somehow I doubt it."

"Why's that?"

"I write horoscopes."

Sara missed a gear, grinding as she started up the hill on Fremont Avenue. "Horoscopes. Ah. So…you really are sort of a fortune teller full time." In a few more blocks she'd be done with this nut job.

Gino pointed to a loading zone. "You can pull in there. I'm sure there's nothing closer. Thanks for the rescue."

He opened the door, and then let it sag shut again. "Just a minute. Can I give you some of this cake?"

"Really, you don't have to."

Gino cut into the box with his pocketknife. "But I want to, if you'd like it. To thank you. And I don't even know your name." He slid a flat round cake out of the package and peeled back layers of plastic wrap. The dense pastry held together as he cut it in half and slid it onto a piece of cardboard from the packaging.

The fragrance was intoxicating. "Sara Shore. Thanks for the cake."

"*Buon appetito*, Sara. I better go. Somebody is waiting up for me." When she glanced up, surprised, he grinned. "Houdini. My cat."

"Oh, I love cats." Sara checked her enthusiasm. This was supposed to be her getaway. "But can't have one where I live."

"Well, if you want a cat fix sometime, you have my address in your system now." He smiled, sincere. "Thanks again for the ride. Goodnight." He slid out and closed the door.

Sara set her navigation for home, turned up the volume, and followed the directions for every turn. And between the turns she thought of Gino. He'd given her a gift—the cake with an aroma that made her salivate. "Turn right onto 15th…" He had a cat named Houdini. "Turn left onto 65th…" Heck, he'd even invited her over to meet the cat—and without any pressure. "Turn right onto 28th…" The smear of makeup he'd missed by his ear was endearing, somehow.

She searched the block and squeezed into a parking space with only inches to spare. *Don't fall for the cheesy fortune teller*, she told herself. Unexpected, a sense of despair rose in her. Would she ever be able to fall for someone, anyone, she could really share her life with? How could she, when she had to keep her guard up? She had sworn off relationships because her secrets always got in the way, but she hadn't felt this much regret about it in a long time.

Sara swallowed the lump forming in her throat, and carried the cake like a treasure into her tiny house. The taste was as good as the aroma had promised, and she fell asleep imaging another slice for breakfast.

✳ ✳ ✳

Wishing he had just asked for Sara's number, Gino was glad he had the name of her friend from the party, Britt. He remembered Sara's eyes lighting up when he mentioned his cat. He called Britt, and she was glad to give him Sara's number. He reached Sara a couple of days later. She jumped at the chance to cat-sit while he visited family in Italy, and that gave him the excuse to meet her for dinner and make the arrangements.

They'd talked for hours, and even had a second dinner filled with friendly banter. Gino tried to teach her a few Italian phrases, and Sara entertained him with stories of investigations she'd helped with at work. She drew a definite line at friendship, though, and would not go beyond. So far, Houdini seemed to be the big attraction. But Gino hoped for more than just a friend.

Three weeks after meeting her at the party, Gino invited her into his apartment to show her the setup and give her a key.

"Here's the email from my cousin Lia. If there's a cat emergency, you can call my cell, or Marco's number—it's here too." Gino handed Sara the email. "I get back June twenty-first, so you don't need to check on Houdini that day."

Sara sat in an oversized recliner, and the big golden tabby rubbed against her legs, then jumped into her lap. Gino looked from Sara to his suitcase next to the door. He and his cousin Marco would have a great time, just like his high school summers in Italy. Marco, a couple of years older, had taken him to beach parties, night clubs, hiking on Mount Etna. But he couldn't help wondering how much more fun he'd have if Sara went along.

He looked out the window for the taxi. "What will you do while I'm gone?"

"Work, of course," she answered slowly, "and I'll be here every day to feed Houdini. My brother, Paul, is coming up from Portland to take me to a new club opening. And I'm going geocaching with Britt."

"Geocaching? What's that?"

"It's a kind of outdoor treasure hunt, using GPS to find caches—hidden containers—or set up hidden caches for other people to find. Anyway, Britt and I are volunteering at a big Geocache Bash. Probably not as exciting as sailing in Italy— but I'll try to keep this guy alive for you." She scratched Houdini's ears. "And I can show you how geocaching works when you get back. You'd be surprised at the caches all over the city." She gave Houdini a big snuggle. Gino felt a pang of envy toward the cat.

He usually dated clingy girls, girls who believed in astrology. After a few weeks, they bored him, but he tried to keep his dating life simple. Until he met Sara. She enjoyed his company without throwing herself at him. If anything, she kept her distance, yet managed to be friendly and interesting. But something about her kept him hoping.

"Here," she said, setting Houdini aside and reaching into her handbag. "I got this book for you—a birthday present. To read on the plane, or when you're sailing."

Gino took the paperback. *Journals of an Astrologer*. He turned to the back cover. *The first English translation of the only known work by medieval Italian astronomer, astrologer, and medical doctor Niccolo Bonamico de Salerno.*

"Wow, looks interesting. We'll be sailing past Salerno, where this guy lived." He tucked it in his backpack. From her, a book on that subject surprised him. Sara made no secret of her disdain for astrology. "Thanks. What would you like from Italy?"

"You don't need to bring me anything." She rubbed Houdini's ears as he curled in her lap again.

At times they seemed to be connecting, and then she just cooled off. Maybe three weeks apart would be good. He went to the kitchen, and pulled a bag from the cupboard. "Here's Houdini's food. And some treats." The cat jumped to the floor at the rattle of food, and Sara followed him to the kitchen.

Sara frowned at the half-empty bag. "Is that enough for three weeks?" Houdini weaved his way between their legs.

"I think so." Gino pulled a twenty out of his wallet. "If it runs out, just get another one. The litter is down there too. Thanks for watching Houdini. I appreciate it."

"Well, I'm going to love the kitty time."

A honking horn drew him to the window. "Taxi's here." He handed her the keys, more reluctant to say goodbye than he could remember from any other trip.

"Bon voyage, Gino. And happy twenty-fifth—make it good!" Swishing her long dark hair behind one shoulder, she stood and held Houdini close.

"Thanks. I'll call you to see how things are going." Grabbing his bags, he headed out the door. When he looked up as the taxi drove off, Sara stood in the window holding Houdini and waving one of his paws.

✳ ✳ ✳

At the baggage carousel in Catania, his cousin Lia saw him first and began to wave, setting aside her natural reserve. They exchanged kisses on each cheek. Marco's excitement erupted in a blur of Italian, punctuated by smiles and an occasional cuff on the shoulder, but Gino caught most of it.

With a degree in Italian, he quickly adapted to Marco's high-speed banter, except when he threw in some Sicilian dialect to trip him up.

Lia tended to keep her head down and watch things over the top of her glasses. But when it came to translation, her confidence shone—she pushed the trendy narrow rectangle frames up on her nose and assumed an air of authority. She spoke to him mostly in English, barely accented.

"Gino, I'm so happy to see you again!" She took his arm. "Marco will have you on the boat, so I'm claiming you today."

Marco tried his English. "Okay. Tomorrow—we sail."

Gino reached for his suitcase, but Marco batted his hand away.

"No, no. *Prego*, I take it." Marco took the suitcase and Lia led them out into a brilliant blue afternoon, eighty degrees.

Crammed into Marco's Fiat, they sped up the coast past lemon and olive groves on one side and the Strait of Messina on the other.

"We sail there," Marco said in English, gesturing to the northeast. "Around the foot."

Lia rolled her eyes. "The *toe* of the *boot*, Marco," she said, and then switched back to Italian. "Use Italian—Gino will understand you perfectly." Marco made a face that said he was used to unwelcome advice from his bossy younger sister.

At Taormina, Marco swerved off the main motorway and up a winding road. Gino peered ahead to get the first glimpse of his grandparents' house. Cars crowded the driveway, and a young cousin stood lookout on the porch between massive pots exploding with red geraniums. By the time Marco parked, a stream of people flowed toward them, surrounding Gino in a flood of Sicilian love that brought a lump to his throat.

Behind the house, long mats of woven cane covered an arbor providing shade, and a light breeze kept the temperature comfortable.

Some forty aunts, uncles and cousins crowded around long tables on the tiled terrace. They laughed and visited together above the fluttering edges of the white tablecloths, sucking the meat from olives grown in their own groves and drinking wine made in his *nonno's* barrels. Platters of fresh white mozzarella, chicken cutlets layered with roasted red peppers, ravioli filled with ricotta and mushrooms, and mussels with gaping shells spilling out fragrant broth, disappeared and were replenished. His father's sister, Felicia, clapped her hands and gestured panic-stricken toward her daughter when any of the serving dishes dropped below half-full. When Gino thought he couldn't contain another crumb, *Zia* Felicia sidled up to him with an enormous dish.

"*Il dolce.*" Her broad smile revealed a gold tooth. She lifted the cover from a tiramisu, and the smells of brandy and coffee and sugar started his mouth watering again.

Marco's father, *Zio* Beppo, stood at the end of the banquet table and raised his glass in a toast to their sailing trip. "*Un buon viaggio e una grande avventura, dovunque vi tira il vento.*" Gino nodded his thanks for his uncle's good wishes: To a wonderful trip and a great adventure, wherever the wind blows you.

2. Your passion for travel will take you farther than you expect.

ON THE DECK OF MARCO'S twenty-one-foot boat, Gino watched his cousin navigate out of the harbor at Capo d'Orlando. They headed past the boulders of the jetty into the morning sun. The temperature rose, and the deck rocked gently. He stretched his legs out on the bench, leaned his back against the cabin, totally relaxed. Soon they were out of the harbor, under sail, in search of the Greek ruins that dot southern Italy's coast.

Along the coastline, hills rose green and lush with occasional groves of bright lemon trees or silvery olives, medieval castles crowning the heights then falling away to palm-shaded villages by the water.

Gino thought of Sara, stuck in the Seattle rain while he enjoyed this glorious sunny day. When Marco dropped the anchor about three hours later, and mentioned lunch, Gino helped him put together simple sandwiches.

After lunch, they sailed on to Vibo Valentia, and in the early evening Gino found his way to the Greek city wall. Greek history and legend fascinated Gino. He had explored the Greek ruins on Sicily during almost every visit, but never on the mainland. Now Marco dawdled behind, smoking and tapping his foot, while Gino imagined himself in ancient Hipponion, where Greeks set these walls in place almost 3,000 years ago.

As night descended, they found a trattoria for a simple pasta dinner, then retired to the boat with a bottle of wine and anchored offshore. The light clinking of the rigging kept time with the distant sound of salsa music from a night club near the marina.

"Gino, do you have a girlfriend?"

"There's a girl I met about a month ago, Sara," Gino began, and told Marco about her. "But she's more a friend and not a girlfriend—not yet. What about you?"

Marco rolled over. "I want to get married, but I can't afford it."

"The girl at dinner last night? She's the only girlfriend you've ever had when I've been here – what do your parents say about you getting married?"

"Mama says save money, look for a house." Marco turned to him with a mournful half-smile. "Papa says sell the boat and find a house now, so he can rent my bedroom to tourists."

"No! There must be some other way."

"No, because Paola likes the boat too. She wants us to keep it." He flicked a cigarette away into the water. "What about your parents? Do they like Sara?"

"They haven't met her. Seattle is a long way from St. Louis, and usually I visit them. They've only been to Seattle once, for my graduation from the university. And like I said, she's not a girlfriend."

Gino honestly hated to hear that lingering hope in his parents' voices whenever he mentioned a girl. They already suspected he'd go to hell for writing horoscopes. The only redeeming quality they saw in his life right now was his membership in the Sons of Italy. But he knew what his parents really wanted – grandchildren.

Gino gazed up at the Great Bear prowling the northern sky and sensed Marco's gaze on him. He tried to sound offhand. "Maybe we'll get serious, but I don't know."

Marco lay back and propped his hands behind his head, elbows out. "Sometimes you can tell if she's the right girl in just a few days. Maybe hours."

Their laughter faded into the warm dark night. But something about Sara did feel right to Gino, even though she showed no interest. "Where will we go tomorrow?"

"Tomorrow we'll find more Greek buildings for you at Paestum. In two days, Sirenuse, the sirens' islands."

Gino remembered joking with Sara about those islands when he dubbed her "Madame Sirena" the night they met. He dozed off thinking about what gift he might find for her near Sirenuse, on the Amalfi coast.

✵ ✵ ✵

Sara left work early with a pounding headache and caught the bus to Gino's apartment. Humidity had been rising all day, and clouds piled up against the Cascade Range, threatening thunder and lightning. She could smell the approaching rain as she walked the last block and unlocked his door. Houdini rubbed against her legs eagerly, and Sara stroked his tawny back as she looked around Gino's living room. On a bookshelf she noticed a framed photo of Gino in a cap and gown, and what had to be his parents on either side. Clearly a happy moment for all three, unlike her own graduation, which her mother didn't attend. Her father made it, only because Paul agreed to stay with her mom. She replaced the photo, pushing away her own sadness, and turned back to Houdini.

"Let's get you some dinner." She rinsed and filled his bowls. She usually played with him for a few minutes, but she wanted to be home before the rain started. A hot bath should help get rid of the headache.

She got off the bus two blocks from her one-bedroom converted garage in Ballard. Big drops were starting to fall. Her laptop bag bumped against her side, matching the throbbing headache. *Get home, close the shades, run the bath,* she repeated in her head as she ran. Indoors, she could block the lightning and thunder from her life, and avoid another "event" as her first shrink used to call them.

Just as her key slid into the lock, a flash of lightning drew her shadow in stark black on the door. Before she could turn the knob, she saw Gino, there in the black spot that was her shadow. Wet and tired, he wasn't on a boat. He was moving away, going somewhere he didn't want to go. Disoriented, she reached toward him but her wrist twisted as it hit the door, hard, and she fell where the black shadow had been. The image had vanished, but she still saw it in her mind. Gino looked confused, a little panicky. Other men hemmed him in, pushing him along. Where was he?

Damn the lightning. She slumped against the door, heart racing, and tried to gather her thoughts, but images of Gino kept intruding. She reached for her purse which had fallen into the faded tulips, and the computer bag that lay on the path behind her. Her keys still dangled from the doorknob, and she managed to let herself in, despite shaky hands and weak legs.

Gino was in trouble or would be soon. But where? Walking along a stone wall, with men around him. Like a prisoner.

She pushed the door shut but still hugged her jacket, shivering. Sinking onto the couch, she grabbed a tissue and wiped her face, but tears kept welling over. She hated these visions, showing her things she'd never been able to change. And the image she saw didn't really make sense. Another thunderclap shook the air, and she shuddered, squeezed her eyes shut tight, and waited for the lightning to end. It wasn't just seeing the vision, she realized. Gino was in trouble, and she cared about that, more than she expected or even understood.

When she opened her eyes, the storm had moved north, the rain now a lighter mist. Even so, she closed the shades, pulled the drapes, and turned on a soft lamp. With a Yo-Yo Ma mix playing on her iPod, she ran a bath.

The soothing cello and lavender bath oil soon had her breathing deeper. But the scene would not leave her alone: stone walls, torches, knives. Had Gino been kidnapped, or was he about to be? He should be on the boat. She would call him in a couple of hours, when it was morning in Italy. She'd feel much better when she heard his voice.

In her robe and slippers, she brewed a cup of herbal tea, and sank onto the sofa. Then she leaned forward, head in her hands, unable to push back the image that had knocked her to the ground. Gino needed help. She knew that much. And he probably didn't even know it yet.

But that wasn't the real problem. A sob caught in her throat as she thought through fifteen years of visions. The real problem was, people died in her visions.

Marco handed Gino the binoculars. "She called you twice already. Why do you think she's not interested in you?" Marco grinned and elbowed him in the ribs.

Gino refocused the binoculars on the sunny green headland to the north, then slowly followed the coastline until Praiano came into view, dotted with houses right up to the cliff's edge.

"She's just worried about something. And had some questions about my cat." Gino tried not to read too much into Sara's calls. "She is following our route on a map, and wanted to know where we're going next."

"You see?" Marco tapped Gino's chest. "She's following you, even from across the world. She must be in love with you."

"I wish it was true, but I doubt it. Where are we heading?"

"Look, you see Capri at the left, and the tiny bits closer— they are the sirens' islands."

Gino's imagination danced with images of the Greeks who had sailed these same waters in ancient times.

"Sirenuse!" Gino glanced at the sun. "Do we have time to go around them?"

Marco shrugged. "Sure. Then we'll anchor off Praiano. See there?"

A round tower rose near the top of a cliff. They had sailed past dozens like it, part of the system of protection from Saracen raiders in the Middle Ages. The ground floor gleamed with fresh stucco and white paint, though. Through the binoculars Gino could see a couple of tiny figures at the base of the tower.

Gino focused again on the little islands, called Li Galli on the modern maps, rising out of the sea as they drew nearer. A square tower topped the largest island, and the villa that his guidebook claimed had belonged to a famous dancer named Rudolph Nureyev.

Marco steered around the south side of the island, and the two smaller islands came into view. Shallower water in the center shimmered like an aquamarine gemstone. "Can you hear singing yet?"

"Very funny," Gino called back over his shoulder. Seabirds screeched along the cliffs.

"Help me with the sail, and I'll motor in closer."

Gino thought about his 'Madame Sirena' and snapped a couple of photos with his cell phone for Sara. She had asked him yesterday to call her from the Amalfi coast. He'd call tomorrow morning, when it was evening in Seattle.

"Can't we sail into the center? There are a couple of motorboats in there now."

"It has a strong current. That is a graveyard of ships. Maybe Homer knew the danger and made a story of the sirens to keep sailors safe."

Gino looked into the clear shallows. "I don't see any ships."

"The current moved them away a long time ago. Big ships don't pass so close now."

The shipping traffic going in and out of Naples stayed far out in open water. A sightseeing boat came around the islands and revved its engines heading toward Capri.

"I want to swim in there."

Marco rolled his eyes, but nodded. "Remember the current."

They had drifted near the small island called La Rotonda. Gino stripped to his Speedo and dove in. *I'll swim to the cliff*, he thought, glad for calm water. The island rose steeply, with no beach at all.

He swam fifty yards or so, about half the distance, and turned onto his back for a look. The sky and sea met in a hazy white rope of light. Marco stood watching him with the binoculars, and Gino thought he waved, but the sun sinking behind Marco made it hard to see.

He rolled lazily in the water and began to kick again when he heard a clear sweet tone drifting across the water. The wind? The light breeze wasn't strong enough to make the sound. As he swam toward the cliff wall of La Rotonda, the note faded in and out, and Gino paused again, listening for the source. Just a few yards from the cliff, swimming into the turquoise shallows, a splash startled him and he choked on a mouthful of seawater. With a hard shake of his head, his dripping hair flew back. A long dark line on the sea floor brought to mind a mast. A shipwreck?

"Gino!" Marco's voice rippled across the water. Gino turned as the boat slid around La Rotonda and out of sight. *Touch the island so you can tell Sara you did*, Gino told himself, feeling a little spooked, and then get back to the boat. The sun almost touched the horizon now. He closed the distance with four strong strokes, and the rough cliff scraped his arm. As he gripped the rock and took a deep breath, the tone sounded, deep and vibrant, closer but still elusive. Beneath him the sea floor glowed like a light through a window, some strange reflection of the setting sun, and he dipped his face in to see if the source was clearer underwater.

A sudden cold current pulled at his legs, and the reflection winked off, then on, off, and on a little faster. His hand lost the cliff wall. He felt himself moving toward the larger island. He flailed for the surface but couldn't feel or see it. The current twisted him like he was circling a drain, dragging him across the shallows and into deeper water. His lungs burned, and he let out air bubbles but couldn't see which direction they went. A constant ringing in his ears could be the tone but might be water pressure, though he'd never heard such a thing before when he swam. The reflection flashed again, almost like a strobe in the dark water, and the pull dragged him down. He had to get a breath but still couldn't find his way up. Then the water and current and sound all faded to black.

✷ ✷ ✷

On Friday night, Sara and Britt paused near the entrance sign to Carkeek Park. They checked the coordinates on Sara's handheld GPS, and Sara stirred the ivy under the sign with one foot.

"It's right here," she said. Her anxiety about Gino had her on edge. Sara had hoped that geocaching would help her focus and forget, but not today. Even Britt's oblivious cheerfulness irritated her.

Britt pushed a fern aside. "Got it!" She pulled the cache, a small coffee can, from its hiding place, and peeled off the plastic lid. "Here's the log."

Sara entered their information in the logbook while Britt stuffed a baggie of coins in the cache. Britt always loved the cute things left in a cache, but for Sara, geocaching was about finding things right where they belong. The exactness of the GPS locations felt satisfying. Today, though, the vision of Gino kept pushing to the forefront, distracting her, reminding her that someone was definitely not where he belonged.

Sara pushed the can back into the brush below the sign. Trees towered above them, and the air cooled fast under lowering clouds. "That's it. Let's go."

Britt puffed along behind her. "Yeah, we'll be back early enough tomorrow as it is."

"Ten isn't all that early." It would be evening in Italy at that time. She hoped she wouldn't miss a call from Gino if he tried her in the morning. If he didn't call tonight.

"It's early for me." Britt grinned.

Sara forced a laugh. With the caches set up, suddenly she felt weary. "Do you mind if we skip the dinner out, and just pick up something? We'll be out again tomorrow night with Paul."

Britt perked up at the mention of Sara's brother. Half an hour later they sat on the couch at Britt's condo, the big cardboard platter of nachos between them. All the jalapenos piled on Britt's side, and all the guacamole on Sara's, and they each had iced tea on the coffee table. Sara wanted most of all to go home, curl up in bed with her phone handy, and wait for Gino to check in with her. But she and Britt hadn't seen each other in a couple of weeks, and she knew Britt wanted to catch up.

"So you're cat-sitting for Gino, huh? Have you been to any more of his fortune-telling parties?" Britt wrinkled her nose and flashed a teasing grin. Her spiky blonde hair gave her a waifish look that Sara envied, but knew she could never pull off.

"No. He keeps kidding me about becoming his assistant, but that's not my kind of work."

"Work?" Britt snorted. "Is that what he calls it?"

"Well, he gets paid pretty well for it. Does that make it 'work?'" Sara recognized her unexpected defensiveness, and something must have come through because Britt backed off.

"Does he have…potential?" Britt had a glint in her eye, and Sara smiled.

"He's a nice guy. He's fun. Italian, but not a mama's boy." She paused, loading another chip with guacamole. "He's interesting, but I'm not interested. Doesn't make much sense, huh?"

Brittney cocked her head. "So you like him."

"I do like him, but really, Britt. Me and a fortune teller? You know me better than that."

"So, what's interesting about him—besides killer good looks?"

Sara munched a chip, taking some time. "He's proud of being Italian—but not proud in a bad way. He loves the culture and history, and his family. And he keeps his apartment neat. He's not a slob." She picked up another chip and loaded it with guacamole. "It's not just all about him either. He's great at conversation, and wants to know about my interests too." She grinned at Britt. "Although I haven't convinced him the geocaching is a fun way to spend time."

"So is something else going on? You've seemed a little out of it today."

Time for a diversionary tactic. Britt didn't even know Sara had visions, and she wasn't going to start by sharing this one. "Oh, a long week at work, I guess. I am feeling pretty wiped out tonight."

Britt's tone changed. "Did he ask about your family?"

Sara searched among the nachos, and mumbled. "Sure, he asked."

"And?"

"I told him we're not close. I told him my brother and I get together now and then." There were things about her family that even her best friend didn't know, though Britt knew enough to realize that something about Sara's estranged parents always became a sticky point in relationships. She couldn't avoid Britt's eyes, and finally answered her unspoken question. "Look, we're not dating, we're not 'together.' If we do get together, I'll tell him about them." If I ever see him again. Sara rummaged in her purse and pulled out a clipping. "Remember I said he's a writer? Well, here's what he writes."

Britt held the clipping closer to the lamp. "Eugene Xavier. What?" She slapped the paper down on the table. "That's Gino?

I've seen his horoscopes before."

"Apparently a lot of people have, but who believes this bunk? He just doesn't seem very serious."

"You've only known him, what, a month?"

"I don't mean about me. His astrology books are just gathering dust on the bookshelf. He makes it all up, like it's a big joke to him."

"Well, I think he's adorable, and he seems like a lot of fun. But I know other things are important to you. You know my rule. When you see the red flag, you stop the car."

Sara took a long drink of iced tea. "Maybe it's just a yellow flag, but I don't want to be just another fling—for him or anybody. If he gets back, we'll see."

"What do you mean, 'if he gets back?' Is he thinking of staying in Italy?"

The strain of keeping her secret hit her hard, again. "*When…* I mean *when* he gets back." She stood and grabbed her jacket. "I need to get home. I'll pick you up about 9:15."

Sara tapped the GPS on her dash, setting it to home, even for the ten-block trip. A woman's confident voice called out each turn, comforting Sara with the knowledge that everything was right where it belonged. Almost everything.

3. In a dark time of life,
mysteries may be revealed.

EARLY SATURDAY EVENING, Sara and Britt walked from the bus stop to the Italian restaurant to meet Paul. She managed to grab a nap after geocaching all morning, but under the weight of worry about Gino, she still felt tired. And he hadn't called yet, like he said he would.

"Paul," she called when she saw him getting out of a cab.

"Hey, sis," Paul said with an awkward half-hug. "Nice dress."

"You like it? I just bought it last week." She pulled a teal pashmina around her shoulders. She'd been thinking about Gino when she bought the black spaghetti-strap dress. But maybe he'd never see it. "Will it be okay for the club?"

"What *doesn't* fit in at a club in Seattle? You look great. You too, Britt." He held the restaurant door for them. "I'm glad you could make it." Paul's flirting interest in Britt was no secret.

"Good to see you again, too. And thanks for including me in the club opening. There's been a lot of hype about it."

He nodded, then turned back to Sara. "And you said you're taking care of some guy's cat. Who's he?"

"Gino—he's a nice guy, lots of fun. But we're not dating." She shrugged. "I just met him last month, so don't really know him that well." She pushed back the image of Gino under guard, and men goading him with daggers.

While Paul put away a plate of veal marsala, Sara steered the conversation to the night club Paul had designed, the Bell Bottom. The owner insisted on an updated 1980s theme.

"All the time I spent researching the design, I kept thinking of Marie. She would have loved it," Paul said with a grin. "Remember all that Madonna and big hair?"

Paul kept eating, but Sara struggled to swallow the last ravioli which seemed stuck halfway to her stomach. The mention of Marie sent an emotional shock wave through her. She picked up her water glass with a shaky hand and sipped until she felt steadier. Britt and Paul chatted on, oblivious.

Paul had gotten over the car wreck that killed their sister thirteen years earlier. But Sara had known the accident was going to happen, and she couldn't think of it without a haunting guilt that she should have stopped Marie, somehow, with what little power a nine-year-old had. The mention of Marie's name still made her feel powerless physically, and weak in her soul. But it only made Paul nostalgic.

An hour later, they scrunched into a half-moon booth with the club manager, Brian, who might have had one too many energy drinks. His foot kept the beat on the pedestal of their table, putting ripples in their drinks like a scene from the movie *Jurassic Park*. The room filled earlier than usual thanks to a lot of promo, and Paul and Brian talked about the traffic flow and the bar's seating capacity. A group with an ABBA sound kept the dancers moving, swaying, having a good time.

"Great job, man," Brian said above the noise as he unfolded his lanky frame and stood up. "I'm going to check upstairs." He lifted his chin toward a balcony that circled the dance floor, and worked his way through the crowd toward the stairs.

"Great job, man," Sara mimicked, grinning at Paul. The margarita relaxed her, and she slid the pashmina off her shoulders. "I'm going to check out the ladies' room."

The line came out the door of the ladies' room, and as Sara waited, she thought Paul should have planned a bigger space for it. But she knew his answer already. You get away with what the zoning will allow.

When she came out fifteen minutes later, the band left the stage, and a deejay took over, prepping some music. She was about ten feet from their booth when the music started with a sonic boom and the pulse of a strobe light.

Sara lurched toward the table, squinting to block the flashes, and caught her foot on a chair. As she staggered and caught her balance, she heard a guy behind her say, "Had enough yet, honey?" and a pouty voice reply, "Don't honey her!"

She eased into the booth, eyes shut, groping for her pashmina. "Paul, let's go outside." This was why she didn't spend much time at clubs. She could see flashes right through her eyelids, and wondered how anybody could dance without falling over.

Paul reluctantly broke off a conversation with Britt. "You want to leave? I thought we'd stay longer, maybe dance…"

"No! The strobe is going to make me sick. I'm sorry, let's go." She covered her eyes and put her face down on the table. Like lightning, between strobe flashes a vision of Gino appeared. She saw him in a stone room. With a look of terror, Gino faced a rat on the floor.

Paul asked Britt to hold their table, then took Sara's arm and led her to the door.

"Coming back?" the bouncer asked.

As she said, "No," Paul nodded and flashed his pass.

The cool air outside cleared her head, and within a few minutes, she could blink her eyes without seeing flashes. But her heart still pulsed in her ears. Was Gino a prisoner in some dungeon with rats?

"What's the matter? You're shaking."

The more she tried to calm down, the more her hands shook. "Let's just sit someplace quiet. There's a coffee shop open up the block."

"I don't get it. You felt fine earlier."

She heard the disappointment and annoyance in his voice. *I'm acting like a crazy person*, she thought, and that upset her even more. She'd spent years after Marie's death trying not to be the crazy person, years her mom made her go to therapy. And here she was again.

But she couldn't get the images of Gino out of her mind. The swords and daggers, the damp stone walls and now rats.

She sat across from Paul in the near-empty coffee shop, and when she ordered a cup of decaf, he said, "The same." They waited in silence, watching the waitress pour their coffees.

As she wrapped her hands around the steaming mug, she said, "Paul, remember when I started high school, and I talked to you about that girl you were dating—the girl with the heavy makeup?"

Paul took a sip then stared into the cup in distaste and poured in three creamers. He looked up, wary. "Yeah. You mean about her dad beating her up?"

"Right. And I knew about it before it happened." She paused. "And I knew she was going to die. But you weren't dating any more then. And I knew Mom would freak out, so I didn't say anything. I didn't know it would be suicide."

Paul shifted in his seat and glanced around mostly empty room. "I thought you grew out of that."

She gave a mirthless laugh, then took a deep breath. "No. I didn't." She kept her eyes glued to Paul's face as he looked up. "It's not the kind of thing a person outgrows."

"So it happened again? In there?"

"Yes. It usually comes on when there's lightning." She paused. "A couple of days ago a storm brought it on. A strobe can cause it, too."

He stared at her, and she couldn't tell if it was pity or fear in his eyes. "What did you see?"

Tears flowed down her cheeks, and she grabbed a wad of napkins from the dispenser and pressed them to her eyes. "I saw Gino, Paul. He's in trouble, but I can't figure it out."

"What do you mean, he's in trouble?" He shook his head when the waitress headed toward them with the coffee pot.

Sara turned her face toward the wall, bringing the scene back to her mind, and dabbing at more tears. "I mean, what I saw looked like men kidnapping him. And then tonight, he was afraid, terrified, of a rat."

Paul's skeptical frown deepened. "Did you try to call him? Doesn't he have a cell phone over there?"

"I talked to him twice since then. He sounded fine, says they are having a great time." Paul shrugged with a look that said, *So what's the problem*?

"But I expected a call today and didn't hear from him. If he does call, what can I tell him? 'I'm worried because I had a vision of you imprisoned in a dungeon.'"

"A dungeon? Sara, come on!"

"That's what it looked like. Usually whatever I see makes some kind of sense—I knew that one of my college professors would have a heart attack on the steps of the library building. I saw it two days before he died, but he was about a hundred pounds overweight. It wasn't a total shock."

"So, what did you tell this Gino?"

"I told him to be careful." She swallowed a sob, and took another napkin. "I told him his cat misses him."

Paul took her hand, then dabbed mascara off her cheek with a napkin. "You said he's in a dungeon. A castle or something?"

"Some men are keeping him in a stone room. I don't know where. It may not even have happened yet, but Paul, it's real."

He sat in silence for a minute and looked at her, frowning. "I didn't think this happened to you anymore. How often do you get these visions?"

"Sometimes three or four times in a year. I never know what's coming. I just try to block them out, but that doesn't always work."

"So, what could you do about the things you see? Can you help somebody?"

"I tried with Marie. When I tried to explain to mom and daddy, they decided I was sick. Mentally ill. That's what I got for trying to help. Some shrink looking at me like I'm something he's read about in a medical journal."

Paul watched her for a minute, waiting for more. Then he shook his head. "Crazy."

4.

To make the best impression,
always dress for the occasion.

ROUGH, STRONG HANDS GRIPPED Gino's shoulders, and a sharp smack on the back started him gagging on seawater. Two men pulled him up the beach a few feet from the water's edge, then backed away, leaving him on his knees in the gravel. He dropped to all fours and coughed. His throat ached from retching.

In the darkness, he could smell sweat and leather. Where was he? At the sound of a harsh command, someone thrust a flaming torch toward him. Gino turned his head away, squinting in the glare. The man with the torch asked a question in a dialect Gino couldn't understand. The sound of it brought his high school Latin to mind. The man's long hair was tied back loosely, and he had deep crow's feet around his eyes. He wore a belted tunic over some kind of leggings. The others wore rough baggy shirts and knee-length pants, and most of them had bare feet. They looked like extras in a pirate movie.

Two more men came forward out of the dark, calling 'Ruggero,' and the torch swung toward them while the leader talked. They repeated a word with urgency. One of the men stepped closer and took Gino's wrist in a tight grip, pulling his arm into the air.

Gino's bare knees ground into the gravel beach, but he tried not to move as the men surrounding him shifted, looking him over. The man called Ruggero pushed the torch closer and examined Gino's armpit, then pointed his chin toward the other arm, and someone grabbed his other arm and pulled it up. Apparently satisfied, the man dropped his arm and Ruggero turned his gaze on Gino's shoulder.

With a start, Gino noticed blood seeping from a wide scrape. He remembered swimming to La Rotonda, grazing his arm on the rock wall, and seeing Marco's boat slip out of sight. Then the current pulled him down. He craned his neck. Faint moonlight on the water revealed no boat, no islands.

"Marco? Where is Marco? Do you speak English? *Parla inglese?*" The five men offered no answer as they stood around him in the pool of torchlight on a narrow gravel beach, perhaps twenty feet wide between the rock walls of a small cove. They talked among themselves, and Gino rolled the words around in his mind. He understood a word now and then, drawing on faint memories of Latin, his fluent college Italian, and his family's Sicilian dialect. Their speech seemed a mashup of all three, clearly some form of Italian, and he began to understand more and more words. Two men fixed their eyes on Gino and gripped the long knives in their belts.

The subject of their discussion was clear—all five stared at his bright blue Speedo. They shook their heads, laughed uncomfortably. After a question to Ruggero, they walked around Gino in a wide circle with the torch, viewing the garment from all angles.

Ruggero spoke again, gesturing to the cliff, and two men hoisted Gino to his feet and pulled him stumbling across the gravel. The small of his back ached from kneeling, but he took a few steps. "Wait! What about Marco?" He turned back to the water, but a firm hand spun him around to face a man holding a dagger. Gino took one step back, then followed the other men.

Near the rock wall, the torchlight revealed a set of steps about eighteen inches wide cut into the rough cliff face. High above them a voice called out, and one of the men answered. Gino caught the word *torre*, tower. Another torch flared to life and Ruggero assigned it to the last man in line. Then Ruggero led the way up, gesturing for Gino to follow.

A night breeze raised gooseflesh on his bare back as they climbed. Gino leaned against the gritty wall on his right, and away from the dark vacuum of space on his left where waves shushed on the gravel beach. Now and then a loose stone clattered into the void, and Gino heard warnings muttered along the line of men on the narrow steps.

Gino's quads burned by the time they reached the top. Stars twinkled in the blue black of night. A quarter moon hung low in the sky, but the faint light revealed that they had reached a round tower rising inside a network of wood posts and poles, a crude scaffolding. Smooth slabs of tufa rock covered the bottom eight or ten feet.

Gino took his bearings as the men gathered at the top of the cliff. The plastered walls of houses—perhaps fifty of them—reflected pale in the moonlight on the hillside above the tower, which stood on a point of land in a wide bay. To his right, low hills stretched toward a headland. And three small islands that hadn't been visible from the beach formed a ring in the bay, lighted by moonglow. Li Galli—he recognized them immediately. The islands of the sirens.

"Ruggero," Gino said, and the man spun around to face him, eyes narrowed. In slow and careful Italian, Gino asked, "Where are we? What place is this?"

Ruggero's eyes registered a surprised understanding, and he glanced around at his men before he spoke. Some of them understood too. "This is Praia," Ruggero said. "Praia of Salerno."

Praia. Praiano. How could it be? There were no cars, no throbbing night club music from the clifftop bar. Had the power gone out? Had the current carried him away from the main town? The houses were all dark, and except for this bunch of thugs, the place seemed abandoned.

The town he had seen from Marco's boat was twice this size, but he couldn't see much detail now, in the dark. That tower looked like the same one he had seen through binoculars, with tourists walking around the base. He must have become disoriented. Here, a cart of quarried stone stood near the scaffolding, and the torchlight revealed a large square heap of rough timbers. Yet it stood on the same promontory above the sea.

"My God. Oh my God." With rising panic, he looked up and down the coastline. What had happened to him at Li Galli?

Ruggero watched him in silence for a moment, and then said, "Who are you?"

"My name is Gino. Gino Calabrese."

Ruggero nodded to his men and gestured toward Gino. "A Calabrian." The men relaxed, and all eyes were on Gino.

"No, I'm an American. My name is Calabrese."

"American? Where is that?" Ruggero frowned hard, then his eyes narrowed. "Are you a spy from Aragon?" Ruggero's hand brushed the handle of a knife in his belt.

Gino raised his hands, shaking his head. "No, no. America. The United States."

Now Ruggero shook his head. "I don't know that place. Who is your king?" With a glance he directed his men to encircle Gino.

"King? We don't have a king."

Ruggero muttered something, and whispers passed between the men. "An emperor, then?"

"We have a *presidente…*" he began, but could not find an Italian way to say the name. What was the matter with these people? They looked like a pirate gang, here in the prime tourist area of southern Italy. Gino looked past Ruggero at the tower, the medieval watchtower he had seen from Marco's boat. His stomach knotted, and he struggled for a deep breath.

He glanced out at the islands again, and back at Ruggero. "Please tell me, who is your leader? Your…your king?"

"Our Queen is Joanna of Naples—who also rules *Calabria*, no? Look, it's cold. Come into the tower."

Queen Joanna? Italy had a prime minister, some womanizer according to the news, unless they elected someone else recently. They hadn't had a monarch for more than fifty years.

Panic began to rise. Gino thought he might hyperventilate. His feet felt like stone but the men goaded him along. He began to shiver, and not just from exposure, though he still wore nothing but his Speedo. What had happened to him, and where was Marco? Gino kept glancing out toward the islands where he had last seen the sailboat slip around the far side of La Rotonda. Nothing moved on the water. The dark shadow of the coastline showed no twinkling village lights, and no taillights of cars heading up the coast highway toward Sorrento.

Pebbles littered the stone pathway and bit into his bare feet every few steps. As the torches cast more light on the scaffolding, Gino saw the rough wood poles lashed together with grassy ropes. That couldn't be safe.

Ruggero entered first into the round room lighted by flaming logs on a wide hearth. Gino was startled to see a woman tending a steaming pot, and when she glanced up at his near-nakedness, her brows shot up and her mouth dropped open. With apparent effort she redirected her gaze to Ruggero, speaking rapidly in a low voice, and gesturing toward a pile of blankets. The youngest man grabbed one and threw it around Gino's shoulders. The rough-woven wool tore at his scraped shoulder, and he winced, pulling that arm out and wrapping himself toga style. The trickle of blood had nearly stopped.

"Anna." Ruggero urged her to look at the scrape. She said something, and Ruggero nudged Gino toward her.

She looked about mid-forties, with the beginnings of gray at her temples. As she applied a salve to the scrape, her dark brown eyes kept glancing to his face, and each time she drew back, wary and fearful. The men watched until she paused and, with an impatient sigh, rattled off a speech that got them all moving.

One scrambled up a wooden stair to the floor above. Ruggero stirred the pot with a great wooden spoon, and two others set wooden bowls, chipped ceramic cups, bread, and wine on a table. The other man remained near Anna, and Gino could see the fuzz just sprouting from his young face. Judging by the adoring look she gave him, he was probably her son. He held a thin stick in the cooking fire, and lit a lamp hanging from the ceiling.

Soon the man returned from upstairs with clothing—a pair of knee-length pants like they all wore, a loose shirt, a belt, and a leather vest—which he tossed on a bench. Ruggero said something about eating, but Anna broke in with a sharp, "No!" She spoke too fast for Gino, but her gestures said she wouldn't feed them until this naked man put some clothes on. She wrapped a shawl around her shoulders, lifted her head high, and put one foot out the door before turning to Ruggero. "I'll wait outside."

When Ruggero handed him the pants, he realized they were two separate pant legs. He turned one piece, trying to figure out the front and back, when Ruggero stopped him and pointed to the Speedo. Gino frowned, and Ruggero pointed again. "Take it off. Anna will wash it."

In the tense silence, he peeled off the Speedo, dropping it on the floor, and brushed the beach grit off his butt. He pulled on the pant legs, which had no apparent means of staying up. Gripping the pants with one hand, he slipped the shirt over his head and tried to tuck it in. Laughter erupted behind him. Red-faced, he shrugged at Ruggero, who burst out laughing and grabbed the belt. With a quick move he had the belt around the shirt, with the pants pulled high enough underneath to stay up.

"*Grazie*," Gino said, as he pulled the vest over the shirt. He turned a tentative smile to the others, who seemed to relax a little. He struggled to mimic their accent, hoping he would be understood. "I'm sorry, Ruggero. I am confused. Maybe I hit my head on the rocks. Who is the pope now?"

"The pope? Pope Clement? What place are you from that doesn't even know the pope?"

"We do, Ruggero, we know the pope in my country too. Maybe I could go to Rome. I might find someone there to help me find my cousin Marco and get back home."

"You won't find Pope Clement's court in Rome. They remain in Avignon, as you must know."

Avignon. "Holy cow," Gino muttered in English. Popes in Avignon? He wracked his brain for some church history from the required class at Bishop Dubourg High School. Only one connection was certain: The popes were in Avignon before Christopher Columbus. Before the printing press. Before the world as he knew it. A weak feeling hit him in the intestines.

Forcing a smile, Gino turned toward Ruggero. "Thank you for the clothes, and for helping me. Please, tell me your names."

Guido had beefy shoulders and short curly hair. The wiry one with a high forehead and a crooked grin was Federico, who had helped Guido pull him from the sea. Gino guessed they were both in their thirties. The other two were Anna's sons, Arnaldo, maybe twenty, who smiled tight-lipped as if his teeth hurt, and Andrea, the younger one, whose straight hair fell to a blunt line at his shoulders. They directed Gino to a bench against the wall, next to Ruggero.

"Mamma," Andrea said, remembering that Anna waited out in the dark. He knocked over a stool hurrying to the door. She looked Gino over, confirming that he was properly clothed. Her eyes flicked to the damp Speedo on the floor.

Soon they were eating chunks of bread and a thin soup seasoned with bitter greens. When Arnaldo filled their cups with wine, Ruggero raised a hand for quiet. "Now," he said, turning to Gino and settling in on the bench, "tell us how you found your way to Praia. Were you taken as a *schiavo*?"

Gino didn't know the word, but the five men waited for an answer. Even Anna, seated on a stool near the fire, watched him through narrowed eyes. "Was I taken…?"

"Look, here." Ruggero pulled Gino's loose sleeve up and pointed to a bluish tattoo on his uninjured shoulder. "Whose mark is this? Who owns you? Have you escaped?"

Gino's mother had warned him that he might regret getting that tattoo. The Greek figure for Gemini looked like a Roman numeral II with the top and bottom bars curved away from one another. He had it done two years ago, to celebrate the success of his column.

Ruggero seemed to think the tattoo marked him as a slave. Did Ruggero know anything about astrology? Gino always got a kick out of telling people that in the Middle Ages, even popes and kings had astrologers, but thought better of joking now.

"It is my birth sign."

Ruggero waited for a moment before saying, "You were born a slave?"

"No, I'm not a slave. Do you know astrology? It's my astrological sign."

The men frowned and murmured among themselves. Ruggero repeated the word slowly, like a question. "Astrology?"

"The stars. Astrologers study the stars."

A light of understanding brightened Ruggero's face. "You read the stars?"

Anna crossed herself, muttered something that sounded like Latin, and called to Andrea. He ignored her and focused on Gino.

Ruggero leaned forward and the other men drew closer around the table. "Did you study in Salerno? With the masters of astrology at the university?"

"No. I learned a little about the stars in another place, far away."

Arnaldo spoke up, his voice surprisingly deep for his slight build. "Can you tell us if we will be safe?"

"Safe? What is the danger?"

"The same danger that threatens all the kingdoms of Europe. Surely you know of the pestilence. Has it not reached your land too?"

"The pestilence?" Gino flipped through his mental history notes until a thought nearly stopped his heart. "Do you mean the plague?"

Andrea nodded. "You may call it so. We thought you were sick with it and were thrown from your ship to save the others. But you don't have the signs of it."

So that's why they looked me over on the beach. The plague! Gino glanced around the room and pressed back against the stone wall, wary of unwashed men who might be carrying a fatal disease. Could he catch it from someone who didn't have symptoms? "No, no. I have not been ill."

"What happened to you, then?" At Andrea's eager question, Anna called his name sharply. She crossed herself again, looking toward heaven. With brusque efficiency, she gathered and rinsed their empty bowls, but Gino was sure she didn't miss a word they were saying. Maybe it would be best not to mention Marco and his boat.

"I was swimming, but the current pulled me down. Thank you for helping me."

"And who is Marco?"

Gino backpedaled.

"You called for him on the beach."

"He…he is my cousin. I was in his boat with him, but I wanted to swim, out at the islands—Li Galli." They seemed not to understand. What was the other name for them? "Sirenuse."

Anna's prayer stopped abruptly, and then became a momentary high wail. Even Ruggero's eyes widened.

"You swam out there?" Ruggero squinted at him and drew back as if he were looking at a madman.

Gino shrugged, palms up. "Where I come from, people enjoy swimming in the sea."

"Calabria?" Ruggero looked doubtful, and Alberto stole a glance at the Speedo puddled on the floor.

He couldn't very well tell them he flew in from the other side of the world a few days ago. "My father left Calabria long ago, though I am still known by the name *Calabrese*."

Guido leaned his bulk against the curved wall, tilting his head to one side. He held Gino in an intense gaze for a long moment as his mouth gradually puckered into a frown. "We watched the coast all afternoon and saw no boat." He drank from the cup held in his meaty grip without taking his eyes off Gino.

Ruggero straightened up on the bench, and then stood, keeping his eyes on Gino.

Gino knew he should try to explain. "My cousin is the sailor—I paid no attention. I don't know how we got by you." He chuckled, as if sneaking by them was a joke, but the men just watched him with suspicion, then turned to Ruggero.

Ruggero shot an abrupt comment to the men, too fast for Gino's ears. Then he turned back to Gino.

"Surely an astrologer can tell us something of when the pestilence will end. Can we safely open the harbor again? Our lord is in poverty with no port fees to collect."

Gino had bluffed his way as an astrologer for almost five years now, and he had a good following. How hard could it be to satisfy these men? He wracked his brain for the dates of the plague, the Black Death, but nothing came to him. He knew a lot more about ancient Greece than medieval Italy. He'd have to rely on the sucker-born-every-minute theory, and come up with something that sounded acceptable without committing to too much.

In the hush that awaited his reply, Gino spoke in the low voice that always drew his listeners to lean closer. "About your personal safety, I can say nothing. Without my charts, without your birth dates and places, nothing. But…" And here he held up his hand with one finger pointing toward the planks of the ceiling. "…I can tell you this much. Your land will recover from this pestilence, and a golden age is ahead, an age of rebirth, a renaissance that will spread to all the countries of Europe." *And long before that happens*, he thought, *I hope to be back in Seattle, if I can find a way.*

Gino watched the men exchange hopeful glances. Gradually they began to nod.

"That is good news indeed," Ruggero said. "But now it is late. Tomorrow we will take you to Signore Ottavio. He will want to hear from you. For tonight, you sleep in the upstairs room, with Guido and Federico."

The upstairs room kept him as secure as a prison cell.

How could he get back where he belonged, back to Marco, back to Seattle and Sara? She would be expecting a call from him in a few hours. Not too likely, he thought. The nearest telephone was more than six hundred years away.

✳ ✳ ✳

Paul sprawled on Sara's couch, asleep. She watched him from her bedroom doorway, and thought about starting some coffee, but decided to shower first, to give him an extra half hour of sleep. And give herself time to think of what to say to him this morning. She knew he still questioned the whole clairvoyant sister thing.

She toweled her hair, then pulled on her yoga pants and a lightweight hoodie. In the Sunday morning silence, she jumped at the sound of her cell phone ringing by the bed.

"Hello?"

A woman's voice she didn't recognize said, "Is this Sara?"

"Yes."

"Oh, Sara," the woman said, rolling the r. "This is Lia Calabrese, in Sicilia. Sicily."

Sara sunk onto the bed, her dread like a brick in her chest. "Yes?"

"I have to tell you, something has happened to Gino." Lia's voice broke, and she coughed.

Sara's throat tightened to an ache. "What is it?" she asked in a hoarse whisper.

"He went swimming yesterday, in the Amalfi area, and he disappeared. Marco searched half the night and today, and the *Guardia costiera*, the coast guarders, have searched too. They have found nothing yet."

Sara could barely speak her next thought. "What will they do?"

"They will continue searching. They notified all the nearby harbors in case another boat picked him up. They will keep looking today on the shores."

"Today? And then just give up?" Sara could not stifle the sob. She heard the rattle of her bedroom door handle, and turned to see Paul staring in, yesterday's mousse pointing his hair in a dozen directions. He sat on the edge of the bed, stifling a yawn.

"I'm flying to Naples from Sicily tonight, and a shuttle will take me to Praiano. Marco is so upset, he can't speak of it. I will do everything to help, Sara. Everything."

"Is there anything I can do here? Anyone I should call?"

"We talked to his parents, and they are flying to Italy later today. I don't know who else, but maybe you know some friends. His newspaper people will probably hear of it through the wire service."

A numbness washed over Sara as she thought about making those phone calls. She didn't know his friends. He played bocce ball with guys from the Sons of Italy, and had talked about some college friends. "I might wait for more definite news first. Call me when you get there. Please, Lia. Don't worry about what time it is." Sara stuttered a goodbye, and threw the phone onto the bed.

Paul looked steadily at her. "Tell me."

"They think he drowned! He went swimming off the boat yesterday—about twenty-four hours ago, Lia said. She's his cousin. He never came back."

Paul held her stiffly in his arms while she cried. As her sobs subsided, she wiped her eyes, and balled up her fists in her lap, shaking with frustration. "Did you say anything to her about the castle thing? Maybe there's a castle—"

"Of course there is a castle." She shot him a disgusted glance, unable to curb her irrational feelings. "It's Italy. There are castles all over the place. But he went swimming, she said."

"So maybe your vision was wrong this time."

Sara flopped back on the bed and stared at the ceiling. "No. That's never happened. Every one I've ever had, they've all been true. Why wouldn't this one be? I just can't see *how* it's true, because what I see doesn't make sense to me. I know he's in some kind of trouble, but it isn't drowning."

They were both silent for a couple of minutes, Paul staring at the rug. "Do you think it could help to tell her about it? Maybe they could look in a different place?"

"Oh, Paul, I've spent most of my life trying not to tell anybody." She tried to take a deep breath, but couldn't seem to draw much air. "Who would believe it?"

5. The camaraderie of friends makes life richer.

GINO GRADUALLY WOKE to a dusty smell. What a nightmare! Marco would laugh his head off when he heard about it. He put a hand down to push himself upright, and yelped when a sliver of wood went a quarter inch into his palm. The rough plank floor beneath him smelled of dust. A circle of stone walls rose around him, with long narrow slits open to the light of day.

He wasn't dreaming, then. He had washed up in medieval Italy. And Marco? What had happened out there at Li Galli?

He swore softly as he pulled the splinter from his palm, then sucked the blood that welled up. The leggings he'd been given were bunched up around his knees, and the blanket made him itch. Or was it fleas? He remembered the men last night, talking about the plague. The surrounding walls seemed to close in on him, and he leapt to his feet and brushed wildly at the imagined vermin.

The shuffling of boots and men's voices rose through the floorboards, muted, but he recognized Ruggero's louder call.

"Calabrese, come, take some bread."

Tucking his shirt into the belt holding up the strange pants, he smelled leather and sweat, and wondered who wore them last. Gino went down the stairs. Ruggero and his men watched him descend, but Anna ignored him, tending the fire and stirring a pot. His Speedo was gone.

Leaning toward Ruggero, Gino said, "I need to go outside." Was there an outhouse? Did they just pee off the cliff?

"Come." Ruggero shook his head as the other men moved to join them, and he led Gino into the brisk morning air and gestured toward the cliff.

Gino scanned the hillside behind the tower. Could anyone see him down here taking a leak? The call of nature prevailed.

When he turned away from the cliff and saw Praiano spread across the hillside, another wave of panic rose from his gut. He was ripped away, like a page torn out of a book, from yesterday with Marco, from his life in Seattle, and from everything he knew. Here, an occasional birdsong and the shushing of waves broke the morning silence. In the distance a donkey brayed, pulling a wooden cart. These replaced sounds of car engines, electric fans, boats in the bay. He didn't fit in the new story, this hillside village, these men, and the tower.

After another long look at the islands, Gino strode toward Ruggero, waiting near the tower. "I need a boat. I need to go back to Sirenuse."

"Not today. I am taking you to Signore Ottavio. He will be very interested in an astrologer washed up on his shore."

"But I have to find my cousin. I don't know what happened to him."

Ruggero shrugged him off. "Signore Ottavio will decide."

Inside the tower, the men eyed him with curiosity but said little. After Gino ate some fresh bread washed down with weak wine, Ruggero directed him out the door, and along a path toward the town.

Arnaldo and Ruggero led him up the hillside to meet the signore, and see what was to be done with him. They zigzagged up a narrow dusty track, passing clusters of four or five houses. Behind each group of homes, terraced gardens reached up the hillside. Except for the occasional barking dog, it was nearly a ghost town. Gino sensed that he was being watched, even when he could see no one.

"Who is this Signore Ottavio? Do you all work for him?"

"We work at the port, and Guido is a fisherman, but since the port has all but closed and there are not so many mouths to eat the fish, Signore Ottavio hired us to repair the tower. It was damaged by the earthquake, the one that destroyed the harbor at Amalfi. With the pestilence spreading abroad, he wants a closer watch on the coast."

Ruggero spoke casually, but his eyes took in the whole steep landscape, keenly watching a man tending his lemon trees. Someone had spread laundry to dry on a bank of bushes. He turned several times to mark the progress of a ship passing beyond the Cape of Sorrento. "The bishop in Ravello is paying for it, and the Signore oversees the work."

The houses were simple, with white walls and red tile roofs. Most had a garden terraced into the steep hillside. Gino recognized the smell of basil. His mother grew it in their tiny back yard in St. Louis, and he inhaled that aroma of home. Had his parents heard of his disappearance by now? The thought jolted him, and he turned to look out at the islands again. That had to be the way home, didn't it, the same way he had come? But how could he get there?

When they paused to rest at one of the switchbacks Gino asked, "What kind of man is Signore Ottavio?"

Ruggero took the lead again, talking back over his shoulder. "A man with many worries, like all men in these dangerous times. His wife died of the pestilence last winter, just after the Feast of Epiphany, and he has no sons. Now he and his daughters keep themselves closed up in his *palazzo*, admitting no one who might bring disease."

Gino glanced around at the mention of the plague. How dangerous was this place? "Are people still sick here?"

"I haven't heard of any for a few weeks. But Signore Ottavio still worries." Ruggero shot a quick glance back at Gino. "He may not be happy that a stranger has washed up on his beach."

Gino dredged up a childhood memory of a big Epiphany procession in Sicily one year when his family came over for Christmas. Epiphany would have been six months ago. The plague started at least that long ago.

"Aren't you afraid of the pestilence, too?"

Ruggero pondered this for a few moments. Then he paused at another turning of the path, and gave a half-shrug and one-sided smile. "There are still dangers, but locked up in my house I would starve to death. So, I trust God and the saints to protect me," and at this he crossed himself, "and go about my work."

Gino sighed with relief, and hoped that the plague had now run its course in this area, as Ruggero suggested. But hadn't it actually lasted years? Not weeks or months? His memories of medieval history were so hazy. Maybe it took a couple of years to spread all over Europe, but didn't last that long in one place.

Gino's thighs were burning after a quarter-hour steady uphill climb, but Ruggero showed no sign of slowing his pace. About ten minutes more, and Ruggero banged his walking stick against the wooden gates that closed off an archway where a faded coat of arms hung at an angle.

"Beppe! Open up, I need to see the Signore."

Gino heard a distant voice respond, and wondered what kind of place was inside the walls. Climbing the hill, there had been no sign of a castle, but these enclosing walls made the property prominent among the village houses.

Facing the sea was a view as spectacular as anything Gino had ever seen. The Bay of Salerno spread into the distance, deep blue in the mid-morning sun. Capri seemed to float off the tip of the green peninsula to his right. When he saw the ring of three islands, though, his heart began to pound. What had happened to him out there? What happened to Marco? How could he get back?

The noise of a latch brought Gino's attention back to the gate, where a man, built like a block of granite with thick gray hair to his shoulders, stared out with a deep crease between his bushy brows. He looked Gino up and down a second time before shaking his open palm toward Ruggero with an angry torrent of words. After a few attempts to calm the man, Ruggero stepped inside the gate by himself for a more private conversation—still audible. Gino picked up a few words, but the most urgently spoken word gave Gino a chill.

"…astrologer…" Ruggero repeated. "Signore Ottavio has been seeking an astrologer."

Gino wanted to charge through the gate and grab Ruggero, to tell him 'No, I'm not an astrologer, I'm just a writer making things up.' No one could learn anything about their personal life by studying the stars—not even those who believed in it. And these people did believe it. But he'd set his course. He would have to act the part in person instead of through his newspaper column, and try to bluff his way through. Writing his column felt like providing entertainment, something he enjoyed. But this—this charade felt like dealing in lies. Not a pleasant feeling.

Ruggero appeared in the gate, waving them through. They entered a courtyard of natural stone and hard packed earth from which three lemon trees and a gnarled olive struggled for life. Signore Ottavio's *palazzo* stood about thirty feet beyond the gate. Arched loggias ran the full width of the building on two floors. A third floor, set back several feet, rose above a low wall. A faded beauty emanated from the building, now marred by neglect, with scraggly bushes dying like the dried-out palm plant in his apartment.

Beppe led them to the house, swaying with an arthritic gait as he hurried along. He held out one hand to stop Ruggero, and they waited outside while Beppe went through the double doors at the center of the ground floor. After a few minutes, they heard voices on the loggia above. "Ruggero," a reedy voice called down. "Why are you bringing a stranger to my house?"

Moving back a few steps, they could see Signore Ottavio peering down at them, leaning one shoulder against the stone column of an arch, and tilting his head this way and that with his eyes fixed on Gino. He was tall, with narrow shoulders and a long neck topped by an unusually round head, made so by a sloping forehead, stubby nose, and almost total lack of a chin. His long fingers twined together in front of him, writhing like a handful of worms.

"Signore Ottavio, good health to you." Ruggero acknowledged him with a slight bow, and urged Gino to follow his lead. Gino bowed, and glimpsed Arnaldo bowing quickly and then glancing at the upper terrace.

A buxom young lady with reddish glints in her dark hair leaned over terrace rail. She tossed something over the edge. "Oh, papá, I've dropped something." She covered a smile with one hand. "Tell one of those men to bring it up to me."

"Fiamma, get back in the house!" Ottavio lifted his chin toward Arnaldo, who ran to retrieve the bit of cloth and disappeared through the doors. "Ruggero…"

"My lord, I am sure this man will be of great interest to you. We have examined him, and he bears no sign of disease. My men pulled him from the sea last night." Ruggero glanced at Gino before going on. "He fell overboard from a passing boat, my lord, and I have learned that he is an astrologer, originally from Calabria."

Gino flinched at that description, but Signore Ottavio leaned out to look more closely.

"He does not wear the clothes of an educated man."

"His own clothing was lost in the sea, my lord. We had only our own clothes to lend him."

"I cannot take on the expense of an astrologer in my household, Ruggero. From Calabria, you say?"

"Originally, I believe so. But he has lived in a far-off land for many years. He speaks our language poorly, but well enough."

Gino hoped he could adapt his fluent modern Italian to the language he heard around him.

Signore Ottavio wrung his hands and glanced back into the house, and then to various points in the empty courtyard as if seeking someone to advise him. "No…well…what is your name, astrologer?"

When Gino hesitated, Ruggero spoke up. "He is called Gino of Calabria, my lord. I know you have been unable to consult an astrologer recently. Perhaps God has brought him to you, knowing your concern."

A giggle drifted down from the terrace above, and Signore Ottavio shouted in that direction. "Fiamma! Get back indoors. There are evil humors in the air." He disentangled his fingers and gripped the nearest column with one hand. "Very well, Ruggero. I will speak with him. Leave him, Beppe will bring him in to me. How is work progressing at the tower?"

"Little by little, my lord. We could use more men, but the pestilence has taken so many…"

At the mention of disease, Signore Ottavio's hands clasped together again. "Yes, well, go on now, and I don't want any more strangers brought to my door."

When Arnaldo came out the lower door, Ruggero put a hand on Gino's arm and spoke quietly. "Read the stars for him and he will keep you here—but if you don't serve him well, he will drive you off, or worse."

Gino watched with a sense of foreboding as the gate closed behind them. What did Ruggero mean?

"Signore," Beppe growled, and when Gino turned, the servant gestured impatiently toward the door. He had just become Signore Ottavio's astrologer.

✵ ✵ ✵

The cool air in the ground floor of the house felt good, but Gino perspired. How he could carry out this pretense? He was no astrologer! In fact, it had started as a joke with his college roommate, a journalism major who bet him he couldn't write something that would be published. Within a month, Gino had landed a horoscope column for the college newspaper.

But Signore Ottavio might not be satisfied with the kind of half-mystical fortune cookie drivel that made his column a hit.

Beppe led him past the doorway to a big room where Gino caught a glimpse of wine barrels the size of Volkswagen Beetles stacked against the wall. Dried straw covered the stone floor. From beneath the straw, Gino heard the skittering of a creature.

He yelped, nearly tripping as he spun around looking for it. Beppe paused long enough to see Gino scanning the floor, and dismissed Gino's alarm with a roll of his eyes and a grunt: "Beh!"

He continued climbing a stone stair to a large room that opened onto the loggia where Ottavio had stood talking to them.

Ottavio had secured the shutters, and stood waiting for them near the top of the stairs. Gino had no idea what to say, no medieval etiquette training to help him. He bent slightly forward in an awkward bow. "Thank you for…for hosting me here, Signore." Gino looked around the hall, furnished with benches, a couple of tall candle stands, trunks, and chairs. The cold hearth spilled ash onto the stone floor. Ottavio's look was just as chilly as he surveyed Gino's clothing.

"Your services will be welcome here, Signore Gino." Ottavio turned to Beppe. "Find him some clothing. And show him to a room." With a wave, he directed Gino to follow the servant.

Beppe led him up another stairway, and then another, each in a different direction, until Gino lost all sense of his location. Finally, he stopped before a closed door, and fumbled with a ring of several large keys until he found one that worked in the lock. He pushed the door open, revealing a dim, dusty room with an old bed frame, listing a little to one corner. Beppe opened the shutters on a small window, and the breeze lifted a million dust motes into the shaft of sunshine.

"Wait," Beppe said, and disappeared down the hall.

The bed had no mattress, only criss-crossed ropes that sagged where a knot had come loose. One foot of the bed looked like it had been chewed off by a dog, giving the bed its odd slant. The only other furniture in the room, a small cupboard, contained two bare shelves.

Beppe returned with an armload of clothing, which he tossed across the bed. With a glance around the room and a grunt, he shook his head. "I'll come back with the bedding."

Alone for the moment, Gino looked through the clothing. He held up a medieval version of boxers. Whose had these been? The collection included a pair of long leggings in a blotchy brown, a pea green linen garment that looked something like a graduation gown, a mustard-colored sleeveless tunic, frayed at the hem, and smelling of musty wool. As he picked up the tunic, a pair of pointy leather shoes clattered to the floor through the bed ropes. They held the shape—and odor—of someone else's feet.

Apparently, these were the clothes of an educated man. He held up the pea green gown. Dust from the bed clung to it. At least the belt would keep it from dragging on the floor. What he wouldn't give for a pair of jeans and a T-shirt! But his clothes were gone, even his Speedo, along with everything else he knew. He swallowed the terror that rose up in him and wondered if he should change clothes now or wait for Beppe.

Better to wait than be caught undressed, he decided, and crossed to the window. Instead of looking toward the sea, as he hoped, this window faced toward the back of the property, perhaps east or southeast. But his thoughts were still on the islands, trying to grasp what had happened to him, and how to get back. Li Galli seemed his only hope. If he could satisfy Ottavio with some kind of predictions or encouragement, maybe Ottavio would help him return to the islands.

The door banged open behind him as Beppe struggled to get through it. His arms surrounded a shapeless cloth bag, and only when he dropped it on the bed did Gino recognize it as a straw-filled mattress of sorts. Gino grabbed the clothes and set them out of the way, then helped spread the mattress over the ropes. Beppe tossed two flimsy blankets onto the ticking, and glanced from Gino to the pile of clothes.

"Dress yourself now. Signore Ottavio will meet you downstairs when he is ready." Beppe turned to go.

"Beppe," Gino said, "where should I wait?"

"The great hall, of course. Where he spoke to you before." Beppe huffed out, shaking his head.

Gino turned for a closer look at his new wardrobe. The clothes he already wore seemed like a better idea to him, but Signore Ottavio had other ideas.

Before long, Gino stood in the great hall shifting from one foot to the other. The wool leggings itched, and threatened to fall down with every movement. He wanted to sit down. But what was the protocol?

Now he took more notice of the room. Four large wooden chairs, elaborately carved and dark with age, sat in pairs in front of the hearth. The largest one—Signore Ottavio's, probably—had a cushion of threadbare reddish damask. The long dim room was eerily quiet, aside from a distant voice or footsteps echoing from another part of the house. Gino was tempted to open the double doors leading to the loggia. The stuffy room needed airing, but he didn't want to anger Ottavio by letting in "evil humors" that supposedly lurked outdoors.

He saw no sign of a wood supply, unless they stored it inside the gigantic wooden chest at the end of the room. Could firewood be that valuable, or was something else stored there? A fancy metal lock secured the chest, and four metal straps bound each corner. A basket of sewing materials lay abandoned on the floor beside it.

A couple of flies toured the twenty-foot length of the room from end to end at about shoulder level. At the other end of the room, a wide board leaned against the stone wall, with benches and what looked like two sawhorses pushed up against it. As Gino considered this strange furniture, a movement caught his eye. The pointed face of a rat poked around one end of the wide board, its nose twitching.

Gino froze. The rat took a few steps and stopped at the foot of one sawhorse, sniffing and nibbling at a crumb on the floor. That must be the dining table, Gino thought, as the rat inched along finding more food. The rat's body stretched to eight or ten inches long, and Gino's skin crawled as he thought of the fleas in that dark gray fur and the plague spreading through Europe.

Then the rat turned toward Gino, raising its forelegs off the ground a couple of inches and sniffing the air, staring with gleaming black eyes. It crawled forward another foot and sniffed the air again. And then it ran straight toward him.

With a yelp, he leaped back, looking around for some weapon. He grabbed a large floor-standing candle stand, but it weighed more than he expected and scraped loudly across the stone floor as he swung it at the rat. The rat zig-zagged at the noise, and then headed toward the stairs to the lower floor.

As the rat scampered down the stairs, Gino shuddered. His heart pounded, and he could feel his pulse all the way to his fingertips. That rat, with its fleas, could be spreading the plague right here in the house, while Signore Ottavio worried about the dangers of fresh air. Shaken, Gino set the candle stand upright, but the frayed end of his sleeve tangled in a curlicue of iron. He yanked at it to free the sleeve, and the iron stand fell over with a crash. As he pulled it upright, he heard the scuffling of footsteps at the far end of the room.

There, near the dining table, stood Signore Ottavio with three girls peering from behind him.

Gino stared back at them, and realized that one legging had slipped down below his knees and his gown hung askew from his lunge for the candle stand.

"There was a rat," he said in a weak voice, pointing toward the stairs.

6.

A new acquaintance is a cause
for hope—and caution.

A S THE HEAT ROSE IN GINO'S FACE, the three girls
erupted in laughter. Ottavio turned. Holding the sides of his
robe wide, he flapped them like the wings of an angry goose,
herding his daughters out of sight. Gino yanked the legging up
and straightened his gown. He put the candle stand back in its
place. He heard Ottavio in the next room, trying to stifle the
feminine laughter, punctuated with protests of, "But Papá, didn't
you see…"

After a couple of minutes, Ottavio stuck his head in. After
assuring himself that Gino was fit company, he waved a hand to
signal his daughters, who entered the room with a decorum that
required obvious effort. They avoided eye contact.

"Signore Gino, I would like to present my daughters." His
stern look kept another outburst at bay. "Lady Alessa."

A girl stepped forward, a girl so unfortunately like her father
that Gino felt sorry for her. A dark green dress hung loose on her
skinny frame, and her chinless head bobbed on a thin neck as she
acknowledged their guest. Her black hair hung loose and lank,
tucked carelessly behind her ears. She glanced at Gino and then
looked back at the floor, but Gino saw her large brown eyes, turned
down at the sides in a perpetually sad expression.

Gino bowed briefly, hoping that was an appropriate response, but Ottavio held a severe gaze on his youngest daughter, and didn't notice.

"Lady Patrizia." With boldness the middle daughter stepped forward, meeting Gino's gaze before making her curtsy. Just a little shorter than Gino, she had regular features and a pouty little mouth that could be pretty if she softened her haughty expression. Her dress strained across her breasts, and hung shorter than the other girls' dresses, as though she'd outgrown it.

"And my youngest daughter, Lady Fiamma," Ottavio said through clenched teeth.

Fiamma took two steps forward, and turning so her father couldn't see her face, she flashed a dimpled smile at Gino. Two combs held back her wavy auburn hair, but it swirled around her shoulders and down around her ample breasts, which were pushed up by her square-necked dress that seemed a bit too small for her. She looked him up and down as she curtsied, and just as he began to bow, she thrust her hand toward him. "A pleasure to meet you, signore," she said.

Gino took her hand, uncertain what to do next. Should he kiss it? No, he decided, and made a more elaborate bow instead. "And you, Lady Fiamma," he answered.

Ottavio began to fidget and hissed, "Fiamma! Enough!" When Fiamma flounced back to her sisters, he continued. "My daughters, this is Signore Gino, a guest with us for a while. He is a Calabrian astrologer."

"Signore Ottavio," Gino said, "it's a pleasure to meet your delightful family."

"Thank you, yes," he said, as though lamenting a sad fact, "but all girls. All needing dowries soon." He continued to shake his head, and gradually the motion ceased and he looked with hope at Gino. "You can help me. Now, my daughters, leave us to talk, go back to your stitchery." Fiamma trailed behind her sisters, and with her hand on the doorframe, swung a wide circle as she left, keeping her eyes on Gino until the last possible moment.

"Come, please, have a seat." Ottavio indicated the chairs by the hearth, directing Gino to a slightly smaller chair while he took the chair with a threadbare cushion. "Ruggero did well to bring you here. I do need wisdom, Signore Gino. Perhaps the stars will tell me where to find a dowry for Lady Patrizia, and how things stand with Lady Alessa's betrothal."

"What about Lady Fiamma?"

"Three dowries? No, I could hardly expect such a miracle. No, I am thinking that a convent might be best."

A convent, for Fiamma? She would liven up the place, Gino thought. "Does she want to be a nun?"

Ottavio peered at him with a bug-eyed curiosity. "Does she want to? I have no idea, but without a dowry, she cannot be married. She might stay here with me as long as I live, but after that, where else can she go?"

"There must be interested suitors for such a charming girl."

"With no dowry? No one is such a fool. Alessa is betrothed, thanks be to God, and was to be married last winter when the pestilence struck." He looked off into a dim corner and began to twine his fingers. "Her mother died, you know, last winter, and I agreed with Signore Tomasso—Alessa's betrothed—that we must wait until after Easter. Tomasso lives in Amalfi, a fine man whose first wife died two years ago. His youngest son died by the pestilence before the new year—," and Ottavio stopped his writhing fingers long enough to cross himself quickly, "and one daughter. And the priest died, Signore Tomasso sent word in March."

Gino thought of Alessa, her big dark eyes looking so hopeless. "It must be difficult for Alessa, delaying her wedding, and separated from her fiancé. Does she miss him?"

"Miss him?" Ottavio's hand fluttered to dismiss the idea. "Why should she miss him? They met but once, at their betrothal a year ago. They will have time together after they are married."

"She's marrying a man she has met only once?" He had read about these customs in history books, but hearing a man speak of his daughters this way, girls he had been introduced to just moments before, disturbed him.

"They know one another well enough. She knows he can provide for her, God willing, and he knows that she has a dowry—such as I have scraped together in these difficult times—and will inherit a share of my estate as well, since I have no sons."

Gino wondered what Alessa thought of this mercenary arrangement, or if her opinion mattered at all. "When will they marry?"

Ottavio turned his eyes, wide with anxiety, to Gino. "I don't know. I expected to hear from Tomasso after Easter, but no news came. So last week I sent Beppe's son to Amalfi with a message for him. He was to be back in four days, but it has now been eight days, and we have heard nothing." Ottavio put a hand on Gino's arm. "Look into this for me, tell me what the stars have to say. Have I brought the boy to harm, sending him at an improvident time?"

As if I would know, Gino thought. Maybe it would be best to just come clean, tell him I can't read the stars. Maybe I can make myself useful somehow. He thought of the life he'd had until yesterday, and swallowed hard. Could he even find a way to get back there, back to Seattle? Back to writing his column, and back to flirting with Sara, his beautiful cat-sitter? Maybe if he dove in at Li Galli again, he would be taken back the way he'd come. "I'm sorry, Signore Ottavio, but I—I can't help you."

"What?" Ottavio pulled himself erect in the chair, his neck even longer than before, and red blotches appeared on his face. "And why not? That's why I welcomed you to my home!" His voice was strained, and his Adam's apple poked out.

That flash of anger brought Ruggero's warning to Gino's mind: If you don't serve him well, he'll drive you off, or worse. Ottavio wrung his hands and paced, but Gino didn't want to see that man who might throw him out—or worse. Better to keep bluffing—he'd made a career of it.

"What I mean, Signore Ottavio, is that I have none of my equipment, my—." What would an astrologer need? "My charts, my books, were all left behind. I truly want to help you, but what can I do without them?"

Ottavio absorbed the news, then slumped in his chair, staring into the cold ashes. "Of course. Fortune is against me in this, as in everything."

"Note everything, Signore. I believe I can help you with one thing—the pestilence."

Ottavio narrowed his eyes. "How can you help with that? No one has been able to stop it."

Gino licked his lips and swallowed hard, hoping Ottavio would believe him. "In my land, we have found that the fewer rats there are, the less disease among the people. If you can get rid of the rats, I think it would help you too."

"Rats? What have they to do with it?" Ottavio paused. "Is that why you chased the rat?"

"Yes, Signore. All of us would be safer without them."

Ottavio grunted softly. "And how many in your family have died from the pestilence?"

"No one."

7. Hearts entwined know no distance.

SARA JOLTED AWAKE AT THE SOUND of the phone. She had waited all day to hear from Lia again, and now her clock said 11:42 p.m.

"Lia?"

"Yes, Sara. I am in Praiano. I'm afraid there is no more news."

"Nothing?"

"Uncle Nick, Gino's papa, is flying over here. The search will go on for a little longer, anyway."

"How is Marco?"

"Oh, he is so upset, I made him take a sleeping pill. He has not slept in two days."

Sara could hear the strain in Lia's voice. "Is he still on the boat?"

"We have a hotel room. He could not stay on the boat—he kept thinking of Gino there. I don't know if he will even be able to sail home."

Sara dragged her quilt out to the couch and curled up with it. Maybe she should take a sleeping pill too. She doubted she could get back to sleep, even with a pill. She took a deep breath. "Lia, is there a castle in Praiano? Some old stone building like that?"

Lia paused. "Of course, the town has many stone buildings, but not a true *castello*. There is a stone watchtower, very old. The coast has many watchtowers that used to guard against the Saracen raiders. Why do you ask?"

Sara bluffed. "Oh, he talked to me a lot about historical places like that before he left. I just thought if he got to land somehow, maybe he'd …" She faltered, knowing this must seem trivial, even absurd to Gino's grieving cousin. But Sara needed to know what her vision meant. "Maybe he'd want to see one."

After a long pause Lia said, "Gino…he won't visit them on this trip, I think." Her voice broke, and after a pause, she said, "I need to go now. I want to check with the searchers again. I will call tomorrow."

"Oh, Lia, I wish I could do something to help."

"Say a prayer for Gino, then. I'll call you again soon."

Sara sat wrapped in her quilt for a long time, thinking of Gino, of his determination to seek out the best Italian food in Seattle, even if it meant visiting dozens of restaurants. Of the friends he talked about, the guys he played bocce ball with and of how hard he'd worked to get ahead on his column before his trip began. He did have a lot of good qualities, in spite of his phony fortunes and silly turban. Sara had rebuffed his personal interest in her—no holding hands or hugs—but now she remembered the warmth of his hand as he opened her palm when they met at the party. His attentiveness whenever they met. And the way he put her at ease with his kindness and witty conversation.

She found herself wishing for another chance to hold his warm hand, and wondered if they would ever laugh together again.

✳ ✳ ✳

Monday morning came much too early for Sara. Her eyes burned after the sleepless night, and she slopped half of her coffee on her pants as she shoved open the door to Magarry and Phillips Investigations. "Sorry I'm late."

Grady Magarry glanced up as she passed his office door, and did a double take. "You're lookin' a little peaked, darlin'."

She mumbled a reply as she pulled open her bottom desk drawer with one foot and dropped her handbag. She laid her laptop bag on the desk, and gazed mournfully at the remaining half of her latte.

When Grady had called her 'darlin'' on her first day of work, she found it a little creepy. But he behaved as a gentleman, and she came to realize he meant nothing suggestive by it. She'd worked with him for two years and liked the work a lot, liked finding the answers to questions raised in their investigations, and found satisfaction in writing up the final reports that made everything clear.

Grady's partner, Jackson Phillips, had retired months ago, and their long-time bookkeeper, Fay, came in three afternoons a week. Otherwise, Magarry and Sara were the whole staff. Fay used Jackson Phillips' old office, and Sara worked in the reception area.

Magarry's chair thudded against the wall behind his desk, and he appeared in the doorway of his office, working a toothpick across the width of his mouth as he appraised her. "Didn't sleep much. Had a bit of a cry, too, I'd say." He combed his fingers through his rusty Brillo pad of a beard.

Once in a while Magarry pried like this, in a fatherly way. Sara tried to make light of it, in spite of her brain fog. "Am I under investigation now? My calendar says we're working on the Padgett case today."

Magarry pulled the toothpick from his mouth and flicked it into the trash. "And you are right about that. What did you find in the surveillance video?"

Sara covered her eyes with one hand, her elbow on the desk, and hoped her threatening tears wouldn't overflow. She'd taken a morning off last week, and told Magarry she would review the video over the weekend. But with all that had happened, she never gave it a thought. "Sorry, Grady." She pulled her laptop open. "I'll do it now." Magarry stood in the doorway for another minute or two, apparently waiting for her to spill her guts, but she focused on finding the videos, and by the time she clicked the play button, he was back at his desk.

The Padgett case started like most of the faked car accidents Magarry investigated. But it changed when Irene Padgett died a couple of days after the rear-ender. Her insurance records showed a whiplash claim fourteen months earlier treated at a shady clinic on the east side, and that red-flagged this accident for the insurance company. Magarry already interviewed the driver who hit her, a Russian with a thousand-dollar jacket and an expired visa. He lived in Bellevue with people the police knew pretty well.

Magarry had learned that most of Padgett's family spoke Russian, and there'd been more anger and argument than concern for her. He started thinking there might be more to the case than a faked medical claim gone wrong. So he convinced a couple of convenience store owners near the accident site to let him see their security video for that night.

When she hit the play button, the first grainy images Sara saw showed the entry of a former gas station, taken from the end of the building. The accident took place in the middle distance, about fifty yards down the block, Sara guessed. She started the film about ten minutes before the time of the accident, and struggled to stay focused on the search for clues: Did either of the cars involved drive by before the collision, anything that would suggest a plan rather than an accident? What witnesses were in the area, besides those they had already talked to? Anything unusual about the traffic, the activity on the sidewalk? They rarely investigated a case involving death. This was the first since she'd worked for him, so she didn't want to miss something important.

Her eyes itched, and her mind kept wandering to Gino. How could he have just disappeared? Who might have him hidden in a stone room? She hoped he would be found soon—but more than that, she found herself near tears again, hoping for his return.

She grabbed a tissue and blotted tears while pretending to blow her nose. Dragging her thoughts back to the video was like dragging a sixty-pound suitcase up a flight of stairs, but she kept at it. She couldn't let Magarry down. After a few minutes of pause-and-review, she was still five minutes away from the actual accident. She stopped the video and refilled her coffee with Magarry's high-test brew. *I'll just watch it through the accident*, she decided, and look at some screenshots.

Sipping coffee, she let the video run, saw Irene Padgett's car coming toward the camera, then something glinted across the screen, like light on a mirror. Sara flinched. Watching the silent images gave her an eerie feeling. No crash sounded on impact when Padgett's car leapt forward, struck from behind. No screeching of brakes as the brake lights came on in the traffic headed away from the camera, and no gasps from people on the sidewalk, just their open mouths. Padgett's car rolled to a stop against the curb.

What light had flashed? Sara toggled the video back thirty seconds and watched again. The camera angle didn't give a clear view of the car behind Padgett's, but it looked like the headlights flashed—at least the one she could see—just before the collision.

At the flash, Sara winced and closed her eyes. Her panic rose, knowing what was coming. She felt like the blood drained from her head. Magarry's face came to her mind, looking something like a mug shot, with a label at the bottom. A bruise darkened his forehead, but something didn't seem right for a mug shot. His eyes were closed. And behind him, not a wall, but floor tiles. Like a photo from the morgue.

"Magarry!" She didn't realize she'd spoken aloud until his chair banged the wall as he got up.

"What is it?" He rushed toward her, frowning, eyes fixed on her face. "Sara, you look awful. Are you sick?" He glanced at the video. "Did you find something?"

In fact, she felt sick, exhausted, and more than a little teary. The roof lights on a police car pulsed in the video image, and she pushed the laptop screen almost shut. She didn't want to see any more flashing, and didn't know what to tell Magarry.

He pulled up the laptop screen and shifted it his direction. "What's on the film?"

Sara turned away from the image, away from the flashing light, to face him. "It looked like the driver flashed his headlights just before he hit her. Magarry, what's on your schedule today?"

He fiddled with the video, and she saw the flash out of the corner of her eye. He watched the collision, and people gathering around Irene Padgett's car. "Who's this guy?" Magarry pointed to a man pulling open Padgett's passenger door, looking toward the car that hit her, and then sliding into the seat beside her.

"Isn't that the guy who called 911? We've got a statement here somewhere." She shuffled through a file.

"No, that's this guy coming from across the street. Off duty paramedic or something. See, he's on the driver's side, getting the traffic stopped."

Sara watched a few more seconds. The man in the passenger seat looked up and down the sidewalk, then got out and scanned the area before walking to the other car. He reached through the passenger side window—did he hand something off?—and then walked away, his back to the camera, hunched into his pea coat. "Who is he, then?"

"Good question." Magarry had another toothpick working its way across his mouth. "I'm going duck hunting today." That's what Magarry called following someone. "The Russian ducks. See what they do when they think nobody's looking."

Sara's heart lurched, the image of Magarry in the morgue fresh in her mind. She grabbed his arm as he started toward his office. "Wait a minute."

Magarry turned a quizzical look on her. "Is there somethin' you need to tell me?"

She fumbled for thoughts, and then words, as she slid her hand off his arm and nodded toward the laptop. "Doesn't it look like something is up on this video? I think those guys are dangerous, Magarry. Let's try to find out who got into Irene's car, before you go out following them."

"How we gonna do that, darlin'?" Magarry pointed his beard toward the laptop. "He left the scene before the cops showed up. Nobody even mentioned him in the reports I read. Do you remember anything?"

"No, but he was in the car when the paramedic got there. Maybe you can talk to him."

"I will. He's on my list."

Sara took a long slow breath, trying to clear her head and calm her heart. "Will you try that first? I just think it would be good to know more about that guy in the pea coat, how he fits in, before you start trailing anybody. I mean, if it *was* intentional, these guys are murderers, right? Maybe they weren't just out to collect phony doctor bills this time."

Magarry rubbed his beard and nodded. "Well, when you put it that way." He leaned over her desk, looking her full in the face. "I guess you'll let me know what else is on your mind in your own time, but how about I look through the video and make notes. And how about you take a bus back home and get some sleep."

He was right. She was in no condition to work. And now she could add visions of Magarry in the morgue to her worries about Gino. "I'll make it up. Maybe I can work tonight for a few hours. And don't you have a bulletproof vest in that back closet? These look like bad guys, Magarry. Maybe you should wear it."

He glanced toward the closet door and rolled his eyes. "Don't worry about me, darlin'." He checked his watch. "Why don't you come back about four, and we'll have a working dinner. Then you can stay as late as you're feeling up to."

In his chilly room that night, Gino layered his clothes on top of the thin blankets, and finally relaxed into a warm spot on the straw mattress Beppe had carried up. He came back to an alert tension at the sound of scuffling in the hall. Could it be another rat? It seemed to come as far as his door, and then stop. He listened intently, and then heard a very soft tapping on the door. Way too polite for a rat, but the whole household had gone to bed.

After a pause, louder tapping, then a whispered, "*Signore!*" in a decidedly female voice.

Gino froze for a moment, and then flung his covers off, grabbing for the green gown. He wrapped it around himself as he hopped from one foot to the other on the cold stone floor. He couldn't see his shoes in the dark, but felt his way to the door in time to hear another whisper.

"Signore, please open the door."

"Who is there?"

"Oh, Signore Gino, it is Fiamma. I need to talk to you."

Gino didn't understand many things about where he'd found himself, but he had no doubts that Signore Ottavio did not want his daughter going into a man's bedroom in the middle of the night.

"Lady Fiamma, can we talk tomorrow? It's late—"

"It is very important, Signore. It must be private."

Great. An urgent secret message from a teenage girl. Gino lifted the bolt as quietly as he could, but the scrape of iron still sounded loud in the silent house. As soon as the door moved, Fiamma pushed her way through, glancing back along the hall as if someone might have followed her. Gino backed away, and she handed him her candle, shut the door and set the bolt without a sound. As if she had done this before.

She wore a wide shawl wrapped around her shoulders, and under the shawl a white shift covered her to her ankles. The smooth curve of her hip under the linen made it clear that she wore nothing else.

"Lady Fiamma, what do you want? I don't think your father would want you to be here."

She giggled softly. "No, but I wanted to talk to you." She glanced around his room, and then sat on the edge of the bed.

Gino remained standing. "You said it was something important."

"Why did you make my father so angry today? Why did you refuse to read the stars for him? Have we not enough money for you?"

"How do you know what we talked about?"

Fiamma cocked her head to one side and smiled, then took her earlobe between one finger and thumb and waggled it in his direction. "I have ears."

"Then you know that I did not ask for any money."

"True, but people do not always say what is on their minds."

Fiamma looked around the room with a frown, and began rummaging through the blanket and clothing on the bed, pulling some of it around her. "Is this all that Beppe gave you?" she asked. "It's cold in this room."

The sight of her considering his bed set off several alarms in Gino's head. "Then maybe you should go back to your own room." His own feet were like ice, and he wanted to get back into bed himself, but not with her in it.

"But I came to tell you—I have something for you. Something you need."

"You do? What is it?"

"Two books and a big chart of the stars. The other astrologer used them—or pretended to—last year."

"The other astrologer?"

"My father went to Salerno and brought him back last year, before the pestilence came, to find the most propitious time for Alessa's marriage. That went well enough, but when he heard rumor of the pestilence, he looked to his charts again, and told Father that it would not touch our household." Fiamma faltered for a moment and her lively cheer faded. "Then mother sickened, and Alessa. And mother was carried off by it, and Beppe's younger son, too, and lots of people in Praiano." She squeezed her eyes shut and pressed her shawl against them, and looked back at Gino. "You must have seen how empty the town is now, when you walked up."

"It seemed quiet, yes, but I didn't think...I'm sorry about your mother, Lady Fiamma. Where did the astrologer go?"

She looked up at him through her dark lashes and shrugged nonchalantly. "Father had him tied hand and foot, and carried off to our friend the bishop in Ravello. The bishop questioned him and proclaimed him a charlatan. We heard that he was executed soon after."

A chill crept up Gino's back. She might have been talking about a deer killed by hunters. But he had been a man, a man who had probably used this same room, slept in this sagging bed. And Signore Ottavio must have known it could cost the man his life when he sent him to the bishop. "A charlatan?" *Like me*, he thought. "And not an astrologer at all?"

"I don't know, Signore Gino. But when Father sent him away, I saw that his books were left behind, and I hid them so I could look at them later. Of course, I have no learning in letters, so the writing meant nothing to me, but the drawings are curious. I embroidered some of the symbols onto a bit of linen." Her dimples flashed again, and she animated every statement with her hands. "Some of my best stitchery, too! But Alessa made me pull it out. So I hid it away with the books, and showed her another scrap of linen so she would think I tore it out. You can have the books, and then you can read the stars for my father."

Not likely, Gino thought, but he could not tell her why— that even if he believed in that tripe, he wouldn't know the first thing about how. His horoscope column focused on quirky vagueness, and lately he'd added an Eastern flair which went over well with his readers. But for Ottavio? *Add a little zen to your life today* wouldn't satisfy a man who had his last astrologer tried and executed for a bad prediction. Still, maybe the books would come in handy somehow.

"You're very kind to let me have them, Lady Fiamma." Gino stifled a yawn. "Now please go. It's late."

She stirred, as if to stand, but then sat back and looked up at him. "Signore Gino, where are you really from? You say you aren't from Calabria, but you call yourself a Calabrian. I don't understand it."

What could he say? "My home is in a very distant land. I'm sure you have never heard of it. Can't we talk about this another day?"

She continued to look at him with a wide-eyed wonder. "Beppo thinks your family sided with Aragon in the war and left Calabria to live there. And now you fear to identify yourself because your family turned against King Roberto, or his father." Fiamma leaned forward and whispered, "Gino, are you a spy for the King of Aragon?"

Shaking his head, he laughed softly. "Please, Lady Fiamma, of course not. I'm not a spy. I sailed here with my cousin and had some kind of accident. That's all I remember. Now hush so no one hears us, and please go back to your room." Gino took the candle and went to the door. He carefully lifted the latch and peered out into the darkness, listening to the silence.

At the touch of Fiamma's hand on his arm, he jumped, pulling the door back hard against his foot. His yelp of pain brought her hand to his mouth.

"Shhhh, Gino," she whispered, gazing at him in the way his cousin Lia called *sheep's eyes*.

"Good night, Lady Fiamma. Now go!" He slid away from her touch, and gently pushed her out the door. Holding a finger to his lips, he repeated her "Shhhh." He closed the door and set the bolt, still not as quietly as she had when she entered, and then moved through the darkness back to the bed. He pulled the green robe off and spread it over the rumpled mess of blankets and clothes, sliding in under them and hoping for a warm spot. The scraped foot didn't seem to be bleeding.

After a long time, he warmed up again and start to relax. A draft came through the shutters, carrying a hint of lemon scent, and he thought of Sara and the lemony fragrance she wore. A surge of heat flowed through him, and then despair. How would he get back? Was Marco searching for him? Sara might know by now that he was missing. Gino drifted to sleep imagining his own memorial service, and dreamed of Sara alone on the narrow prow of Marco's boat, weeping and tossing flowers into the sea near Li Galli.

8.

The right book will unlock
mysteries of the universe.

THE NEXT MORNING, Gino woke with a jolt. After a panicky moment of staring around the strange room, he remembered it all. Not a bad dream. The bedroom door had long iron hinges, and a piece of straw stabbed him in the back.

He came downstairs to the great hall, and found Ottavio just going down the stairs to the ground floor.

"I have to go out to the stable and find Beppe. God protect me from what foul things might be abroad." Ottavio crossed himself. "There is a bit of bread on the table for you."

Gino sat at the end of the table nearest the windows, and pulled one of the shutters open a few inches. He inhaled deeply, and took in the sliver of view. The scent of lemon perfumed the warm air.

"Signore Gino!" Fiamma spoke in a stage-whisper and placed a cup in front of Gino. "I had to tell you—the books will be in your room, against the wall behind the cupboard."

"What should I tell your father about where I got them?"

"Tell him you found them there, in your room. He will just think they were there all the time."

At the sound of heavy shuffling footsteps, Fiamma stepped away. "Your wine, Signore Gino, as you asked." Then she hurried to the doorway that apparently led toward the kitchen. A rotund woman had come that far, and looked with suspicion from one to another, wiping her hands with the edge of her apron.

In a voice that could charm snakes, Fiamma said, "That's exactly what he wanted, Marianna. Exactly!" Gino took a drink of the wine and smiled. She stepped lightly past the cook and into that part of the house that appeared to be off-limits to Gino.

When he returned to his room, Gino looked behind the cupboard. The books and chart were there, as Fiamma promised. The giant volumes the size of newspapers, with hardened leather covers, creaked and crinkled when he opened the stiff pages. The thick brown hand-lettered text meant nothing to Gino, even if he had been able to decipher the elaborate script. He'd forgotten his high school Latin long ago, and none of his studies included lessons on reading medieval writing.

Setting the books aside, Gino unfolded the chart and carried it to the window for more light. Around an outer circle, the familiar constellations of the zodiac trailed one after the other with their pinpoints of stars, and outlines of the bull, the ram, the crab, and the rest, each surrounding its starry foundation. In the center of the chart, several concentric circles formed an elaborate pattern. Gino remembered similar images from his early dabbling in astrology. He hadn't looked at them in a couple of years.

The narrow outer circle showed the 360 degrees marked off in 30-degree groups and labeled by fives. The next circle named the months, one with each 30-degree segment, and a tiny colored image—an axe, a haystack, a flower—representing some activity for the month. Within that the signs of the zodiac alternated with the calendar months, and within that another ring of numbers one to thirty in segments of twelve degrees.

His eyes burned from staring at the details of the lettering and images, but none of it meant anything to him. What could he tell Signore Ottavio that would satisfy, that would make Ottavio willing to help him get back to Li Galli? The way back home must be from the islands, Gino thought, the same way he ended up here.

But if he made something up—suggesting a date for Alessa's marriage or a prediction of safety that proved untrue—the wrong guess could cost his life. A disturbing thought of the other astrologer hanging from the gallows came to his mind and gave him a chill.

One thing was becoming clear. He'd have to follow through with the plan, and give Signore Ottavio some kind of 'reading.' He would concoct something as vague and benign as possible, that still might satisfy him. Meanwhile he would look for a chance to return to Li Galli, and a way to get there.

He carried the books and chart to the great hall, but the dining table was gone. Then he realized the top board leaned against the wall, just like it had been when he saw the rat. He chose the only other large flat surface, the top of the trunk, and spread the books out there. He opened the chart again. Each corner contained a scene, images he hadn't noticed before. He pulled one of the shutters ajar for better light.

Two of the scenes showed a person lying on a bed, with what Gino supposed was the doctor nearby. Dark spots marked one patient's skin, and a bowl on a table close to him held similar spots. Leeches? This looked like medieval medicine, all right. The other patient appeared to have a head injury, and the doctor held a jar partly filled with something.

In another corner of the chart, a man carried a cross mounted on a stick, and held a small creature in the crook of his arm. Gino turned the page a little more toward the light. The animal looked like a rat to him. Gino couldn't help himself. He scanned the room from end to end, remembering the rat he'd seen the day before.

The fourth corner showed a woman being comforted by a nun in front of a building with arches across the front. Somebody's version of a hospital? It jarred him to see priests and nuns illustrating an astrological chart. He remembered the men in the tower asking him if he'd studied astrology at the university in Salerno, and that seemed a little strange too, now that he thought about it. He didn't remember any astrology classes in the course catalog at the University of Washington.

Hearing a rustling on the stairs, Gino turned to see another rat mount the top step and speed toward the kitchen, following its twitching nose. He groaned softly. The rat paused and peered at him before disappearing past the doorway.

He determined one thing at that moment. If the rats were going to be guests in this house, he wouldn't be staying. He'd find somewhere else to go, some excuse for getting out of here. Ottavio's hospitality wasn't worth the risk of bubonic plague.

From the ground floor, Gino heard Ottavio giving Beppe some instructions

before starting up the stairs. "Good morning, Signore Gino," he said with his usual downcast look.

"Signore Ottavio, I just saw another rat. What can be done to get rid of them?"

Ottavio dismissed the question with a wave. "When Beppe's son returns, he can catch them. Beppe is too busy with other work."

"I don't want to stay here with rats in the house. And I need to return to Sirenuse—my cousin's boat is out there, probably anchored where we can't see it. I have to return." Gino hoped it was possible, but how could he get Ottavio to help him?

Ottavio frowned and shook his head. "You think a rat is dangerous? Rats are everywhere! But those islands—that place is a graveyard of boats. I wouldn't risk my men to take you there. You would all be lost!"

What leverage do I have, Gino wondered. Then he remembered the books. "Look what I found in my room. I didn't know you had books of astrology."

"What? What are you talking about?" Ottavio rushed over, his mouth gaping open in a dark O. He touched each of the large books, opening the covers and peering with a pained frown at the lines of text.

Gino slid the chart toward him an inch or two, and he picked it up for a closer look. "They are! They are astrology books, just what you needed, Signore Gino." Ottavio ruffled the pages of one book again, barely looking at the contents, then slammed it shut and turned to Gino, gripping him by the shoulders. His quarter-moon smile showed darkened teeth. "Now you can read the stars for me! You found these books in your room? This is a miracle! Surely God wants you to reveal what to do."

There it is again, Gino thought. Nobody at home thought God wanted them to read their horoscope. But a suspicion had come to Gino that he had to test.

"Signore Ottavio, I have a question for you." Gino opened the nearest volume and ran his finger across the text of a couple of pages as if searching for something. Then he stopped. "Ah. Here. I want your opinion of this."

Ottavio blinked a couple of times and licked his lips. "Let me have a better look." He pulled the shutter open wider, throwing more light on the page. His head weaved back and forth as he looked over a couple of lines. Then he glanced at Gino, and looked back at the lines again. "Hmm. Interesting. I'm not sure what to think."

"I have never read anything by this man," Gino said, pointing to words on the first page that looked like they might be a name. "Do you consider him reliable?"

"Well…it must be so." Ottavio closed the cover gently this time, and shifted his glance from one corner of the room to another before looking back at Gino. His voice held a hint of pleading. "God has provided them, don't you see? We must trust in him to reveal the truth to you."

"But what about these statements I showed you?" Gino opened the book to a different page, but pointed to about the same place on the page as he had before.

Ottavio looked at it for just a moment, then began bobbing his head with a sage expression. "It's a mystery. And God will reveal the answer to you! Surely this is your calling, your life's work."

This will make things easier, Gino thought. He can't read Latin any better than I can. Gino filed that fact away, hoping he could find a way to make use of it.

* * *

Sara hopped off the bus at ten to four, rested, hungry, and ready to work. The image of Grady Magarry she'd seen when she watched the video troubled her mind until she saw him rummaging in a file cabinet as she pushed through the office door. Relief flowed through her, but how could she convince him to be careful when she didn't know the source of danger?

"Did you reach that paramedic today?"

Magarry half-turned toward her, a file folder clenched in his teeth. He marked a place in the file drawer with one hand, and continued riffling through files with the other. His guttural response sounded like a negative reply to her.

"Can I help you find something?"

He flipped through a few more files, gestured his impatience, and shoved the door shut. Taking the file from his mouth, he said, "No, this'll do." He squinted her direction. "You're some improved, darlin'. You hungry?"

"I need some comfort food, Magarry. Fettuccine alfredo would be perfect."

About thirty minutes later the fragrance of garlic bread accompanied the delivery guy through the door, and Sara had her desk cleared off and ready, with a chair pulled up for Magarry, and a list of cases they needed to discuss. But when she opened the Styrofoam box, the fettuccine brought Gino to the forefront of her thoughts again. Magarry methodically quartered his three big meatballs with a plastic knife. When he laid the knife aside, she said, "I need to tell you something."

He speared a piece of meatball and paused to look up at her, waiting.

"I told you I'm cat-sitting for a friend, a guy who went to Italy?"

"I remember."

"He's missing."

"Isn't he still in Italy?"

"He's missing in Italy. Gino's missing. They think he drowned." She poured out the story as her fettuccine cooled. She didn't bother trying to stop her tears this time, and Magarry listened without comment, chewing his meatballs slowly.

Finally, after she told him about Lia's latest phone call, she stuck a plastic fork into the fettuccine and twirled a few noodles, but didn't lift it to her mouth. She wouldn't be able to swallow past the lump in her throat.

Magarry put his fork down too. "So he's missing and presumed drowned."

Sara slumped back in her chair, shaking her head. "Yes, but…" How could she tell him what she knew, from her vision? "I just don't think it's true," she finally said.

"You don't *want* to think it's true?"

"Of course I don't, but that's not why. I just have such a strong…hunch about it." She shrugged apologetically. "It doesn't sound like much to go on, does it?"

Magarry rubbed a napkin over his whiskers. "Frankly, no. But in the couple of years you've worked here, I've come to respect your hunches. You have a good sense about things."

His faith in her brought some comfort. "What do you think I should do?"

"Hm. I don't see a clear next step for you, darlin'. Keep your ear to the ground. Keep talkin' to that cousin of his. Something will come to you, and when it does, that's what you do." Magarry balled up his napkin and closed the Styrofoam tray. "Now I'm gonna nuke your noodles, and I'd like to see you eat a couple of them while we go over that list of cases."

Sara nodded and tossed another sodden tissue in the trash. "Thanks, Magarry. Thanks for listening." She still couldn't imagine telling Magarry about her visions, and pushed away the thought of Magarry on a gurney in the morgue. Could she pass that off as just a hunch too? She felt desperate to tell somebody the whole truth. But who could she trust not to call her crazy?

✳ ✳ ✳

Two days later, Sara and Britt sat cross-legged on Sara's bed, facing each other. "They gave up the search yesterday." Sara's throat ached.

"I'm so sorry." Britt reached out with a hug, and Sara lay her head on Britt's shoulder, letting her tears soak into Britt's T-shirt.

"Gino's dad is flying home soon, to St. Louis. They'll come out here in a few days, he said." Sara sat up straight and tried to pull herself together. "I'm going to bring Houdini over here. His dad asked me to keep him, because they have a dog in St. Louis, and they don't want a cat. And it's too hard to keep going to his apartment. His dad's going to mail something to me—a gift Gino bought for me, Lia said."

"It's all so heartbreaking. Just disappearing like that. If they found something, at least there could be some closure."

Sara looked away. Sun filtered in through the madrona branches. She had to tell Britt, and hoped their friendship could take it.

"The thing is, Britt," she began, then paused and took a deep breath, their eyes locked. "I know he's not dead."

Britt started to speak, to talk sense to her, but Sara held up her hand to stop her. "I know I sound like a complete maniac, but I have to tell you." Sara paused, barely able to breathe, heart pounding. "I've never told anyone except my family—and they didn't believe me." She stalled, clearing her throat. What would Britt say? "I know he's not dead because I have been clairvoyant since I was a little girl, and I've seen Gino alive."

"Clairvoyant?" Britt stared slack-jawed for a few seconds, then shook her head. "You…What? You are the most straight-arrow person I know! If that's true, how could I not know it?"

"Because I've spent my whole life hiding it and denying it with all my strength. You know I had an older sister who died?"

Britt nodded.

"Well, you don't know the whole story." Sara told her about it, the lightning, her vision, the car accident, and the months of psychiatric effort to "fix" her. They brewed tea and sipped at it as Sara told her all the rest: the other visions, and hiding from lightning storms and strobe lights and failing fluorescent tubes. How even her brother Paul doubted her, when she told him after they left the club in such a hurry a few days earlier. Finally, a quiet settled between them. In her soft clear voice, Sara said, "I can't keep denying it, knowing Gino is alive somewhere, in trouble. How could I live with myself if I just gave up?"

Britt gazed at the ceiling, deep in thought for a few moments. "It sounds like this gift, or whatever, it's not going away." Then she turned to Sara. "But what can you do with it? How can you help Gino?"

Sara crumpled, sobbing and hugging a pillow. "I don't know," she wailed. "I don't know enough! But I can't just let him go. I don't want to let him go. He has to come back!"

Britt stood up and massaged Sara's shoulders for a couple of minutes. Then she huddled close to her on the bed, a co-conspirator. "What if you tried to find out more?"

Sara grabbed a tissue and wiped her nose. "What do you mean?"

"I mean, you've been doing all you can to stop having visions, to avoid them. What if you opened up to them instead, pursued them, even? If you don't know enough, maybe you could learn more. Maybe you could meet with somebody else who sees the future, or one of those psychics that find missing people."

Sara stared at her. "Do you know how crazy that sounds?"

Britt put a hand on her arm. "I know you've been told it's crazy. I'm sure there are lots of wackos and frauds among the psychics and fortune-tellers out there. You said even Gino just makes his stuff up. But maybe some of them have the real thing, some kind of gift like you, and just use it the best they can."

"I don't know."

"Look, I'm not saying go open a shop reading tea leaves at the back of a tattoo parlor in the U District. But if you think learning more about Gino's…" Britt cast about for a word. "…situation might help, then I think you should do it."

"You do? You really believe me?"

Britt took Sara's hands in both of her own. "I do believe you. I don't think you would make this up, and I don't think you're crazy. You, my friend, are amazingly strong to do what you've done all these years, and you are amazingly brave to talk about it now. To think about changing things."

Sara threw her arms around Britt. "Thank you so much. Thanks for just believing me."

✳ ✳ ✳

Gino dreamed of rats that night, disease-bearing, flea-infested rats chewing on one foot of his bed, chewing their way up to him as he tried to knock them away. He woke in a cold sweat. The rats he had seen downstairs, and heard scuffling through the straw, seemed to be tattooed on the insides of his eyeballs. The green tunic he wore to bed itched. He tried to calm his heart with some yoga breathing.

"Signore Gino?" Fiamma whispered, tapping on his door.

He decided to ignore her, feign sleep, and hoped she'd go back to her room.

"Signore, I heard you call out. What's wrong? Gino?"

The tapping persisted and got louder. She'd wake up the whole house if she kept it up. He slid out of bed, keeping the covers in place to preserve the warmth, and opened the door a crack.

"What do you want?"

In the flickering candlelight, Fiamma's smile faded, and her brown eyes widened, threatening tears. "I wanted to talk with you."

"Lady Fiamma," he said, trying a little softer tone, "can't we talk tomorrow? It's the middle of the night. I'm tired."

"But I heard your voice. You were calling out." She put her hand up to the door as if to push it open further, but Gino held it steady with just a three-inch gap.

"I had a bad dream, about rats."

"Rats?" She laughed softly. "Why are you so afraid of rats?"

He looked steadily at her. Maybe she could help him keep them all safe. "In my country, Lady Fiamma, wise men have learned that rats are connected to diseases like the pestilence. When we get rid of the rats, the disease goes away. Rats could even be connected to my death." The story rolled off his tongue with conviction, like it always did when he did his fortune-telling act at parties. But here, his life might depend on their belief in him.

Fiamma glanced along the hallway floors, then gasped and pushed against the door.

Caught off guard, Gino backed away and grabbed for his robe on the bed as she slipped in and closed the door quietly.

He spoke in a stage whisper. "What was it? A rat?"

She turned, leaning her back against the door, and shook her head quickly, putting her fingers on his lips with a very quiet, "Shh."

She listened intently with her head tilted back and lips parted. When Gino took her hand from his mouth to whisper, "What was it?" her warm fingers curled around his. Her candle glowed steadily in the still air, highlighting her collarbones and the soft hollow at the base of her neck. *She's fifteen years old*, Gino told himself, stepping away from her.

Loosening his fingers from hers, Gino leaned near enough to whisper, as she concentrated on listening for sounds in the hall.

"What did you see?"

"Light down the stairs. Someone else is there." She turned to press her ear against the door, and a wave of auburn hair fell across the thin linen shift.

Gino realized he needed to get her out of here, and fast.

She turned to face him. "It sounds like they're gone."

"Who's gone?"

Her shrug didn't convince Gino, and when he narrowed his eyes, she said, "Maybe Patrizia."

"You better go, Fiamma. Don't come here at night. We'll talk tomorrow, after breakfast."

She reached for his arm, letting her shawl drop from one shoulder. "But Gino, I can't. Father said we should stay away from you, leave you to do your work."

"Maybe you should obey him, then." He picked up the trailing end of her shawl. "Here, cover up. And go back to your room."

She smiled at his touch, tilting her head to one side. Then her expression changed. "But Signore Gino, what about the rats? Are you in danger?"

"We may all be in danger. I told your father, but he doesn't think the rats are a problem."

"What do the stars say?"

"It's not always easy to interpret them."

"But now you have the books! That will help you, and you can help father too."

She trusted him, and he hated to disillusion her. "There are other tools I need."

Fiamma's shoulders sagged. "You mean the books won't help?"

"What I need is an astrolabe." *And you better not have one hidden under your mattress*, Gino thought.

"What is that?" Hope filled her voice.

"It's used to show the positions of the stars. I also have to observe the stars myself. I need access to the terrace at night."

She frowned and her gaze fell to the floor. "I don't know about that. I don't think Father will allow it." Then she brightened again. "But I could meet you in the great hall and lead you to the terrace, when everyone else is sleeping."

Gino held up both hands and took a step back. "No. No, Lady Fiamma. I will have to convince your father, and get his permission. I can't sneak around behind his back like that. And neither should you." He moved to the door, eager to send her back to her room.

"Signore Gino," Fiamma whispered, moving near him again. "I will help you in any way I can."

"Then go back to your own room. Why doesn't your father want you or your sisters to speak to me?"

"You're a stranger, Signore Gino. Who can speak for you, tell him that you can be trusted? Nobody. So he has to wait and see for himself."

"But what is there to be afraid of?"

Fiamma laughed. "The things everyone fears from strangers. Violence, theft, disease, deception. And since my mother's death, these things are much more real to him. To us all."

"To you all? Then why are you not afraid of me, too?"

A smile came to her lips as her gaze drifted from his curly hair to his bare feet, and back to his face. "Oh, Signore Gino, there is something very different about you. But what is it? I feel like I have to know, and it is hard to learn when you are afraid."

"I hope your father will learn to trust me, too, but if you are found sneaking to my bedroom at night, he will do to me what he did to the other astrologer. Now go." He pulled open the door and peered out. "No one is here. Go back to bed. I need sleep if I'm going to do anything for your father, your family."

Fiamma said nothing more, but stepped out into the hall with her candle.

9. Turn your regrets into opportunities.

A WEEK WENT BY, a week of Gino poring over the books, making a show of studying them, and trying to avoid the rats that made their way up to the living quarters almost every day. Had Marco given up searching for him by now? How long did they search for someone missing at sea? He needed to be back in Seattle soon, finishing his next batch of columns. Instead, he lay in bed past breakfast time, with no desire to get up. What were the newspapers saying about him? What could they say?

We regret to announce that syndicated astrology columnist Eugene Xavier is missing and presumed drowned off the coast of Italy. Sources report that while swimming off a relative's boat during a vacation, he disappeared. An extensive search turned up no sign of him, and foul play is not suspected. The end.

His parents would be in shock, and Marco would be feeling so guilty—not that he had any blame, but he'd feel responsible anyway.

And what about Sara? His parents didn't even know about her. But Marco did, and he hoped Marco and Lia called her. She'd be worried when she couldn't reach him. She had been worrying about him the last time they talked, but he wasn't sure why.

What he wouldn't give to talk to her right now! Not here in this run-down *palazzo*, but over a pizza and wine at Via Tribunale in Fremont, at a booth in the back where they could stay a couple of hours. He'd quit making fun of the geocaching thing she did, and ask her why she liked it so much. He wouldn't let her blow off the questions about her family; he'd ask her what went wrong. He suddenly felt desperate to see her again, to find the key that would open the barrier she kept between them. To be more than friends.

He'd taken his own family for granted, he realized. At times he felt smothered by their interest, but it occurred to him that the distance he kept, the rarity of his phone calls, actually hurt his mom's feelings. And had he tried to have a serious conversation with his dad in the last three or four years? He didn't know what his dad wanted to do when he retired, how his parents had coped with the empty nest, what the two of them did in the evenings. Did they still go to Mass on Saturday night, or had they just done that when he lived at home, to do their duty to the church, make sure he knew the Catechism?

If I can find my way back, Gino vowed to himself, I'm going to do things differently.

He had spent the past week dodging Lady Fiamma, who followed him to the loggia, watched from a distance when he went to the privy, and trailed after him into the dimly lit hallways whenever she could do so unseen.

The previous night she had come to his room again, asking about his progress, and eager to gaze at his shaggy black hair. If he'd met her in his teens, he'd have been crazy about her, flattered by her interest. At twenty-five, he felt like an older brother, and her longing looks gave him the creeps.

As he dressed, Gino resolved to keep Fiamma away somehow. Then, as he stepped out of his room, he heard a commotion. Shouting echoed up two stairways from the main hall. Signore Ottavio's voice, normally a high trill, had deepened with what sounded like anger. As he came down the first flight of stairs, he heard Fiamma's voice. She sounded indignant, and a little out of breath.

A few steps down the second stairway, out of sight from the great hall, he stopped. He could hear them clearly.

"What does it look like I'm doing? I'm taking this out to Beppe to get rid of it."

"Put that filthy thing down!"

"Fine. I'll throw it off the loggia."

"Fiamma! Put it down! Where did you find a dead rat?"

After a pause, Gino heard a tall shutter scraping the floor as it opened and then closed again.

"I didn't find a dead rat. I found a live rat, and killed it with this." He heard the sound of wood tapping on stone.

Then a new voice joined in, one of the sisters, Gino assumed.

"What has brought on this interest in killing rats? You paid them no attention before." Her last word was the bait, and Gino cringed when Fiamma rose to it.

"Before *what*?" she asked.

After a derisive laugh, the sister said, "Before your friend the astrologer came."

"Fiamma, what is this?" Signore Ottavio's voice, tinged with suspicion, sounded like he might erupt into violence. "I told you to stay away from him, let him do his work. Patrizia, what do you know about this?"

"Father, all I've done is killed a rat," Fiamma said, cutting off her sister's reply. "It's more help than she has been."

Her sister laughed harshly. "You just killed a rat because *he* tried to kill a rat. Do you think to impress him with your skill?"

"Father has told Beppe to keep the rats out, but he does nothing about it. Nothing! Did you ever wonder why Signore Gino wanted to kill that rat? Maybe they are more dangerous than you think."

"Girls!" Signore Ottavio's screeching voice cut off Patrizia's retort.

In the moment of silence that followed, Gino barely breathed. He wanted to creep back up the stairs, but feared that they would hear him, that he'd be caught eavesdropping. Could he continue down the stairs as if he were just coming from his room, and pretend he had heard nothing? After all the yelling, it didn't seem likely they'd believe it.

"Father—" Fiamma started, but Ottavio cut her off too.

"No, Fiamma. I won't hear it. Go to your room. I'll talk to you later."

"But—" Gino could hear the sob in Fiamma's voice.

"By God's mercy, Fiamma. Go now!"

Her footsteps receded as she ran from the room, leaving Ottavio and Patrizia in an uncomfortable silence. Gino could imagine Signore Ottavio wringing his hands and pacing in nervous steps that seemed too small for his long frame.

"What more do you know, Patrizia? Has she been bothering the astrologer?"

"I…I'm not sure, Father."

"Have you seen them together?" Ottavio's voice rose with his exasperation.

"No, only at meals, when we are all together."

"Then what were you talking about a few minutes ago? Are you just digging for trouble where there is none?"

Patrizia stalled, mumbling something, until Ottavio shouted, "Speak up!"

"She left our room last night."

"Do you know where she went? Perhaps to the privy."

"She took a long time."

"How long?"

Patrizia seemed reluctant to speak, or maybe she paused to calculate the time in her head. "Almost an hour, I think."

Gino heard a long sigh from Ottavio. "Did you think to go look for her? Perhaps she felt ill."

"Fiamma is never ill, Father. I did look—in the privy, in the kitchen, and in the great hall."

"But you didn't check at the astrologer's room?"

"No, Father!" Her indignation softened when she continued. "But I listened at the stairway," she said, and Gino saw her arm swing back to indicate the stairs where he now stood, "and heard nothing."

For some reason that didn't satisfy Ottavio. "Nothing at all?"

"No…it seemed too quiet."

When the hand touched his shoulder, Gino startled so badly that he nearly yelled, but he caught himself with a gasp. Fiamma stood on the step behind him. Her eyes were red, and the trails of her tears ran to her chin. She beckoned Gino back up the stairs. If he didn't go, she might try to whisper something to him here, and her father would probably hear them.

Instead of going toward his room, though, Fiamma opened a door at the top of the stairs. Gino had assumed it led to another room like his, but instead the open door revealed a narrow passageway with a low ceiling.

"Where does this go?" Gino asked when Fiamma had closed the door behind them. But instead of answering, Fiamma threw herself against him, sobbing silently. He put his hands on her shoulders and gently moved her away. "Come on, Fiamma. Don't cry."

"Your language is so beautiful," she hiccuped, and then he realized that he had spoken to her in English. And suddenly she kissed him with an eagerness that pushed him stumbling backward.

"No," he said, shaking his head. He pulled away, taking her arms from around his neck.

"Signore Gino," she breathed, gazing at him like he was her favorite rock star.

"Please, Lady Fiamma," he said, holding her hands together in front of his pounding heart. "You don't understand. I can't do this." Tears welled in her wide, trusting eyes, and he reached up and wiped his thumb across her cheek to stop the flow.

Just then the door they had come through opened wide, banging against the stone wall, and Signore Ottavio stared at them, his face reddening in the dim light. Gino stepped back to distance himself from Fiamma, but she turned to stand beside him, hooking her arm around his and pressed against his side.

"Marianna!" Signore Ottavio's high-pitched shout sounded almost like a scream. Behind him, from the other end of the small hallway, Gino heard heavy steps and panting breath.

"Yes, my lord?" Marianna asked as she took in the scene.

"Tell Beppe to prepare three horses for a trip to Amalfi." Ottavio spoke to Marianna but his eyes never left Fiamma and Gino. "And pack Lady Fiamma's things in the small trunk."

Fiamma let out a small scream and ran to Ottavio. "What are you doing, Father? Please don't send me away."

She peered up into his face, but Ottavio stood impassive against her pleas. Then he shook his head.

"You must go eventually anyway, Fiamma. The Sisters of Santa Susanna will take you for a small gift. You know I don't have enough for a dowry."

"The Sisters? Father, no!"

Gino watched as Fiamma crumpled on the floor, gripping Ottavio's robe and wailing. When Ottavio could not shake her off, he leaned over and slapped her face, and Gino felt the blow.

10. Sometimes your comfort zone
doesn't contain everything you need.

THE NEXT FRIDAY WHEN SARA came home after work, a package was stuffed in her mailbox. Sara took in the St. Louis address, the Calabrese name, the light weight as she hefted it. She dropped her laptop bag on the couch and pulled the box open and emptied it onto her kitchen counter. A lump rose in her throat at the sight of the book she gave Gino to read on the trip. Inside the front cover, Gino had printed 'From Sara, birthday trip to Italy' in neat square lettering. She laid it aside and unwrapped crumpled paper padding a three-inch square box. Inside on a bed of cotton lay a gold locket with a cameo on the front. A mermaid carved in pale pink stood out against a darker pink background, and she held a little harp on her lap. Sara had never seen one like it, and when she opened the clasp, a little paper fell out. In the same neat lettering she read, *for Madame Sirena*.

"Oh, Gino, where are you?" she whispered. She imagined him bringing her this locket after his trip, and her hug of thanks would turn into a warm embrace. She had always kept him at a distance to keep her secret. But if Britt could believe it, maybe Gino could too. Because she didn't want to push him away any more.

She carried the book and locket to the couch, and snuggled into her fleece throw. The creases and dog-ears showed that Gino had started reading the book. Journals of an Astrologer. Comforted by holding something Gino had held just a couple of weeks ago, she wondered what Niccolo Bonamico of Salerno had to say about the future.

She skipped the academic introduction, and turned to the last corner Gino had marked, at page 42. Sara let herself slip into the medieval astrologer's world.

> From the time our gracious and beloved Queen Joanna was crowned, when I was twenty-five years old, I made it my aim to serve her, though my father wished me to follow him as a master of the medical arts, teaching at the university in Salerno. I had studied diligently at the university from the age of seventeen. My father opposed my purpose to leave Salerno, but I excelled in my medical studies and hoped to find a way to Naples, to the queen's household. I vowed to maintain that purpose, however long it might take.

Sara skimmed through Niccolo's medical training, and his growing desire to go to Naples, where the queen suffered through her own trials. She became the top suspect in her husband's murder.

About seven o'clock, hunger drove Sara to the kitchen, still holding the book open as she peered into the fridge, opened a couple of cupboards, and then grabbed the jar of peanut butter and a spoon and went back to the couch and read on.

> Fortune smiled on me when our Queen Joanna's cousin Louis, Prince of Taranto, became her husband. Members of his household, sailing in the spring of 1348 from Taranto to Naples, landed in Salerno seeking a physician for the seneschal, near death with a fever, and my father was chosen from among the university masters, and drew him back from death. As he recovered, my father entrusted me more and more with his care, and I became well acquainted with the seneschal.
>
> The prince possessed an impatient nature, and they dared not delay in continuing the sea journey to Naples.

The seneschal, comfortable now with my services, invited me to Naples to serve his family. The enormity of my good fortune was barely to be believed. A connection to the royal household itself!

Sara scraped another spoonful of peanut butter from the bottom of the jar and marked her place with one finger while she flipped to the book's index, looking for Joanna. A long string of page numbers followed her name—*might as well just keep reading the book*, Sara thought. But when had her reign started? Sara tapped her smart phone and found the Wikipedia entry. Joanna, born in 1328, became queen in 1343—fifteen years old. If the astrologer was twenty-five years old the year of her coronation, then he was twenty-eight by the time she married that cousin, Louis of Taranto. She turned one page in the index and found his name, with far fewer references.

Before Sara could flip back to continue reading, another entry in the index made her gasp: Li Galli. Where Gino disappeared. Sara scanned the page that referred to Li Galli, running her eyes over it twice without finding the words. Frustrated, she flipped to the pages on either side, and saw that a chapter began on the previous page. She picked up Niccolo's story there:

The journey from Salerno to Naples is not a great distance, and should have been uncomplicated. Who could have foretold the strange events? The stars revealed nothing to me, and I left Salerno two weeks before midsummer, glad to leave the plague-ridden city behind, although nearly every ship in port brought news of death wherever they travelled. But with this also came good news, the departure of the queen's Hungarian cousin, her late husband's brother who disturbed the peace of our entire kingdom. He fled back to his own cursed land. Rumors reached us that our queen would soon return to Naples, and I purposed to be there when she arrived. Such was the year of our Lord 1348.

Among my companions were two strangers speaking a strange tongue, men I suspected as spies and enemies of the Kingdom, for every moment they huddled together, casting furtive glances at other travelers, and giving every impression of plotting and scheming. These men I avoided but watched them carefully. Other men of importance traveled with us, too, clearly having heard the same news we celebrated, namely that our Queen would soon be in Naples, in her rightful place over us again.

We also carried a family from Praiano, a father and daughter with two servants, traveling with a Calabrian man, or so he claimed, although he spoke like no Calabrian I have known. He had a strong interest in the islands along our sea route, those rocks known as Sirenuse.

A footnote identified Sirenuse by the modern name, Li Galli. Gino had been right about those islands – they had been famous for centuries, even though Sara had never heard of them before she met him. Sara searched the index and read snippets here and there, pulling her throw around her as darkness descended outside.

Sara closed her eyes and held the book to her chest. After she and Britt had talked about what to do next, she'd done some research on psychics in the area. Two or three had seemed legitimate enough to contact, and all wanted to have something the missing person had used recently. Now she had the book, and Gino's gift to her, the siren pin. Now she could set up a meeting. A warm blanket of hope brought her deepest sleep in weeks.

Ottavio waited with his arms crossed and his mouth pinched into a tight line. Fiamma moved away from him, sliding a few feet toward Gino before standing. Ottavio's handprint stood out in bright relief on her cheek.

Gino reached out to help her up, but she flinched and then looked at him, all the trust gone from her eyes. She brought her hand up to cover her quivering chin.

"Lady Fiamma," Gino said softly, and reached for her.

She took a step back, turned a brief glare on her father, and then looked at Gino. "You can't help me now," she said in a husky voice, and ran toward the far end of the hallway.

Gino watched her go, and then looked back at Ottavio. How could a man hit his own daughter that way? Ottavio watched Fiamma leave, absently rubbing his palm against his thigh. His face relaxed into a smug expression, some satisfaction with the way he had handled the girl.

Anger rose in Gino, rushing through him like a flash flood, and it pushed him a step closer to Ottavio. "Why did you hit her?" he demanded.

Ottavio's eyes widened. "What do you mean?"

"What good will it do to hit her, to hurt her that way? She's your daughter, for God's sake!"

From the door to the stairway, both men heard a snicker and turned to hear only the scuffle of retreating footsteps. Patrizia, Gino thought.

"Maybe you should send *that* troublemaker to a convent," Gino spat as he pushed past Ottavio. He had to get some space before he hit the man.

But Ottavio grabbed Gino's arm as he started up the stairs to his room. "And what should I do with you? A guest in my house who has lured my daughter to his room at night? A man who claims to know the meaning of the stars, but says nothing to show it is true?" He took a step closer to Gino and looked down at him with narrowed eyes. "What do you have to say for yourself? Are you good with a sword, Signore Gino? Beppe! Bring swords!" He shouted these last words down the stairway.

Gino's mouth went dry. "I swear to you, signore, I did not lure her to my room."

"Beh! Why should I believe a stranger over my own flesh and blood?"

"Lady Fiamma told you that?"

A flash of uncertainty broke Ottavio's glare. Beppe's heavy tread sounded at the bottom of the stairs, and they both turned to see him staring, his mouth hanging open. Marianna stood behind him with a sticky ladle in her hand.

"Swords, I said!" Ottavio screeched at Beppe.

Beppe frowned and strained forward squinting. He looked Ottavio and Gino up and down, and then spoke to Ottavio in a stage whisper. "Surely not, signore?"

Ottavio stepped back, drawing himself up to his full height. But he repeated Beppe's once-over of Gino, and paused before taking a long breath in. "Bring out the swords, I said, and get them cleaned and ready. I didn't say I needed them now. I'll be needing them—for a journey."

And I did not claim to be an astrologer, Gino wanted to say, but he sighed with relief that a sword fight was apparently off the table, for now. Forever, he hoped. He wished he could just walk out, get away from Ottavio and his morose household, and find a way back to Li Galli. Maybe whatever weird whirlpool that sucked him here could also take him back. The bay would be full of tourist boats, and he would be rescued.

When Gino worked parties in Seattle, he found that people paid more attention if he held a steady gaze on them as he spoke. So he faced Ottavio full on, and looked slightly down at him from one step up the stairs. "Signore Ottavio, I will tell you the truth, because unless you know it, I cannot help you at all. I began to study astrology several years ago, but I didn't complete those studies, and instead I began to work as a writer." So far Ottavio tracked with him, looking a little doubtful but staying focused. "I cannot remain here giving you false hope that I will be able to reveal the future to you. I would like to help you, but I do not have the skill."

"You have led me on! Why should I believe you didn't do the same with my daughter—foolish woman that she is?"

"Woman? She is a child, Ottavio. Girls are all foolish at her age."

"A child? She is ripe as a plum, ready to bear children. If I had the dowry for her, if the pestilence had not taken my wife and caused such widespread death and misery, Fiamma would probably be married already. She's just the age a man wants his wife to be."

Gino looked Ottavio straight in the eye again. "Not me, Signore. Such a thing is not done in my country."

Ottavio pulled his head back and tilted it to one side with a skeptical frown. "You would marry an old woman? Are you married, Gino?"

"No, I'm not. But a woman is not old at fifteen, or even twenty years old."

"Not old enough? I'm glad not to be one of your countrymen. My wife was sixteen when we married and ready to be molded to my liking. An older woman is not so pliable, you know."

Gino wasn't prepared to discuss what he knew or didn't know about the pliable natures of women at various ages. "As I say, I have never been married. But when I do, it will not be to a child like Fiamma. I did not seduce her and have no interest in her."

"Ahh, Fiamma." Ottavio locked eyes with him for a long moment, and then sighed heavily. "Very well, then. I believe you, Gino. But did you tell her to kill the rats?"

"No, but I did tell her, as I told you, that the rats are unhealthy. You would do well to get rid of them—you'll be safer from the pestilence if you keep them out of the house."

"But the rats are not diseased. Some of them die, as any creature does, but most are as healthy as I am!"

"They appear to be, Signore Ottavio, but you know things are not always as they appear. You have seen my own efforts to keep the rats out. The danger from them is very real."

"And Fiamma tried to help you because you told her of the danger?" A hint of sympathy crept into his voice.

Gino nodded. "I think so."

Ottavio looked down the narrow hallway, and then pulled the door shut. "I will miss her. She reminds me so much of her mother." He spoke almost absently, and then looked around and seemed surprised to find himself with Gino at the top of the stairs.

The thought of sword fighting was behind them, much to Gino's relief. But now Fiamma occupied his thoughts again. As Ottavio turned to go, Gino said, "Excuse me, Ottavio, but where are you taking Fiamma? Where is this convent?"

"In Amalfi. Not far—a half-day's ride. Now I need to see about the horses."

Ottavio almost reached the great hall at the bottom of the stairs when Gino called down to him. "Could you find an astrologer in Amalfi? And maybe you will find Beppe's son too, and learn what has happened to Alessa's future husband."

"The barons of Amalfi have their own astrologers. I would probably have to go to Salerno to find one, and that is too far to travel these dangerous roads."

"Salerno?" Gino knew Salerno had a bigger port. Perhaps someone would be willing to take him to Li Galli, if they were sailing from Salerno to Naples or Sorrento. "Could I go to Salerno for you? I could try to send back an astrologer who could help you more than I have. And I may be able to get some news of my cousin."

"The man whose boat disappeared at Sirenuse? Don't hold false hope, Signore Gino. If the sirens called him, you won't find him in Salerno."

Gino ran down the stairs to where Ottavio stood. "But I have to try. I need to go back to my home. And I could go with you as far as Amalfi. Wouldn't a bigger group be safer?"

Ottavio wrung his hands and paced, but Gino couldn't tell what troubled him so much. Gino guessed the time as mid-morning, from the slant of the sunlight coming through the shutters. Only two or three hours until Ottavio and Fiamma would be leaving. With the morning's tension easing, Gino's stomach began to growl, but he remained standing at the entrance to the great hall, with the smells of hay and wine barrels drifting up from the ground floor. At least there were no rats in sight.

Ottavio's pacing finally wound toward Gino, and came to a stop. "I will take you with us, but when I leave Amalfi to come home, you will be on your own. If you find an astrologer who wants to come here, I will be grateful, but I have no money to send with you, so I can't really expect that." Ottavio paused, glanced briefly at Gino, and then said, "I suppose I should be glad to get rid of you, bringing such trouble and disappointment as you have."

"You could simply have a fisherman take me out to the islands so I can search for my cousin."

"I would be considered a murderer for leaving you there, to certain death! Even if it is your wish to go."

Gino's shoulders slumped. He had no money or means to hire a boat—and the fishermen here would certainly have more loyalty to Ottavio than to take him. "Amalfi, then."

11. Not every journey ends at the
intended destination.

GINO SAW NO SIGN OF FIAMMA the rest of the
morning, and she didn't come downstairs to eat with the
family at midday. Ottavio gave Gino a leather pouch something
like a medieval messenger bag, and he took it to his room to pack.
He had only the rumpled tunic he'd been wearing to bed and the
linen shirt and pants Ruggero had given him in the tower. He
wondered if he would need a blanket, or if Signore Ottavio would
let him take one. They were so threadbare, Gino would have been
embarrassed to donate them to Goodwill.

He hadn't arrived with much, and as he looked around the
room one last time, he felt a sense of relief, in spite of the fact that
he didn't know where he would be sleeping next. Would there even
be a bed, or a roof over his head? He grabbed the shabby blanket,
folded it as flat as he could, and stuffed it into his bag.

This might be a chance to find his way home, even if they
were going to Amalfi first. With more sea traffic there, he might
get back to Li Galli. Gino started down the stairs with more hope
than he'd had since Ruggero's men dragged him from the sea.

As he entered the great hall, Gino heard male voices that
sounded a little familiar. He heard Ottavio asking about progress
on the tower repairs. Arnaldo answered him, and his brother

Andrea stood beside him, looking around the large room with an admiring smile.

"Signore Gino!" Andrea said, "I'm glad to see you again."

Arnaldo sulked, and Gino wondered what Ottavio had told him. Had Ottavio mentioned Patrizia's accusations? Arnaldo wouldn't like that, and he'd be unhappy about Fiamma leaving for any reason.

"It's good to see you too," Gino said. Then he noticed Anna standing near the door to the kitchen, wearing a sheepish expression. She fidgeted with a small bundle, and took a couple of awkward steps toward Gino. She made a small curtsy and mumbled 'signore' without looking him in the eye.

"Hello, Signora."

She looked down at the floor. "You were probably wondering, my lord…I meant to help you, but…I'm sorry…"

Andrea stepped in and took the small linen bag from her hands. He pulled out what had once been a piece of brilliant blue spandex. Gino lifted it from Andrea's hands. There were scorch marks, and the fabric had melted in a couple of spots, puckering wildly out of shape.

"She tried to wash it, Signore Gino, when she boiled our shirts, and it seemed to get bigger. Then as it dried by the fire…I don't know what happened." Andrea apologized, and Anna looked humiliated by the thought that she had destroyed Gino's mysterious garment.

Gino held up his old Speedo, trying to distinguish the leg holes from the waist, and a smile spread across his face. He snorted softly, and then began to chuckle. "Don't worry about it, Anna. I have another one."

Anna gaped wide-eyed at that, and Gino hurried to add, "Not here—it's at home." She stepped back, skeptical but relieved. Gino laughed again at the image of her stirring his Speedo in the cauldron of boiling water.

"What's this, Gino?" Ottavio sidled up to him, frowning at the wrinkled blue spandex.

"Oh, it's my old clothes," Gino said, tucking it into his leather bag. He turned to Andrea again. "Say hello to Ruggero and the others when you go back."

"We're staying here. Didn't you know? Standing guard and helping Beppe clear out the rats while Signore Ottavio is away."

Ottavio broke in. "And now we must leave. The horses are ready, and Marianna packed us some bread and filled a wineskin for us."

"But where is—" Gino began, but Ottavio interrupted.

"Meeting us outdoors."

Half an hour later, Gino gripped the reins of a brown and white horse with a bad attitude. On the uneven ground, the mare's steps flung Gino from side to side, and with Fiamma on the ridiculous sidesaddle they couldn't go much faster than walking anyway. Gino would have preferred walking to riding this horse with its ears laid back, but after the argument between Ottavio and Fiamma over the sidesaddle, he didn't want to make waves. The sword hindered him in several ways. It dragged him to the left, and the hardened leather scabbard kept hanging up on the back edge of the saddle. He would certainly put a gash in his own leg if he ever had to draw the thing.

They were only a mile or two from the gate of Ottavio's *palazzo* when the road turned to the left, curving around the hogback ridge on which Praiano stood. Gino tried to rein in the mare, but she turned her head toward him and bared her teeth. As he jolted on, Gino turned for a last glimpse of Li Galli. The road curved directly away from the islands, which were soon out of sight.

Ottavio led the way, followed by Fiamma, and then Gino as rear guard. They wound along the coastline, into ravines with trickling creeks shaded from the sun, then back onto the stony hillsides covered with shrubby bushes. There were plenty of spots where bandits could hide, but houses were spaced pretty regularly along the way, too, with lemon and olive trees planted on the steep slopes. Even the vegetable gardens were terraced so steeply that Gino saw a man standing on one terrace and tending the plants on the level above him, about waist high.

At midafternoon, they were high above Conca dei Marini, and they took a break in the shade of an olive grove. Ottavio shaded his eyes, searching for a glimpse of Amalfi from various spots nearby.

"There it is, Gino," he called, pointing down the coast. "The ride will be easier once we descend a little."

Gino leaned against a tree, pulling one knee and then the other to his chest in hopes of unkinking his back. "How much longer?"

"We'll be there before dark, and we'll get a good meal at the convent. There should be news, too, from other travelers."

Fiamma glared at her father, then turned away from them to lay down on her cloak, spread like a picnic blanket under an olive tree. Some of her hair escaped from the little crocheted bag she had tucked it in, and the wisps curled around her face. Even with a scowl, her beauty radiated. But he still couldn't think of her as a woman, as Ottavio did.

Ottavio tore chunks from a loaf of bread for each of them, and passed Gino a wineskin. Then he walked to the edge of a ravine a few yards away to relieve himself.

"Gino," Fiamma whispered, the first words she had spoken for hours. Gino turned, but she kept her eyes on her father. "Take me back with you, Gino. I'll help you get back to the islands, and go to live in your land. Don't leave me in the convent." Her whisper faded as she took her bread and bit into it. Gino heard Ottavio tramping back through the grass.

"So you've decided to speak again?"

She turned a sullen gaze on her father. "I asked for a drink," she said, sticking her hand out to Gino. He passed her the wineskin.

✻ ✻ ✻

The sun nearly touched the western sea by the time Ottavio stood at the gate of the convent just outside Amalfi, waiting for a reply to his knocking. Gino wanted to dismount too. His hips felt all but dislocated, and he couldn't tell if he still had use of his feet. But Ottavio shook his head, so Gino waited in the saddle, squirming and aggravating the horse.

Gino hated the look of disdain Ottavio cast on Fiamma. He gripped the reins of her horse as if she might gallop away to escape her fate.

Fiamma bit her lip and shifted in the saddle. She glanced from one gate to another up and down the street. Was she hoping to find an escape route? Her eyes glistened, but somehow she kept the tears from falling, and Gino felt a surge of pity. He began to hope that no one would come to the gate.

When no one answered his knock, Ottavio banged his fist against the gate, then spied a rope hanging over the crossbeam. "This should do," he said, giving it a yank. A bell clanged on the other side, and Ottavio rang it a second time, and shouted over the wall, "Travelers need your hospitality, Sisters."

"Patience," a husky voice replied, but instead of the gate, a tiny window within the gate opened to reveal a doughy face with a mustache that would answer the prayers of an adolescent boy. But this face wore the headgear of a nun, and her shifting gaze took them in with suspicion.

"We need lodging and an evening meal, Sister," Ottavio said in a voice a full octave higher than the woman at the gate.

"I am sorry, signori, but we have no food and cannot take in guests this night."

"But I am seeking a place in your community for my dear youngest daughter." Ottavio's head bobbed and his Adam's apple slid up and down as he spoke. Fiamma caught Gino's eye, and he glimpsed the hope on her face.

The mustached woman turned her face in the small opening, and stared for a moment at Fiamma, who gazed steadily back at her. "She has a calling to serve God?" the woman asked with obvious skepticism.

"She has a need to be protected from the world."

"And she has no dowry to protect her?"

"What is that to you?" Ottavio sputtered. "I would speak to your abbess about it."

"You are right, signore, to ask for the abbess, but she cannot attend. She is taken ill, like so many in these hard days."

Ottavio stepped back two steps, then another, before squeaking his one-word question. "Pestilence?"

"I cannot say, signore, but she's abed, and two of the other sisters as well."

Ottavio scrambled onto his horse before she finished speaking, and turned abruptly to retrace their steps.

"God's blessing, signori," the deep voice muttered wearily, and the little window slammed shut.

Ottavio rambled about the pestilence as he rode back the way they had come. "We passed the monastery, should have stopped there first," he said, glancing anxiously at the sun sinking into the sea. It wasn't far, and they didn't have to wait, because one of the monks peered out into the street as they approached.

"Brother, we seek your hospitality for the night. Myself and my daughter, and a Calabrian traveler."

"Greetings in the name of our Lord, and I'm sorry to say we have every corner filled tonight. So many of the lodgings have closed you know, with the pestilence, and crop failures. I wish you God's blessing, but I've just returned myself from trying to buy more food, and we haven't enough for the guests who are already here, even with the brothers fasting for their sake." The man backed through the gate, closing the gap as he spoke, until it closed tight, and a bolt slid into place with finality.

As the daylight faded, they could barely see one another or the street before them. Like Praiano, Amalfi lay against a steep hillside, and the zigzag roads were a tangle of hairpin turns and narrow alleys. Ottavio led the way down from the upper edge of the town, letting the horse feel the way slowly in the darkness. They seemed to be wandering.

Gino cleared his throat. "Do you know of another place to try?"

Ottavio said nothing, but continued down the hill toward the more densely built up area of the city.

After a few moments, Fiamma spoke up. "Father, what about Uncle—"

"No!" Ottavio yelped. They continued in tense silence to the next tight curve. Gino wracked his brain but could not remember any mention of an uncle. Then Fiamma spoke so softly that Gino barely heard her.

"But is there anywhere else to go?"

✳ ✳ ✳

The dark square before them lay silent. Ottavio stared at the palazzo looming three stories high across the cobbles, chewing his lower lip while he rearranged his grip on his horse's reins. Gino looked back at Fiamma. She watched her father intently, almost holding her breath. All three startled and the horses shied sideways when the gate banged open matched by a burst of harsh laughter. Two men stood in the open gateway, and the shorter one pushed a torch higher and peered out.

"There are latecomers in your piazza, Don Carlo," the short man said.

Ottavio pulled the reins and his horse stepped back into deeper shadow. In a low voice he said, "We shouldn't be here." Fiamma reached for him, and her whispered reply was interrupted.

"Who goes?" the taller man called, and another man stepped into the circle of light, his hand on the hilt of his sword.

To Gino's surprise, Ottavio urged his horse forward a couple of steps, leaving Fiamma reaching for his arm. "Carlo?" His voice quavered.

The tall man put a hand out to restrain the swordsman, and then took a step closer. "Ottavio? Is that you?"

"It is."

"It's your voice I hear, but come closer, brother. Let me have a look. Enzo, bring another torch."

Ottavio dismounted, and indicated with a nod that Fiamma and Gino should do the same. He crossed the square like it was a frozen pond he doubted would hold his weight, with Fiamma at his side, each leading a horse.

Gino had no chance to ask questions. This must be the uncle Fiamma had mentioned, but why was Ottavio so tense? As they came closer to the gate, Enzo arrived with the second torch, and Gino took a closer look at Ottavio's brother.

The two were nearly the same height, with the long neck and rounded head of some forebear they shared. Carlo had thick hair flowing from under a velvet cap and cut blunt at the shoulder, more muscle on his frame, and a long wool cape held by a brooch with two jewels that gleamed in the torchlight. With just a glance from Carlo, his guard placed the torches into standards on the wall. The short man who had spoken first now frowned deeply as he stared at Fiamma. But Carlo leered at her with a half smile.

"I see you've brought your daughter, Ottavio. That is a convenience I did not expect. My brother saved you the trouble of fetching her, eh Tomasso?"

For the first time, Ottavio took his eyes off his brother, and jerked his head to stare at the shorter man. "Tomasso!" Ottavio's mouth fell open, and he sputtered but no more words came out.

"My lord," Tomasso said, turning to Carlo and shaking his head, "this is not…"

But Carlo wasn't listening. Instead, he gloated in some triumph that Gino failed to grasp. Gino turned to Ottavio, and recognized fear on his face, and in his shaking hands. What kind of bad blood had come between them?

"Here is my long-lost older brother, and I am keeping him standing at the street." Gino could hear the sarcasm in Carlo's voice. "Come into my home—you know it as well as I do! And a special welcome to your beautiful daughter Alessa. Tomasso, you were too modest in your description of her."

"No, Don Carlo, I tell you, that is not her. That is not Lady Alessa," Tomasso hissed.

"Not Alessa?" Carlo turned to Ottavio, his eyes narrowed. "Who is she, then?"

"I present my daughter, Lady Fiamma, my youngest," Ottavio said with a slight stiff bow, and Fiamma dipped in a brief curtsey.

"Fiamma." Carlo's enthusiasm suddenly turned to vinegar.

Carlo waved them all through the gate, where a boy took charge of the horses. Gino tried to get his bearings, glad to be ignored in the hostilities. A crest similar to the one over Ottavio's gate hung above the door, sporting fresh paint. If Ottavio was the older brother, why had Carlo inherited the family home?

A servant held the door open to them all, and Carlo watched with a half smile as they entered a great hall with geometric marble paving like the Cosmati tile work Gino had seen in churches, and heavy tapestries on the walls. Clearly, Don Carlo had the money in the family.

Ottavio faced Carlo as the door closed behind them. "We seek shelter for the night only. We arrived late and could find no other place. Could I find one night's rest in my ancestral home?"

"So you were not bringing Lady Alessa for the marriage you arranged?"

Ottavio's face reddened. "What is my daughter's marriage to you, Carlo?" He flung an arm toward Tomasso. "And why should I bring her when I had no word whether you lived or died with the pestilence? You didn't have the decency to send word, no reply to my messages?" Veins stood out along his temples, and his gangly arm felt for his sword.

Tomasso began to speak, but Carlo cut him off.

"Naturally I was concerned, brother, when your servant came to Amalfi asking after Tomasso's welfare. Enzo, bring him here."

"My servant?"

"Orso, he calls himself, and claims that you sent him. Did you not?"

"I did not send him to *you*, but to Tomasso. Have you harmed him?"

Don Carlo laughed with a soft snort. "Do you always think I mean you harm, brother?"

Ottavio hardened his gaze at Carlo. "I have reason enough."

Watching the brothers spar, Gino's wariness grew. In his weeks at Praiano, Ottavio's dealings with him had always been straightforward, even when they disagreed. But some undercurrent of ill intent swirled from Carlo, the sly fox, setting Gino's nerves jangling.

The guard returned, holding a burly young man by the arm.

"Orso, what befell you? We have worried for days." Ottavio stepped forward to put a fatherly hand on his arm, and looked him over.

Gino looked him over too. Beppe's son had his father's thick brows and bear-like build, the appearance that must have earned him his name. Orso glared at the guard, jerked his arm free, and rubbed at his wrists. A bruise faded to yellow on one cheek, at least a couple of days old, and his dirty shirt gaped from a torn seam.

"Signore Ottavio, I'm sorry. I fell into their trap." He glared at Don Carlo and Tomasso.

Ottavio turned to his brother and stretched himself up to his full height. "See here. What are you doing holding my man captive, and what is your business with my daughter's betrothed?"

"This is precisely the question I planned to discuss with you in Praiano, but you have saved me the journey." Carlo now sounded smooth and conciliatory. He gestured to a servant who trotted off without a word. "Let us sit and share a cup of wine as brothers. I have a proposal I hope you will consider."

Judging by the way things had gone so far, Gino doubted Ottavio's interest in anything Carlo suggested. It seemed he hadn't planned to visit his brother at all on this visit to Amalfi. But they sat at benches around a long wooden table and the servant soon returned with cups of wine for everyone. Don Carlo sat at the head of the table, in a chair with the family crest carved into the back. Ottavio sat on a bench to his left, and Fiamma stayed next to her father. Tomasso sat to the right of Don Carlo.

In the tense quiet, Gino noticed there were servants quietly working around the hall. One built up the fire, and another lit a lamp hanging over the table on a long chain. Even Carlo's servants wore better clothes than Ottavio, with none of the stains and patches that were common in the Praiano household.

A tiny old woman carried out a tray of cold meats and set it in front of Ottavio. Gino saw a flash of recognition pass between them, and tears welled up in the woman's eyes as she turned away. Ottavio shifted on the bench and watched her until she disappeared through a doorway. The woman looked ten or fifteen years older than Ottavio. Who could she be? Then Gino noticed Don Carlo's expression—a smug half-smile as he enjoyed Ottavio's pain.

When Gino slid onto the bench next to Fiamma, Don Carlo seemed to notice him for the first time, and he smirked.

"Ottavio, do you welcome your servants at your high table?"

"My servants? You are mistaken. This is Don Gino of Calabria, a guest with me lately."

"Don Gino, my apologies, but your clothing led me to believe…but never mind."

With no idea what to say, Gino simply nodded in acknowledgement. He sensed no good will from Carlo, and doubted the wisdom of spending the night in his home, regardless of Ottavio's family connection.

"Don Gino met with an accident before arriving at my house, and we provided him such garments as we could spare. If my fortunes were better…" Ottavio's voice trailed off, and he looked into his cup of wine and took a swallow.

Don Carlo waved a hand toward Enzo, who stood at the end of the table with Orso, waiting to do Carlo's bidding. "Take that boy out to the kitchen," Carlo said with a frown.

"Wait, brother!" Ottavio bumped the table as he half-stood and reached toward Orso. "I want him here in my sight. Can you spare him a seat at the far end of the table?"

Gino glanced from Ottavio to Carlo and back to Ottavio, who clearly mistrusted his brother as much as Gino did.

Finally, Carlo relented. "Very well, if you insist. Enzo, you join us too—my retainer, brother, as you can see from his manner and dress, not a servant." Carlo cut a slice from the roast, rolled it neatly, and ate it in two quick bites, licking up a bit that stuck to his finger. Then he put his hand on Ottavio's arm. "But you mentioned your fortunes. Perhaps your tide will turn."

Ottavio waited with a wary look while Carlo washed the meat down with wine.

The sight and smell of meat made Gino salivate, stomach rumbling. He pulled a chunk from a loaf of bread. The others cut slices of the roast with their personal knives, but he had no knife. Gino felt the wine warming and relaxing him, soothing the ache in his butt and thighs from the miserable hours on horseback. Then Don Carlo's voice brought his attention back to the brothers.

Don Carlo spoke as though there was no one else in the room. "My wife, Donna Sofia, is barren these many years, brother. We have produced no heir for all the blessings that God has seen fit to give us, not even a daughter."

Gino took another look around the room. Would Ottavio inherit this home if Carlo died without an heir? Fresh straw mixed with lavender covered the floor, and lamplight revealed the room's tapestries, cushioned benches, and brass studded chests. Was this really Ottavio's childhood home? How had he fallen to the level of the broken-down, rat-infested house in Praiano? Maybe some of that was Carlo's doing.

"A few weeks ago, in the course of some other business, Tomasso mentioned to me his betrothal to your—to Lady Alessa. Naturally your family's welfare interested me, brother."

Ottavio braided his fingers and began to twist his hands. "It has never troubled you before," he said. His jaw twitched as Carlo continued.

"Lady Alessa's dowry is so small, and Tomasso is concerned that you may not have found matches for your other daughters."

Ottavio leaned toward Carlo, lifting himself off the bench. "You beggared us yourself! When the earthquake destroyed the harbor in Amalfi, you could have sent ships to Praiano, but no! For two years everything you controlled went to Salerno. And you wonder that my daughters have no dowries?"

"I am ready to make amends, brother."

"You are ready to help only yourself, as you always have. Perhaps you have fathered a bastard somewhere who can be made your heir. Otherwise your wealth, and this house, will come to me when you are gone. I'm sure you pray that won't happen!" Ottavio swallowed more wine and wiped his mouth with his sleeve.

Carlo looked at him intently and nodded. "Yes, I do have one bastard child, a daughter." Carlo paused, then leaned close to Ottavio. "You know it's true, and you know her well."

Ottavio backed away, shifting his body as if to shield Fiamma from Carlo. Fiamma watched the exchange slack-jawed. Across the table, Tomasso's eager face suggested he knew Carlo's plan. Despite his hunger, the roiling in Gino's gut would not tolerate food as he watched the tension thicken between brothers.

Ottavio's voice softened to a pleading tone. "No, Carlo, don't do this wicked thing. Find another heir. Take one of your retainers, or a servant. There are foundlings aplenty. Haven't you done me harm enough?"

The weakness in his voice only urged Carlo on. He answered in a hoarse whisper. "You took what I wanted, don't you remember?" Carlo's eyes hardened. "The woman I wanted."

"She chose, Carlo. That's all behind us, years ago. And she's gone now, dead with the pestilence" Ottavio crossed himself. "Leave her memory in peace."

"She chose unwisely, brother."

"And she paid for it! If you had cared for her. . ." Ottavio's voice broke.

Fiamma gripped Gino's hand, not flirting this time. Her hand trembled. She seemed as ignorant of this old rivalry as Gino himself, and more frightened by it. Gino glanced at the door, wishing he could draw Ottavio and Fiamma back into the street and seek somewhere else—anywhere—for them to stay.

Carlo smirked and sliced off another bit of meat. "I only showed her what she would be missing—even though she fought the lesson."

Fiamma winced, and Gino felt a shudder. Was it hers or his own?

Carlo's gaze softened to a wistful smile. He might have been remembering a pleasant romance of his youth. Then the look vanished, and he turned a hard eye on Ottavio again. "You surprised me, brother, taking her to wife after I sowed my seed in her."

"And may God damn you for it!"

12. Can a stranger bring an end to a family feud?

GINO COULD HARDLY BELIEVE THIS. Carlo had raped Ottavio's wife? Raped, for God's sake! No wonder Ottavio hated and feared him, despite their shared blood. And what offer did Carlo have in mind now?

Fiamma leaned against Gino, tense as a guitar string, and he heard her whisper, "Mama." Gino saw a tear run from the corner of her eye. He put a hand on her back, wary of Ottavio's anger, but Ottavio focused on his brother. Carlo turned his head from one side to the other, and shrugged his shoulders like Gino did when he'd sat too long at his laptop. Ottavio slumped, head in his hands, the picture of defeat.

Carlo tore a chunk of bread from the loaf and paused with it halfway to his mouth. "You see, I only claim what has been mine all along."

"You will ruin her, putting abroad that she is a bastard!"

"Perhaps better a bastard to a rich man than a daughter to you." Carlo chuckled softly. "But I do not propose to ruin her. I could adopt a niece, it's not unheard of. Nothing need be said publicly. Then she would inherit from me."

"And I would not."

"Well, if you insist upon selfishness." With a smirk on his face, Carlo leaned toward Ottavio. "But one daughter would be a wealthy woman. And she would know the truth."

"And if I don't want her to know the truth, then she is simply the poor girl she has always been."

"Oh, no, brother." Carlo's harsh laugh echoed on the stone walls. "She *will* know the truth. And bastard children sometimes win an inheritance, but if you deny me my own daughter, I can find another heir. That was your advice to me, was it not? Maybe adopt Enzo here, or even Tomasso, no matter that he is near my own age."

Tomasso laughed nervously but still watched Carlo with caution.

Fiamma touched her father's arm. "Let's go, Father," she whispered.

"Surely you will stay the night, at least." Don Carlo leered at Fiamma, and turned back to Ottavio. "I insist. You all seem weary, and I have a room for you with pallets and a warm fire. Have some more to eat, more wine, and we'll talk again in the morning."

Ottavio turned to Fiamma and Gino. "I'm sorry I brought you here, even for one night." At the end of the table, Orso seemed ready to bolt from Carlo's hospitality.

"I would rather sleep in a field!" Fiamma whispered.

"Can we find a safe place anywhere else?" Gino wondered how dangerous it might be to sleep under the stars if the four of them were together, but his thoughts were interrupted when Carlo stood.

"I will speed your decision along, brother, so preparations can be made. I have locked my outer gates and do not intend to open them until morning. Here is a board to take, as you have eaten almost nothing," Carlo said, picking up a wooden tray. He took his knife and speared through several slices of meat, moved them to the tray, and set the remaining bread on top. "Tomasso, carry this and follow me."

So they were locked in now, Gino thought as they pushed back the benches, guests in Carlo's prison. The loud scraping on the tiles echoed in his head, and Gino realized he had a major headache. There was more scuffling when Orso pulled away from Enzo.

Carlo led them up a flight of stairs. Ottavio slipped near Fiamma. "We should not have come here. Tomorrow we'll go home."

But Gino could see that Carlo held all the cards. Would he let them go home tomorrow? Or would Carlo keep them until Alessa—his own daughter—could be brought to Amalfi to spite Ottavio? For a man who considered rape a casual thing, perhaps the murder of his brother wasn't such a stretch.

They would need to find a way to escape his grip—and the odds were against them. Three travelers against Carlo's house full of servants and retainers.

Carlo stopped at a doorway, and when Ottavio saw it, his eyes narrowed.

"Yes, brother, it is our old room." Carlo enjoyed his own cruelty for a moment longer, and then herded them all inside.

The room, about fifteen-by-fifteen feet, had only straw-filled pallets on the floor. A disappointment, as Gino had hoped for a comfortable bed after riding that horse most of the day. The one tall window was shuttered for the night, and a fire burning in the corner fireplace gave a little heat and light. At the near end of the row of pallets, Tomasso placed the tray of food on a large flat-topped storage chest.

As Tomasso left the room, he whispered something to Carlo. Carlo told him to wait downstairs, and then turned back to Ottavio.

"I am leaving two servants here at your door. Ask them for anything you need. And tomorrow we can go to the town hall together, and arrange for Alessa's adoption." Carlo turned and left the room, laughing as Ottavio swore at him.

Gino took in the servants. More like guards, he thought. They had daggers in their belts, and looked prepared to use them. They sat on a bench in the hall opposite the "guest room" and one of them took a small piece of wood from a pouch and started carving on it with a short blade. As Carlo's steps faded down the stairs, Ottavio pushed the door shut.

"Ha, look at this," Ottavio said, pointing to the edge of the door.

Gino saw that the latch had been removed—recently, by the look of the wood. They couldn't keep anyone out. But how could they *get* out? With all that had gone wrong today, Gino kept thinking of Sara—her work investigating insurance fraud, and how animated she became when she talked about solving those puzzles. He wished he had her help getting out of this mess, but he'd have to do that on his own.

Ottavio turned and leaned against the door, his eyes closed. In the dim firelight, he looked exhausted, and Gino could feel the weariness in his own bones. Fiamma took the cloak from her shoulders and held it open near the fire to warm it. Then she wrapped it around herself and sat on the pallet farthest from the door. She tugged off her shoes and rubbed her feet.

"I'll stay here next to you," Ottavio said to her, tossing his cloak down on the next pallet. This left room for Gino and Orso, but separated them from Fiamma, which suited Gino just fine, although the conversation between Ottavio and Carlo had taken the spunk out of her. Orso checked the fire, glancing with suspicion at Gino a couple of times. Would Orso help him if he found a way to escape?

Gino looked at the window, set high in the wall. He touched the lower sill, about four feet from the floor. Could they get away without being seen?

"Signore Ottavio, is this window on an outside wall?"

Ottavio shook his head. "It looks down on the courtyard where we came in."

Gino opened the latch, pulled back one shutter, and hiked himself up to lean out. Below the twenty-foot drop, he could make out the shapes of two dogs the size of ponies that lay on the ground looking up at him. One gave a low growl. He hoped to see a ledge that would allow them to get past the dogs, but the darkness revealed nothing.

Gino dropped back to the floor and scanned the room for something that might help them escape. There were blankets on the pallets, but the fabric didn't look strong enough to tie end to end securely. And if they got down into the courtyard, could they get out of the locked gates before the dogs woke Carlo—or attacked them?

"You lived here, Ottavio. Is there a way to get out? What do you remember?"

"I remember my brother." Ottavio looked like he might fling himself out the window just to end it all. "He always gave the orders, threatening me, forcing me to obey him. Nothing has changed. And now he will bring this shame on Alessa too!"

Gino wanted to shake him out of his despondency. "But Ottavio, you did *get* away before, and made a life for yourself in Praiano. We can do it again. The four of us must be able to get out of here."

Ottavio stared at the floor, lost in some grim memory. Finally Gino put a hand on his arm.

"What will become of your daughters if you don't get away from him?"

At that Ottavio looked up at Gino, and then to Orso. "But what should I do?"

"You know this house. How can we get out?"

Orso cleared his throat softly. "Someone here would help you, Signore. They call her Betta, the old woman who served at table tonight."

Ottavio's eyes flashed hopeful for a moment.

"Who is she?" Gino asked, looking from Ottavio to Orso. Orso spoke first.

"When I arrived in Amalfi and found Tomasso's house, he persuaded me to stay a few days, saying he would travel back to Praiano with me after he finished some business. He put me to work around his house, in his garden, and mending a stone wall. After a week, I spoke of returning, but he kept putting it off. He said he had preparations to make for his wedding to Alessa. When two more days went by, I told him I must leave for Praiano. He was angry, and said I must wait for him, but I refused to wait longer than the next morning. I wanted to come home sooner, Signore, but I thought you would want me to bring him to you if I could."

"Of course, you did well." Ottavio frowned. "But how did you come to be here at my brother's house."

"I had never heard you speak of your brother, Signore, but… " Orso paused and looked sheepishly at Ottavio. "Some said your family had renounced you, though you have always been good to me and my father." Orso paused.

Gino's mind focused on escape. "What about the old woman?"

Apparently, Ottavio wondered too. He bobbed his head impatiently.

"That night, as I slept by the hearth in Tomasso's house, two or three men approached me by stealth, and put a bag over my head. They tied me with ropes and carried me to a cart. I could see nothing, but the cart traveled some distance—all within the city, by the feel of the roads. Then we stopped, and the men hauled me indoors and dropped me on the floor of a tiny room. They pulled the bag off my head, but before I could see anything, they slammed and locked the door."

Gino became aware of a soft snoring, and looked around to see Fiamma with her mouth slightly open, and all the anxiety gone from her face. Orso noticed too, and continued in a softer voice.

"I managed to sit up, with my hands still bound. After some time—I couldn't say how much—the latch slipped and the door opened slowly. It was that woman, Betta, looking this way and that to be sure no one saw her, bringing me some bread. She had an odd way of talking all the time without saying anything to me. As she muttered, I heard her say your name, and I began to listen better. She said they never treated you well, and that she would take care of me even if Don Carlo meant to starve me, she would see that 'Ottavio's man,' as she called me, had a crust in his belly. Then she cursed Don Carlo for a wicked man, and that he deserved all the punishments of hell for his wickedness. Then she said…" Orso paused and looked from Ottavio to Gino and back, then leaned forward slightly and whispered. "…she said she would do anything to have you for a master rather than Don Carlo."

Gino grabbed Ottavio's shoulder. "You see, we have an ally!"

"No, not that. I can't put her in danger." Ottavio shook his head, then leaned close to Gino. "And there are two men in the hall blocking our way to her!"

In the silence that followed, they could hear the low voices of the guards in the hall. Orso shook his head. "Maybe there is no way out," he said, and went to the pallet farthest from Fiamma. He pulled a blanket around himself and stretched out.

"How can you give up so easily?" Gino tried to shake off his tension and anger. He leaned against the wall by the window, looking up at the stars and wishing for once that he could really find something useful there.

✷ ✷ ✷

Sara peered out the car window at the sign in the window across the street. *Elizabeth Hayes, Psychic Readings.* She'd hit the road before nine to get to Bellingham. Sara didn't want to risk being seen by anyone she knew, visiting a psychic in Seattle. She took the day off work, saying she had a few more things to clear up for Gino's family. Magarry was very understanding. Fifteen minutes early for her appointment, she sat in her car taking deep breaths, trying to relax.

She'd had a good feeling about Elizabeth Hayes when she saw her professional looking website. And she had such a normal name. That had a strong appeal these days for Sara, whose sense of normalcy had vanished in a flash of lightning a couple of weeks ago. Elizabeth sounded very businesslike on the phone. Now she had to go inside and sit and tell the whole crazy story. At five to eleven, she grabbed the tote bag on the passenger seat and opened the car door.

The storefront windows were opaque glass most of the way up, and a lacy valance covered the clear glass at the top. A distant bell rang as she pushed the door open, and she heard footsteps approaching. The waiting area exuded professional calm, furnished with three chairs, a lush plant, and a stack of travel magazines. Maybe most people who waited here wished they were somewhere else.

The door had barely closed behind her when Elizabeth Hayes came around the partition with a cheerful, "Hello, you must be Sara. Would you like some tea? Coffee?"

Her greeting put Sara at ease. She was older than Sara would have guessed from the website photo, probably close to sixty, with hair cropped short, and nearly six feet tall. Sara followed her around a partition and chose Earl Grey from a basket of tea bags next to a water dispenser for hot and cold water. She dropped the tea bag into a mug of steaming water, and Elizabeth opened an office door.

"Come in and have a seat. So you have a missing person to find?"

Sara had said that much on the phone, trying to keep the story as simple as possible until they met in person. Now she set her mug on an end table and sat on the overstuffed love seat, keeping her tote bag at her side.

"Yes, he's been missing since early June."

Elizabeth sat in a chair that matched the love seat, and leaned attentively toward Sara. "And how do you know the missing man, and when did you last see him?"

"We met in May at a party, and I agreed to take care of his cat while he took a trip. I last saw him the day he left."

"So you'd been dating just a short time—"

"We weren't dating," Sara said, cutting her off with a stronger protest than she intended. "Just friends. He traveled to Italy for a family visit, and he disappeared from his cousin's boat."

She raised her eyebrows. "In Italy?"

"Yes," Sara said, fidgeting with the handle of her tote. "They were sailing along the Amalfi Coast, and he went swimming, and disappeared. They searched for several days, up and down the coast—his cousins told me. Now they've stopped searching, but…" Sara reached for a Kleenex, and fought back the lump in her throat.

Elizabeth cocked her head with interest. "You don't believe he drowned? Why not?"

Sara forced herself to continue. "Because…because I keep having visions of him, and I'm sure he's still alive." Elizabeth said nothing. "I've had visions like this most of my life. And they've always been true, but my family never wanted to hear about them. I learned to ignore them pretty well." Elizabeth showed no sign of skepticism, and Sara told her about her sister, and the psychologist who treated her after her sister's death.

"Describe to me what you have seen in your recent visions," Elizabeth said, leaning back in her chair. "Maybe we can make some sense of them together."

Sara told her about the stone room, and the sense that Gino was in trouble, maybe in a prison. "I'm so worried about him, I tried to focus on him more to see if another vision might come, you know, to give me more information. I never did that before. Then last night, when I turned off a lamp, the bulb popped with a little flash, and another vision came. He was with two men and a girl, running along a trail at the top of a steep bank. Running away from something. They seemed afraid, and…I don't know why, but I think they were going south. Seems weird, but I just have that feeling."

"No, that's good to know." Elizabeth spoke in a matter-of-fact tone that Sara found comforting. "You said you had something that belonged to him? Did you bring it with you?"

Sara reached into her tote bag. "This. I gave him this book to read on the trip. He had started it—there were pages folded over where he'd marked his place."

"You're sure he read it, not his cousin?"

"No, his cousin doesn't speak English."

Elizabeth took the book and held it, closed, running her hands over the cover. She looked out the window, where the branches of a weeping birch swayed in a light breeze. "Yes," she murmured, and blinked her eyes slowly before looking down at the book again. "You've been reading it too?"

"Yes." Sara felt a sudden panic. "Did that mess it up, whatever you might learn from it?"

"No, not at all." She set the book in her lap. "What else do you have there?"

Sara handed her the cameo. "He bought it in Italy. His parents found a note to me in the box, so they sent it to me."

"Ah, a gift for you."

"Yes, the carving is a siren. We had a little personal joke about that."

Elizabeth handed the cameo back, and Sara took it, a little disappointed that no revelations seemed to be forthcoming.

"You said you had a map of the area where he traveled?"

Sara pulled out the map of southern Italy and followed the highlighted line Gino had drawn marking the route they planned to sail. "They took off down here from Sicily, and this–" Her finger slid along the line to Li Galli. "This is where he went missing. Praiano, here, is where they were headed that night."

"That's good. He marked this line on the map himself?" She peered intently at the islands.

"Yes."

"Interesting. The line breaks there, right next to the islands."

Sara frowned and looked closer. "What do you mean?"

"See, it's not one smooth line. It's two separate pen strokes, like he drew one line up to here, then lifted the marker, and put it down again to continue."

"Does that mean something?"

Elizabeth shrugged. "Maybe not, but maybe so." She pulled the map nearer to her, and ran her hand over the line, the islands, and the coast near Praiano, much as she had done with the book cover.

Sara watched her face, every little flex in her jaw and watched her gaze roam around the room as her hands moved across the map, and then back to the book in her lap.

"I'm glad you brought the map. You mentioned that you saw him going south. What is south of the islands and Praiano?"

Sara shifted the map to see it better. "There's Amalfi, pretty close." She checked the distance scale on the map. "About five or six miles. Farther south is Salerno. About another ten miles. Oh! Isn't that...?" She peered at the book in the psychic's lap. "The guy who wrote that book is from Salerno, isn't he?"

Elizabeth looked down and nodded. She frowned and turned the book over, reading the back cover blurb about Niccolo of Salerno. When she finished, she wrapped her long fingers around the book again, and closed her eyes.

Sara held her breath for fear of breaking the fierce concentration on Elizabeth's face. The few moments seemed to last an hour, and Elizabeth opened her eyes again, glanced at Sara, and looked back at the book, scanning the first few pages with some impatience.

"Is something wrong?"

Elizabeth looked up at her. "I have to tell you, this is very unusual. I do get a strong sense of your friend's presence with this book, but it's more than that." She held the book up so the cover faced Sara. "I feel very certain that your friend and this astrologer know—or knew—one another."

Sara looked from the cover to Elizabeth's face. "What? That guy lived six hundred years ago." It made no sense.

Elizabeth just nodded, looking as perplexed as Sara felt.

"Do you think Gino was reincarnated from him or something like that?"

"No. But I think this book has some answers for you. I'm not sure what they will be." Elizabeth handed the book back to her.

Sara took the book, looked at it with a frown, and sat back in the love seat. "That's it? How can that even be possible?"

"I'm sorry, I really don't know. But my sense of it is very strong."

Sara picked up the book, then looked back at the psychic who reminded her of a college professor she had really liked. Was the woman a fake, in spite of her solid appearance? "Your sense of it? That seems pretty vague. Isn't there some kind of scene you can describe to me?"

Elizabeth smiled slightly, looking a little sad. "My psychic sense doesn't come in visions, like yours. That kind of clairvoyance is actually pretty rare." She leaned forward and put a reassuring hand on Sara's arm. "But I can tell you, I'm as confident of the sense I have as you are of your visions."

✶ ✶ ✶

Sara dodged through the I-5 traffic and got back to Seattle before four o'clock. The book lay on the seat beside her, drawing her hand over and over again like a magnet as she wondered what else she would find there. Had she missed something? Nothing in the sixty pages she'd read so far had answered any of her questions about Gino. And what kind of a crackpot suggestion was it, anyway, that Niccolo of Salerno and Gino knew each other? Niccolo lived in the Middle Ages, and might have been an astrologer for some queen. Somewhere in the book, Sara had seen a woodcut picture of her castle.

As that image came to her, just a few blocks from home, she remembered her first vision of Gino, and the stone walls and men with knives. Nothing could have looked more medieval. But if Gino had somehow time warped back to the 1300s—still an unthinkable idea—how could she possibly find him? Her hope of helping Gino melted into despair.

Then the vision of Magarry came back to her, looking like he'd died. He was right here in Seattle. Could she warn him, and somehow keep that vision from coming true?

She jerked the car against the curb and blindly stuffed the book, map, and her sunglasses into her bag. She swallowed the lump in her throat for Gino and clenched her jaw. I will not give up, she thought to herself, ready to call Britt and tell her about the psychic.

As she stepped onto the sidewalk, she noticed a man standing at her front door. The last person in the world she expected to see. She stopped cold.

"Dad?"

He turned toward her, watchful. "Sara."

How long had it been? Five years? "What's wrong, Dad?"

"Nothing's wrong. I'm fine." He paused and brushed wisps of his thinning hair away from his face. "Your mother's doing okay."

A panicky thought rose in Sara. "Where did you leave her?" she asked, glancing around for what might be his car.

"I didn't bring her with me. No, she can't. She doesn't travel any more. I got somebody to stay with her."

Sara stepped forward slowly, the strangeness of the day weighing on her. "I'll get the door." She fumbled with her keys, and pushed through the door ahead of him. "Come in. I'll get us some coffee." She dropped her tote bag and purse in the kitchen, and caught Houdini as he headed for the door.

"You got a cat. You like cats now?"

Sara pushed the door shut with her foot, feeling eight years old again, having to remind her distracted father that she existed. "You're thinking of Marie. She didn't like cats, Dad. But I just got this one a few days ago." She let Houdini go and ran water into the coffee carafe. Her father stood looking around her apartment. Why was he here? "Did Paul talk to you?"

"Your mother wanted me to come up and see you."

Sara stopped pouring water into the coffeemaker and stared at him. She hadn't seen her mother in five years, and didn't miss her. At least, she didn't miss the prying questions, the insistence that Sara get psychiatric help for imagined mental illness, the paranoid ideas that kept her mother living in fear. By the time Sara finished high school, years had passed since she'd heard a kind word or felt any gentle comfort in her mother's touch. She couldn't keep the suspicion out of her voice. "Why?"

Her father looked shaky, and pulled one of the kitchen chairs out and sat down. "She said you needed help."

"She said—what help does she think I need?" How could she know anything about my life? Sara's thoughts flew like startled birds, until her father spoke again.

"She's been talking about it for two or three weeks, 'Sara's in some trouble. Sara's having a hard time. Sara's been crying again.' She never could explain anything more, but I thought I should come and see you anyway." He looked at his hands, the bookshelf, and out the window, then in her general direction. "It's been so long."

No kidding. "Did she talk to Paul? Has he visited lately?" Maybe Paul had called them after he stayed with her. He might have mentioned Gino, but that really wouldn't be like him. But maybe he told them about her vision at the club. She felt too shaky to drink coffee, but finally got the coffeemaker started in case her dad wanted a cup.

"I called Paul yesterday to get your address." He swallowed hard and looked like he might be sick. Like a man beaten down by his life—it dawned on Sara that he might be as beaten down by life with her mother's mental illness as she had been, but she had been able to escape it. Her dad had not. He had chosen to stay. "Paul told me just yesterday about your friend who's missing." He paused and looked directly at her for the first time. "I didn't tell her."

Sara sat on the other kitchen chair and pulled Houdini onto her lap. For a few moments the drip of the coffeemaker and Houdini's purring were the only sounds in the room. She'd given no thought in years to what she might say to her father, and now nothing seemed quite right.

"Are you in some kind of trouble?" His voice sounded strangled, like he forced out a question he didn't really want to ask.

"Oh, I've been having a hard time sleeping, and concentrating at work, since my friend has been missing. I helped clean out his apartment, and I'm keeping his cat."

"You have a good job?"

"I like it. I work for an investigator, in a little office downtown. He's a good guy, and I'm doing okay, paying the bills."

He nodded gently, taking in her words.

"Dad, when did Mom start talking about me needing help?"

"I know the date she first said something. It happened on her birthday. I bought us a couple of cupcakes and lit the candles without thinking. You know, she never did like burning candles. But she looked right at those candles like she was looking through a window at something far away, and then she pushed the plate away and said, 'I can't eat this. Sara needs some help.' She got real agitated like she does, and I had to give her medicine early that night. That happened on her birthday, the sixth of June."

June sixth. The night she'd gone to dinner with Paul. The night Gino disappeared. Her heart contracted like a muscle that's been punched hard. She must have flinched, because her dad reached out as if to steady her, and she instinctively took hold of his arm, to steady herself. "Yeah, Dad, that was a bad day." But how had her mother known? She hadn't even heard the news herself yet. She wanted to ask a hundred questions, but every one of them would bring up the old taboo, the visions, the doctors, and her mother's mental illness.

He patted her arm a couple of times, and then eased back, looking incredibly sad. "What is it, Sara?"

"It's just, well, how did she know? I didn't hear that Gino disappeared until the next day. But somehow…" Sara paused and frowned. "…she knew something was wrong before I did."

Then it dawned on Sara that she really did know, days before Lia called to tell her about Gino's disappearance. She knew the day of the lightning storm. Before it really happened.

Then her question became a demand. "How did she know, Dad?"

His face crumpled. "She just knew." He choked out the words, and turned away from her, holding a hand across his eyes. Blotting tears, Sara realized. "She didn't try to find out—she just knew, like…like…"

"Like me?" Sara could hear the hysteria rising in her voice. Sara bolted from her chair, sending Houdini racing to the bedroom while Sara stormed around her little kitchen. "Like I knew Marie was going to die before she wrecked the car? But Mom made me feel like a freak, like some kind of mental case all those years."

"She always hated knowing things, Sara, and she didn't want that for you, all the problems she has."

He stood and reached for her, but she put both arms out as if warding off a blow, and turned away. "No! Let me be."

He took a step back, and glanced around. "Where's the bathroom?"

She pointed the way, then closed her eyes and took a long deep breath when she heard the door click shut. For a minute or two, her parents were out of her life again, without all the stress, her mother's fears, the pain of her old relationship with them. Houdini reappeared, twining around her ankles. She picked him up, looking around her own space to find comfort in the things she could control. Her own private world. Her bookshelf, her laptop, her kitchen. The chair by the front door—and the bag with Gino's book in it.

She turned away, but the sense of control crumbled. She fought for it, went to the coffee pot and filled two mugs as tears leaked down her cheeks, set the mugs on the table and got a carton of milk from the fridge as her shoulders began to shake. *What could my father possibly do to help? Could he bring Gino back? And if my mother is really clairvoyant, is that what had driven her toward mental illness? Is that my future too?*

The toilet flushed, and Sara grabbed a tissue, wiped her eyes and blew her nose. Her father padded back to the table, and winced when he saw her tear-stained face. Before he could speak, Sara said, "Sit down, Dad. The coffee's ready." She sat, too, and poured a little milk into her cup. "I really don't know how you can help me."

He frowned and bit his lip—*the same way I do*, Sara realized with a shock.

"Paul didn't tell me very much, except that your friend was missing."

"Gino—my friend—has been missing for three weeks, and they've given up searching for him in Italy, where he disappeared. His parents, everybody, thinks he's dead. Some of his friends here are planning a memorial in a few days." Her throat tightened so the next words came out in a whisper. "I don't want to go."

"You've done some hard things before. Got out on your own so young, and took care of yourself." He looked down into his coffee. "We couldn't help you then, either."

"This is different. I just can't go along with it."

His weary eyes met hers. "Because?"

"Because I'm sure he still alive—I just don't know where."

He frowned and then his eyes widened. "You're sure?" He reached tentatively for her hand. "Then it makes sense, what your mother said."

"That you should come and help me?" If it made sense, Sara didn't see how.

"Not that. When I got in the car this morning, getting ready to drive up here, she came out on the porch and said, 'Tell Sara to keep looking. Don't forget, Ray, she can't give up. She has to keep looking.' I guess she meant your friend."

Sara's heart pounded. "She said that?" When he nodded, Sara stood and paced, buying a little time to untangle her whirling thoughts. Finally, a message of hope, but could she trust it? After all, it came from a woman who was mentally ill, the mother who had forced Sara into psychotherapy to 'cure' her clairvoyance. A clairvoyant herself, it now seemed. Or was this message just the product of her unstable mind? "Really, Dad," she finally said, "is this just more of her crazy talk?"

"I know it's hard to trust her. Believe me, I know. I've lived with her for more than thirty years. But there's more to her than that." He paused and drank a sip of coffee. "In her mind, seeing the future was always part of her mental illness. She didn't want that for you. She's been in treatment now, and she's starting to see the difference. This time, she really wants to help. She's still your mom."

She stopped by the table in front of him, her mind still roiling. The emotional longing for a supportive mother clashed painfully in her chest with her fears of what that relationship would mean.

Her dad stood up and faced her. "Look, Sara, I don't know what to think about her seeing things that haven't happened yet, any more than I knew what to think about you telling us Marie would die." He gently took hold of her shoulders, keeping some distance between them and meeting her eye. "But I do know that's what happened. What you said then, it was true. And it didn't mean you were mentally ill."

Sara gave a shaky nod and took a deep breath, letting his

fatherly touch and affirmation sooth her anxious heart. He believed her. Finally, somebody believed her.

He took a step back and glanced at his watch. "I better head back. Long drive, you know."

Suddenly Sara wasn't ready to say goodbye. "Can we go get some dinner before you go?"

"No, I better not. She'll be worried, and I don't want to impose on the friend staying with her." A hint of a smile crossed his face. "And I can get a fast-food hamburger. Haven't had one in years."

True, Mom was always paranoid about fast food. A small spring of compassion trickled through her, for all her father had given up to care for the woman he loved, and for the simple pleasures her mother had been robbed of by her mental illness. Fast food, for example. "Okay, Dad. But thanks for coming up." She reached for him, not sure either of them was ready for a hug.

He returned the gesture with a brief, lopsided embrace and headed for the door.

Sara watched from the doorway, and when he reached the street, she called out, "Tell her I'll keep looking."

He waved and was gone.

13. A deceiver must guard against deception at every turn.

AFTER TEN MINUTES, Orso's breathing was deep and even. Despite his exhaustion, Gino couldn't sleep. He slid down to sit against the wall near the hearth, and looked across the room at Ottavio, leaning against the wall near Fiamma, his face a mask of despair.

"The dogs are the real problem," Gino said. "If we could get rid of them, we might be able to climb down."

"I don't know how," Ottavio said, his voice flat.

"Maybe Betta could let them in." Fiamma spoke softly, but both men started at the unexpected sound.

"I thought you were asleep," Ottavio said.

"My stomach hurts. I need the privy. Where is it, father?"

"At the end of the hall there is a garderobe."

Fiamma got to her knees and began to stand. "Do you think those men will let me go?"

"I think they'll want to escort you," Gino said.

Fiamma's answering glance revealed fear.

"Wait," Gino said. "Maybe you could tell them you need something for your stomachache. See if they will take you to Betta."

"I could ask for some mint or balm. She would have some in the kitchen, I'm sure."

As she stepped toward the door, Ottavio took her arm. "Put your shoes on, and if Betta can help you escape, go. You can trust her."

"Alone? How would I get back home alone?"

"She's right, Ottavio. It wouldn't be safe for her, would it? Even if Betta went with her, with Carlo after them, how far would they get?" Gino paused. "But maybe Betta could get rid of the dogs! You could ask her, Fiamma, while you are getting your mint."

Their whispering woke Orso, who sat up and rubbed his eyes. Gino quickly told him their plan. "She would have to be very sick," Orso said. "Those men have no feeling."

"Then I'll be very sick," Fiamma said. She folded her cloak and held it close to the embers, until Gino thought it might catch fire. Then she pressed it to her face for a minute or two. Then she spit in her hands and ran them through her hair. The effect mimicked the flush and sweat of fever.

Ottavio stood by the door. "Are you ready?"

With a brief smile at the three men, Fiamma gripped her stomach and groaned. "Oh Father, I need help," she cried out.

Ottavio banged on the door. "Help us! My daughter is taken ill."

"Hold on!" After a moment the door opened, and one of the guards, his dagger drawn, growled, "What is it?"

Fiamma moaned again and slumped against her father.

"She's taken a fever and has pains in her gut. That kitchen woman, she must have some mint or balm to ease it." Ottavio patted her shoulder. "She can barely stand. I'll help her along."

"No you won't." The guard barred his way. "I'll take her off your hands."

"Are you willing?" Ottavio turned from Fiamma and looked into the man's eyes. "It might be the pestilence. Her mother died of it."

The men drew back and crossed themselves. Ottavio gripped Fiamma and moved toward the door.

"Not you," the man with the dagger said. After a few whispers with the other guard, he pointed his dagger at Gino. "You, Calabrian, you take her down to the kitchen. Go left at the bottom of the stairs. The old woman sleeps back there."

Gino put his arm around Fiamma's waist as Ottavio backed into the room. Suddenly Fiamma's hand flew to her mouth and she gagged. The guards drew back and urged them down the stairs before closing the door. Gino could feel their eyes on his back as they made their way down the dark stairway. Fiamma continued groaning until they reached the bottom and turned to the left. From a doorway about twenty steps away, a low light flickered.

"That must be the kitchen," she said, standing now without Gino's help.

"Stay close," he said. "The charade may not be over."

With a half-smile, she said, "Carry me, then. I feel faint." She fell against him as they reached the doorway, and he scooped her into his arms.

"Betta!" he called softly, then again in a louder voice. The kitchen fire burned very low, and from a shadowy corner, Betta emerged holding a stick of firewood.

Fiamma shifted in Gino's arms and slid to her feet. "Betta," she whispered, "Please, we need help."

Betta frowned and looked from Fiamma to Gino and back. "You're running away with him?"

"No! My father needs your help, we all do, but the guards would not let my father come down with me. I told them I was ill. We need to escape from Don Carlo. Can you help us?"

"But what can I do?" the old woman hissed, laying the stick on a woodpile near the hearth. "He would surely kill me..."

"Come with us then," Gino said. "But we cannot get through the yard with the dogs on guard."

"No, no, they will give you away to Don Carlo, and chase you down for him."

"Can you let them in, or close them up somewhere?"

Betta wrung her hands. "The dogs won't obey me—they'd only wake him if I approached."

"Please, Betta," Fiamma begged. "Isn't there something you can do to help us? How can we get out?"

Betta's eyes darted to the hallway door, and then to another shadowy corner. "The cantina, the wine cellar below the house, opens out to the kitchen garden—the dogs can't go there."

"Can we get out of there to the street?" Gino asked.

Before Betta could answer, they heard footsteps coming up the hall. Gino hoisted Fiamma into his arms and rested her on the big kitchen work table. "Quick, get her some tea!"

Betta grabbed a small bowl and poured water into it from a kettle by the fire. One of the guards appeared in the door.

"You've been down here long enough."

Betta shushed him. "She's very ill. She needs to finish this draught, and when she's done, he'll carry her up."

Fiamma moaned, and Gino put on his sternest expression. "Lady Fiamma, you must do as she says. Drink the rest of that tea."

The guard walked around the table and looked Fiamma in the face. As Betta tipped the bowl to her mouth again, Fiamma raised up and gagged convincingly, spewing the mouthful of water onto herself and Betta, who backed away and grabbed a bowl and towel. "Lean her forward, Signore," she said to Gino. "Hold the bowl. I need to brew another tonic." She pushed past the guard and began rummaging in a cupboard. "You can see she's still sick. I'll send them back later."

Reluctantly, the guard left the room, and when they heard him climbing the stairs, Betta came back to them. "I have an idea," she whispered.

✷ ✷ ✷

Betta carried a small lamp up the stairs, lighting the way for Gino, and three sticks of firewood. In Gino's arms, Fiamma's eyes were closed, her face slumped against his shoulder, but he could feel the tension in her back and legs. The girl could have made a career for herself in Hollywood.

"Open the door," Betta called softly to the guards. "Don't wake her. We need to build up the fire."

The man who had come to the kitchen laid down his wood carving and stood, then pushed the door open. Ottavio jumped to his feet and crossed himself at the sight of his daughter, as if he thought she might be dead. "Is she better? Is it the pestilence?"

Gino followed Betta into the room. "She needs to rest," he said, and eased himself to the floor near the straw mat, laying Fiamma down as gently as he could.

Right on schedule, Fiamma groaned and opened her eyes, then gripped her abdomen.

"Come, girl," Betta said. "I'll take you to the garderobe."

Gino helped Fiamma to her feet, and Betta steadied her as she walked to the door.

The guards exchanged an uneasy glance. The one who had been carving said, "I'll come along."

Betta shot him a defiant glare, surprising Gino with her vehemence. "You'll wait outside in the hall. She doesn't need your helping hands all over her."

As Betta eased Fiamma out the door, with both guards in the hall, Gino pulled Ottavio and Orso further into the room, out of their sight. "When Betta calls for help, we'll go into the hall. The guard will be distracted, and I'm going to cover his head and pull him into the room. Orso, be ready to knock him on the head with the wood and tie him up with this." Gino pulled a length of strong twine from his sleeve. "And we can gag him with these rags," he said, taking some lengths of cloth from under his shirt. "There should be enough for both of them."

Orso snatched the twine and stuck it in his belt, but Ottavio just wrung his hands, and Gino hoped he wouldn't botch the plan. In a louder voice, Gino said, "Orso, build up that fire for Lady Fiamma." As Orso bent by the fire, Gino pushed the stoutest stick aside with his foot. Orso glanced at Gino with a knowing hint of smile, then pushed the coals around and set a couple of sticks on them.

Gino leaned close to Ottavio. "When the time comes, follow Fiamma and Betta," he whispered.

"I hope your plan doesn't put us all in danger."

"Not as much danger as staying in this room. Do you think your brother will let us go tomorrow, after imprisoning us tonight?"

Betta's voice brought them all to attention, and Gino pushed Ottavio toward the door, whispering in his ear, "Ask the guard if your daughter needs help."

Ottavio complied, but the older guard said, "Not from you," and turned to the whittler. "Go see what the old lady wants."

"Why should I go?"

"I said so. Just go. The sooner we're done with them, the better."

Grumbling, the younger guard set his knife on the floor and ambled along the hall toward the garderobe.

Gino could hear the sound of Fiamma retching as he peered over Ottavio's shoulder. He prodded Ottavio to move into the hallway, and the other guard moved closer. "I said they don't need your help."

The guard put his hands on Ottavio's chest to give him a shove, and Gino stepped aside and pulled Ottavio back so the guard's weight carried him into the room. Gino threw his cloak over the man's head, and Orso struck at the flailing figure as Gino tried to draw the cloak tight without being knocked out himself. The man grunted but didn't shout, and on the third try, Orso connected with his head, and he dropped to the floor.

"He's only stunned," Gino said as he bound the gag. "Quick, Orso, the rope." Ottavio had been knocked down in the scuffle, but got slowly to his feet, gaping as Gino and Orso tied the guard and dragged him to a spot where he couldn't be seen from the doorway.

"Ottavio, look down the hall. Is the other one coming back?"

At that moment, they heard the guard call out, "Hey! Where did you go?"

Ottavio's voice quavered as he peered out the door and said, "Him? I don't know. I think he went downstairs."

Gino heard the guard's steps quicken to cover the long hallway.

"He's coming," Ottavio hissed at Gino as he shrank back into the room.

"Come on," Gino said to Orso. They couldn't let the guard get downstairs and raise an alarm. Gino stepped into the hall in front of the guard. "Is Lady Fiamma feeling better?"

The guard glanced down the stairs and back up the hall, and before he could decide what to do, Gino put a hand out. "Her father is feeling ill too. Come and see."

The guard knocked Gino's hand away.

"Please! I think your friend just went to relieve himself." Gino gestured toward their room.

Shaking his head, the guard grumbled, "All right. What's wrong in here?" He pulled the door open, and Orso waited until he was well into the room before throwing a blanket over his head. Gino grabbed him from behind.

"Orso, the stick," Gino said. A second later the stick grazed his head. "Not me!"

"Sorry," Orso said, and grunted as he brought the stick down on the guard's shoulder.

The guard turned and tripped over Ottavio who tried to slip around them to pull the door shut and keep the noise from reaching the men sleeping in the great hall. As the guard hit the ground, Orso's stick finally connected with his skull and he slumped. Gino quickly gagged him, and Orso tied him with the other length of rope before he came to with a groan.

With both guards bound and gagged, grunting muted accusations at one another from opposite sides of the room, Gino, Orso, and Ottavio crept into the hallway, where Fiamma and Betta waited. "Well done, Betta. Lead the way," Gino whispered, handing her the guards' candle. The five of them slipped down the stairs and into the kitchen.

Betta opened a door in the far corner of the kitchen. "Careful. The stairs are narrow." She led the way down the winding stone steps, cool air wafting up at them as they descended into the cellar.

Ottavio slipped near the bottom stair, but Orso caught him from behind. In the dim light of Betta's candle, Gino saw wooden barrels lined up against the wall to their left, and a winepress on the right, next to a few gardening tools. Betta stopped at a barred double door, and as she fumbled with the candle, Orso stepped forward and quietly lifted the bar.

The door swung out at a light touch, and groaned like a dying man, setting Gino's heart thumping. They stood stock still until the silence reassured them that no one had heard, and their eyes adjusted to the moonlight on the garden.

Gino touched Betta's arm. "What about the dogs?" he whispered.

"This garden is walled off. They can't get in here, but they could still hear us so—" From across the wall, they heard a woof, then a louder bark, and then a frenzy.

Betta pinched the candle, dropped it to the ground, and fled across the garden. Fiamma followed, with Ottavio, Orso, and Gino close on her heels. About thirty feet beyond the last rows of vegetables, Gino saw a gate in the garden wall.

Betta opened it and warned them as they came through. "The trail is narrow. Stay close together."

Shouts of men joined the chorus of barking dogs, and the unmistakable, bellowing voice of Ottavio's brother.

Betta closed the gate firmly, then jammed a stick in the hinged side. She turned toward the path, but Orso frowned at the gate, then picked up a large stone and bashed the latch. He shook the gate, and grinned at Betta when it held fast. Torchlight flared at the cellar doors, and the band of escapees followed Betta along a narrow trail that followed a series of walls on their left. A wooded ravine dropping steeply on their right. The moonlight barely penetrated to the path, and they moved more slowly to avoid stumbling on branches and stones that littered the way.

Behind them, the gate rattled and Don Carlo swore and called, "Fetch the dogs!" over the shouts of his men.

Gino breathed a little easier as he realized the gate held, but they would certainly guess their direction and find a way to cut off their escape. And where was Betta leading them? They were heading downhill, slightly, with undergrowth snagging their clothes. Fiamma stumbled once, but rose immediately and carried on without a word.

Gino guessed they had gone three or four hundred yards when Betta stopped at another gate, and pointed her chin to direct them through it. The narrow alley was nearly as dark as the ravine, but only twenty yards long, and opened up into a street.

Betta moved to the lead and peered tentatively out, holding up a hand for quiet, and that's when Gino noticed the bones she carried. Far in the distance they heard a bark, and Betta turned to the right, threw a bone behind them and another uphill on the narrow street. Then she turned downhill. "Run!"

As Gino made the third turn, the harbor lay before him, and he wished he could give Betta a big hug. Fiamma turned, and reached for Ottavio's hand. As she said, "Look Papa," Gino gasped.

"You're hurt," he said, staring at the blood on her skirt, which stuck to her left knee and shin.

Fiamma looked down, and seemed as surprised as Gino at the blood.

Betta reached as if to look at Fiamma's leg, but checked herself. "The bleeding has stopped now, but it might start up again if I pulled her dress away. When we get to the harbor, I'll tend it. We can't stop." Snarling dogs in the distance sent them all running again, but not before Betta tossed two more bones into the street behind them.

At the last turn, Ottavio looked back up the hill as if he expected to see Don Carlo's men come around the hairpin curve with their swords drawn. "Then where will we go?"

Betta fumbled at her belt, then took Ottavio's hand and slapped a soft leather bag into it. "You find a ship to take us home to Praiano." She pointed her chin at the pouch in his hand, and hinted at a smile. "Carlo will pay for it. He owes you that and more."

"Betta!" Ottavio's voice cracked. "You stole this from Carlo?"

She tilted her head and smiled crookedly. "Oh, did you have the money for our passage?" With a soft laugh, she said, "I find a coin now and then, and put it in there. Carlo is sometimes careless, but I am very thrifty. Consider it the inheritance he cheated from you."

"Come on," Gino said. "They're still following."

Betta took Fiamma by the arm and continued down the street at a trot.

Gino hurried down the last stretch of road leading to the harbor. Moonlight added a romantic touch to the peaceful scene, and thoughts of Sara succeeded briefly in replacing thoughts of Don Carlo and his henchmen who were no doubt out for their blood. When he heard a shout from somewhere in the labyrinth of streets behind them, he sprinted past Orso and Ottavio. "Come on, let's find a ship."

As he passed the women, Fiamma leaned heavily on Betta, and Gino realized she wasn't play-acting this time. He stopped in front of them and looked Fiamma in the face. "We need to keep moving," he said. "I'll carry her. Where should I take her?"

Betta pointed to a two-story building near the dock. "The back door. I know the woman there."

Light spilled out the front door as Gino approached the building from the side. A man stumbled out with one arm around a woman whose lusty laugh carried out across the water before they turned and headed away from the wharf, oblivious to the group coming down the hill.

At the back door, Gino put Fiamma down, and held on until her legs found strength to hold her up. She gripped a pillar that supported the second-floor terrace above them.

Betta knocked on the door, and then said, "Signore Gino, it's best my friends don't see us all. Please help Ottavio find a ship to take us."

Ottavio and Orso were close behind, and Gino turned to intercept them. "Betta knows the barman's wife—they will be safe here," he said, moving them away from the back door, and around to the darkest side of the building, out of the moonlight. "Where can we find a ship to take us back to Praiano?"

"Praiano?" Ottavio bleakly surveyed the harbor. "I doubt any of them are going to Praiano."

"Where would they be going?"

"Naples? Salerno, Messina, maybe even Marseilles? Ships have stopped coming to Praiano. That's my brother's doing."

Gino gripped Ottavio's shoulders and shook him once, startling him. "Look at me," Gino said, "and listen. What will your brother do when he finds us?"

Ottavio sighed and glanced up the hill. "He'd like to kill me."

"And probably not only you. We all need to get away. We've got some money. How much is the passage from here to Praiano? Do we have enough?"

"The price will be high if he has to make harbor only for us," Ottavio said absently, as if talking it over with himself. "And passage for five…" He shook his head as he opened the leather bag Betta had handed him, and tipped the coins into his palm, but in the darkness they could have been rocks. He stepped around the corner into the moonlight and gasped.

"Is it enough?" Gino asked, peering in surprise at the gleam of gold among the silver.

"We could buy a ship with this," Ottavio said, closing his fist on the coins.

Orso took a step back. "Our lives are surely over if he finds us with his gold in your hands."

Ottavio might have discovered a scorpion in his hand as he looked at the coins, quickly slipped them back into the pouch, and pushed it into Gino's hand.

"Not if we can use this gold to get out of here. And how would he know we didn't bring it with us? As long as he doesn't know it came from Betta, he won't suspect it's his money." Gino looked up with a grin, but something drew his gaze past Ottavio. "Damn!" He shoved Ottavio back against the dark side of the building. "They're coming."

14.

A trusted friend listens
and speaks with wisdom.

THE STUFFY AIR FELT SUFFOCATING, and as Sara cranked open the living room window and turned on the bathroom fan to draw in some fresh air, she dialed Britt's number.

Britt dispensed with the usual greetings. "What did she say?"

"She said Gino knew an astrologer to the Queen of Naples about six hundred years ago."

After a short silence, Britt said, "Are you leaving something out? Was she some kind of psycho psychic?"

"Actually, she seemed perfectly normal—until she got to the crazy part. In fact…in fact she seemed kind of like me."

"I'll be there in half an hour with Chinese."

"And Britt?"

"Yeah?"

"When I got home, my dad was here." She heard Britt's sharp inhale. "He's gone now."

"I'll hurry."

Sara changed into her yoga clothes and sat cross-legged on the couch holding Niccolo of Salerno's book, and thinking about Gino reading this story. The psychic's words replayed in her head. *I feel very certain that your friend and this astrologer know—or knew—one another.* How could Gino possibly know a man who lived more than

600 years ago? She was still staring at the cover, when Britt came in carrying two bags, one from The Top Wok, and another with margarita ingredients from the liquor store.

"Food or drink first?"

Sara pulled her gaze from the book with an effort. "Both," she said, hopping up from the couch and giving her friend a tight squeeze. "You're a genius, Britt. I'll get the blender, and you dish up."

With drinks in hand, and plates of almond chicken and Mongolian beef on the coffee table, Britt sat down in the chair across from Sara. "So what's first, the psycho psychic or the long-lost father?

Sara took a deep breath. "I'm still wondering about my dad's visit. It shocked me to see him, but it wasn't all bad. Actually, encouraging in a way. A lot to think through."

Britt eyed her for a moment, then said, "Okay, the psychic, then. How is Elizabeth Hayes like you?"

"Because she knows what she told me sounds crazy, and she's completely convinced it is true."

"So tell me."

By the time Sara reached for the book, the book that supposedly held some key to Gino's disappearance, the margarita glasses were empty. "She is sure that the guy who wrote this book knew—or knows—Gino personally."

Britt chewed some of the crushed ice from her glass. "What do you make of that?"

Sara speared a piece of beef from her plate and chewed thoughtfully. "When I'm investigating something at work, it's usually because things don't match up, something doesn't make sense. So I start with what I know, what I'm sure of, or what somebody else seems sure of, and work from there. Try to figure out what events or circumstances would make the most sense in light of those facts."

Britt nodded, waiting for more.

"So if we know that Gino disappeared in the water, and I know that he's still alive, and Elizabeth Hayes knows that Gino and Niccolo were personally acquainted in spite of being born about 700 years apart, then one or the other of them has to be, like, time traveling. And the fact that Gino is missing from 'now' suggests that it's probably him. Which also, now that I've thought it over, fits pretty well with the visions I have had, the stone buildings, the strange clothes, the daggers and torches."

Britt kept her eyes on Sara, chopsticks hovering above the almond chicken. Sara went on.

"Elizabeth said she thinks the book has some answers for me. I've read a few pages of it, and didn't see anything, but I wasn't looking for anything about Gino in it either. So this," she said, picking up the book and holding it in front of Britt, "is my best evidence at the moment, and I need to examine it thoroughly, and see what it shows me."

Britt set her food on the coffee table, and took the book. "It sounds like a very rational way to approach the whole crazy business." She leafed through a few pages, and glanced at her watch. "It's only six now. How about I blend us another drink, and we read some of it together?"

Britt delivered the second margarita while Sara studied the index of the astrologer's book.

"Okay, where do we start?" Britt sank into the couch and leaned against Sara so she could see the book.

Sara frowned. "I hoped I could find some reference in the index that would help, so we don't have to read the whole book. There's a lot of obscure astrology—obscure to me, at least—that doesn't tell me anything. Lots of references to Naples and the queen and her husband, who this guy calls the prince. The Prince of Taranto, it says."

"I suppose you looked up 'Gino Calabrese' already."

Sara stared at her friend. "Brilliant," she said, flipping back a couple of pages. "Maybe you should have my job instead of me." But she ran through the listings for G and C without finding Gino's name. "There are a few mentions of Calabria, but no Calabrese."

"So what is Calabria? Could that be about him?"

"It's a place, like a province, the toe of Italy's boot." She scanned the page for the first reference to Calabria. "This just says the prince's seneschal got sick as his ship sailed by Calabria. What's a seneschal, anyway?"

Britt reached for her smart phone, and in less than a minute she read: "Seneschal: a steward in the household of a medieval prince or nobleman, in charge of all his domestic arrangements."

"Well, that's all it says about Calabria here." Sara flipped back to the index and turned to the next reference, about halfway through the book. "Listen to this. 'The pestilence began in Sicily, and flew north through the kingdom like the hot winds of Africa.' Then he lists a bunch of places the plague went, and Calabria is one of them. There's a footnote. It says he's talking about the Black Death."

Britt frowned hard and leaned toward Sara to see the book.

Sara met her eyes. "Oh my God, *the* plague. Gino might…" Her voice trailed off and she yanked a Kleenex from the box on the coffee table to dab her eyes.

Britt hugged her, then gripped Sara by both shoulders. "You keep telling me you're sure he's still alive, and you would know if he wasn't, so I don't think you need to panic about the plague. Besides, this book covers a lot of time. We don't know when Gino might have met this astrologer." Britt reached for Sara's glass. "Here, you're neglecting your drink. Want me to look up a couple?"

"Sure, there are three more I think." Sara took a slow sip and looked out her front window at the evening light, fading shafts now coming through tree branches. She calculated the time in Italy to be about 5 a.m. now, the sky just lightening in the east. Gino's cousins returned to Sicily and were struggling with the loss. Lia continued to call occasionally. Would her own life ever be normal again? She felt tears rising and pressed the Kleenex to her eyes until Britt tapped her arm.

"Okay, listen. This is a lot later. From the footnotes, let's see… 1370s sometime. The plague is probably over by then, right?"

Sara forced a smile, but couldn't really get much enthusiasm into her voice. "I guess so. What does it say?"

"'A group of Calabrian barons arrived in Naples intent on an audience with Queen Joanna, and traveling with them, a man who claimed to be an astrologer from the farthest reaches of Calabria. I kept my suspicions to myself, and invited the man to dine with me, and then to view the stars from the castle parapet, as it was a clear winter's night and the sky as a royal garment stitched with thousands of gleaming gemstones. My fears were confirmed when he could not pick out the evening star, and mistook Scorpio for Capricorn. But if not an astrologer, who was this man?

"'When I asked about his home and family in Calabria, he spoke of a village near Reggio, from which he could see the fair shores of Sicily, as one might tell of a beloved homeland. And if that island was his homeland, then he could well be an enemy of our Queen.'"

Britt scanned the page, summarizing as she went. "The barons stayed for weeks, his suspicions grew, one admitted having family in Sicily."

Could this be Gino? Sara wondered what kind of mess he was in.

Britt went on. "He consulted others who were also suspicious, yada yada yada, the barons distanced themselves from him, and—oh!"

"What?"

"'He was no astrologer but a spy for the King Frederick, who would like nothing better than to add Naples to his kingdom, just as his forbears took the island from the ancestors of our beloved Queen. When this treachery came to light, the knights of the royal household dealt swiftly with him, debating only the question of whether or not to return his head to Frederick.'"

Sara felt queasy, but with a few deep breaths it passed. "I know he's still alive. That can't be him. It can't be him."

"Here, what about this? 'The man claimed to be a Calabrian, but I doubted him...'"

"Who is he talking about there?" Sara craned her neck, skimming the page to quickly to absorb anything useful. "Where does that section start?"

"Here, I found the page." Britt began to read aloud.

"'In my father's work, and in the university, I knew many people who studied and practiced astrology, many who served people of high position in the kingdom, and who used their knowledge to help physicians, pilgrims, the owners of ships, and others who needed guidance for healing, safety, and success. God guides the stars, they said, and through them he guides man. Even cardinals and bishops seek God's guidance in the stars, so I am told.

"'But the man who piqued my interest in astrology, and drew me away from my former pursuits despite my success, told me he was not an astrologer at all. Others who knew him told me he was an astrologer, in the household of a lord of Praiano. Not knowing who to believe, I questioned him closely when we met, and he seemed indeed to know little of the science or wisdom of astrology, less than a midwife or a common shepherd might know. And yet he spoke of certain matters with such an air of authority that I could not discount him completely.

"'In short, he was an enigma, truly a riddle to me. The man said he was a Calabrian, but I doubted him from the beginning, having known many Calabrians in my lifetime. He was certainly like none of them. His speech differed from theirs, though he spoke our tongue well enough to be understood.

"'I know now, after pondering the mystery of his brief influence for so many years, that his denial of the astrologers' wisdom made me want to defend the truth of it, and to do that I had to become one of them, to learn their skills and practice their craft myself.'"

Sara waited for more, but Britt read on silently. "Come on, what does he say?"

Britt inhaled deeply, and shook her head. "He's going on about studying astrology for a long time in Naples. Apparently he has a patron in the royal family or household, and his father back in Salerno is angry that he's not doing whatever he did before. 'My father's letters dogged me, as he harassed me to leave off this foolish quest, as he called it, but I could not, and that rift would never be healed.

"'My father died before the plague had run its course. This risk always threatened those in our profession, but the risk did not influence my choice to leave it for astrology. Still, now that I have lived longer than my father did, I wish we could have parted agreeably. Perhaps the next life will give us opportunity to heal that wound.'"

"Nothing else about the Calabrian man?" Sara drained the last of her second margarita. The front window showed their reflections against the dark outside, and she got up and pulled the drapes closed as Britt scanned the next page.

"Okay, here's a little more."

Sara plopped back down on the couch, all ears.

"He says—Oh my God. I think this might be…"

"What?" Sara yelled, grabbing the book.

"I think we may have found him."

15. Take action when the opportunity is at hand.

GINO HOPED BETTA'S FRIENDSHIP with the barman's wife would prove stronger than Don Carlo's influence, because Carlo now headed for the tavern. With their backs plastered against the dark wall, Gino, Ottavio, and Orso looked frantically for a way of escape.

To their right, the town rose among the steep hills. In front of them the waterfront buildings were darkened for the night, the businesses of the port at rest. To their left, about fifteen yards of loose gravel led down to the water. They couldn't reach the wharf, or even the fishing boats pulled up along the shingle, without being seen or heard.

As they listened to the approaching group—Gino guessed there were three men with Carlo—Ottavio began to whisper a prayer. Gino grabbed his wrist to silence him, and they listened as Carlo and his men went into the tavern, and Carlo shouted a question at the barman.

Glancing around again, Gino saw an overturned boat, the kind the local fishermen used, about fifty feet from them, on the upper edge of the gravel beach. It looked large enough for them to hide beneath, if they could get to it and slip under. He tapped Orso and pointed to it, gesturing that they should hide there.

Orso frowned, but as Carlo bellowed another question, Orso crossed himself and ran for the boat. Realizing Carlo wouldn't stay in the tavern once he determined they weren't inside, Gino pulled Ottavio along by the arm, while Ottavio whispered his prayers.

Orso reached the boat first. Gino's heart sank when he saw the twenty-foot rotting hulk. They'd have to avoid the near end of it, where a gaping hole a foot across provided an unwanted window for their hideout. Gino hoped Carlo didn't come out of the tavern with a torch—and even without one, the moonlight could give them away if someone came near enough.

"Here, get under," Orso said, gripping the edge to lift it. A chunk of wood came off in his hand, and a rat ran from beneath it, crossing Gino's foot as it sought another hiding place. Gino shuddered and swore but forced himself to stand firm. Orso managed not to drop the boat on Ottavio's head, as he scooted beneath it. Gino went next and raised his back against a plank seat to hold the side up for Orso. The plank groaned but held as Orso slipped under. Gino eased the boat down onto the gravel. They were folded up like concertinas, but hidden from view.

"What about the dogs?" Orso whispered.

Hidden in the inky darkness under the boat, Gino heard Betta's voice. "Throw it out!" And something landed on the ground, attracting the dogs and setting them snarling and snapping.

Carlo cursed the dogs and shouted to one of his men to leash them and take them home. "They're no help with all these distractions."

Gino sighed with relief and Ottavio shushed him as the babble of voices grew louder.

They must be outside the tavern, he guessed. Their boots crunched across the gravel, but they didn't seem to be coming closer. Carlo argued with someone, but Gino couldn't make out what he said.

Then Carlo began to shout. "My men are going to check the boats. Stand aside, or you'll stand to lose more than your position as port guard."

"But no one has been on the water since sunset," the guard shouted back.

After another indecipherable exchange, they heard Carlo

directing his men to the fishing boats along the shore, and then the splash of paddles. No one came near the wreck where they hid.

As the minutes passed, Gino wondered how they could rejoin Fiamma and Betta. How badly was Fiamma hurt? With Carlo pushing his weight around, would any ship be willing to take them aboard? His muscles began to knot up but he didn't dare try to move. The sound of the shifting gravel would give them away.

Gino strained to hear footsteps on the shingle to tell him where Don Carlo's men were. The sounds grew more distant, and when they paused, Gino assumed they were examining one of the beached fishing boats, or perhaps checking a building farther down the shore.

Then the tavern door banged open, and a noisy group headed for the wharf.

"Give me a couple of coins," Gino whispered. "I'm going to try to buy our passage."

"No, Gino!" Ottavio said. "Carlo will catch you, he'll catch us all!"

"I have a plan, but I will need the money. Besides, Carlo doesn't really care about me, and if he does find me, I'll tell him I parted from you in the ravine. Come on, give me a coin or two." He reached into the dark and nearly poked Ottavio in the eye.

"Stop!" Ottavio said, flinching away from him. "Here, take the pouch. I'm just keeping two coins."

From another dark corner Orso whispered, "How will we be able to join you?"

"And what about my daughter, the women?"

Gino eased the boat up with his back. "Hold this, Orso. I won't leave any of you, but I can get to the boats with these drunkards without being noticed." He eased out, and whispered, "Be still. I'll get you somehow."

As quietly as he could, Gino moved toward the tavern, crouching in the shadows. When he couldn't stay in the dark any longer, he stood upright, trying to pick out the leader of the group heading toward the wharf. They were about thirty paces away, and not moving quickly. Four men, and two of them very drunk. The one who looked most sober urged the others along, threatening their lives, wives, and daughters with a familiar and friendly tone of authority. Gino hoped the man would be as friendly to him.

A glance up and down the beach showed shadows moving at the north end of the beach, near the last of the fishing boats. Stepping into the moonlight, Gino called out, "Think you're leaving me behind?" and staggered toward them, trying to close the thirty paces as quickly as he could.

The group swayed to a stop, and one said, "Who goes?" as they squinted at him.

Gino went directly to the sober man and threw an arm around his shoulder.

"What's this?" the sailor said, trying to shake him off.

Gino quickly pressed a coin into his hand. "I can pay you well for helping me," he whispered, and felt the man's startled response as he recognized the gold coin. Gino looked the man in the eye, and saw a glint of curiosity. "Give me half an hour of your time, and then decide." Then, in a louder voice, "You said you'd take me on."

The sailor paused, then slapped Gino on the back, and pulled him along toward the wharf. "I could never forget such a friendly face."

One of the drunken men squinted at Gino. "But the captain won't like—"

"Oh, the captain will be delighted to see him, I'm sure."

To Gino's relief, the other men accepted his word, and carried on their slurred conversation as they approached the wharf. Their ship hugged the side of the wharf rather than anchoring in the bay like two or three others.

They were about twenty feet from the ship when Gino heard Don Carlo's voice. "I'm very concerned about my brother, Captain. If you see anything of him before you sail, send me word."

As Carlo stepped onto the wharf, Gino turned to hang over the opposite side of the deck, and began gagging loudly as if he would vomit. He listened to Carlo's receding footsteps before drawing his arm across his mouth and standing upright.

"Too free with the drink tonight, eh?" his new friend asked. Gino saw him turn the coin in his hand, and glance up the dock toward Carlo, whose men were gathering in front of the tavern.

"I'm fine now," Gino said.

"Follow me, then. You'd better meet the captain."

"Tell me, what's your ship's destination?"

The man glanced at him with a sharp look of surprise. "Naples, of course."

The slurred voice of one of his companions came from behind as the leader stepped onto the ship's deck. "We are carrying important passengers. The queen's own—"

The leader silenced him with a raised hand. "Get to sleep, the lot of you, and no trouble." His voice softened a bit. "We've had a fine time tonight, but there's an early morning ahead. See that you're fit for it."

The three men disappeared into the shadows, curling up in some kind of medieval sleeping bag on the deck. Gino wondered that any passengers could be accommodated in so small a ship— barely twenty-five feet across the deck. His hope of escape faltered a little. The leader cast him a grim look.

"We'd better see the captain. He'll decide if we keep you or throw you back. Take back your gold, and you can hand it to him if he'll take you on."

Gino found the coin thrust back into his hand, and stared at it in surprise.

"Give me your name."

Gino looked up. "Excuse me?"

"Your name? I should be able to tell the captain your name, and what service you seek to buy from him."

"Gino Calabrese. I need passage to Praiano for four of my friends, and I want to go.." Gino stopped short of naming Li Galli. "I need to travel a little farther."

The man's eyebrows rose slightly at the mention of Praiano— or perhaps the four additional passengers. Then with a brief shrug he started to turn, but Gino touched his arm.

"What is your name?"

"Poldi."

"Thank you, Poldi."

Poldi headed toward the end of the ship nearest the shore. Gino couldn't tell fore from aft in the dark, but he could see the dark line of the mast rising to the cross-beam where a sail hung.

Ropes, barrels, and crates littered the deck, and Gino picked through them, following Poldi to a door. They waited for an answer to his knock.

The wait was brief. The captain had spoken to Don Carlo only a few minutes earlier, and when the door flew open, he glared out, black hair askew and shirt half buttoned, at the next unfortunate man to disturb his night's rest. To Gino's relief, he found that a gold coin still had persuasive powers, at least enough to open a discussion over a stingy cup of some primitive but potent liquor.

"Praiano?" The captain shook his head, and reluctantly pushed the coin toward Gino. "*Assolutamente* no."

When Gino tried to speak again, the captain closed his eyes, put up a hand and said, "No, no, no. I cannot consider your tempting offer, Signore." He took a deep breath and fought off a yawn. "As my crew well knows," he said with an accusing glance at Poldi, "the ship is contracted privately for a delivery we are making tomorrow. We sail directly to Naples, no other port. We have been held up here in Amalfi for three days already, and we cannot take you." Again he pushed the coin toward Gino, eying it longingly before forcing his gaze to Gino's face. "Take it, sir, and look elsewhere."

Gino rose to go, and took one step toward the door when another knock sounded.

The captain spoke a word or two that Gino couldn't understand, but the tone and volume suggested a seafaring curse of some kind. Poldi jumped up and opened the door to a man of about Gino's age wearing a belted tunic and leggings with fine leather shoes.

"I must speak to the captain. It's urgent," he said, looking past Poldi, pausing to look at Gino for a moment, and then meeting the captain's eye.

The captain dragged himself to his feet and nodded deferentially. "I wasn't expecting you until morning, Dottore."

"I beg your pardon, Captain, for this late hour, but I have been called for urgent medical care tonight."

The captain hit his forehead with one palm and raised his eyes toward heaven. "Madonna! Not another delay! We cannot stay longer, Dottore. We must reach Naples tomorrow!"

"Yes, certainly, Captain, I understand. But this patient needs further care, and I think it best if I bring her with us."

"Her? A woman?" The captain's eyes narrowed.

Even in the dim lamplight, Gino caught the young man's expression, the mild flush, the half-smile, the glow of hope in his eyes. "A lady, Captain. And her maid." The doctor stepped further inside, revealing two figures standing on the deck behind him.

Fiamma leaned against Betta, in her most fetching pose, eyes downcast, with the ends of bandages dangling below the hem of her skirt around her injured leg. Betta patted her arm and murmured comforts to her as if she had nursed her from birth. As the captain looked them over, shaking his head, Fiamma slowly raised her eyes, smiling sweetly.

"Please, sir," she began, when her eyes met Gino's, and she gasped. "Gino!" she squealed, and took a couple of strong steps toward him when the doctor caught and held her.

"My lady, don't do yourself injury. Your leg must heal." He looked from Fiamma to Gino and back. "This man is known to you?"

"Yes, he is." Gino could almost see her mind racing, and tried to imagine what she might have told the doctor, and how she might adapt that to fit the new situation. "He is my…my father's… astrologer."

"Truly?" The doctor glanced at Gino with respect, while Gino groaned inwardly.

Fiamma's eyes searched the small room, and she reached toward Gino. "Where is he? Why isn't he with you? Where are my father and Orso?"

"I came alone to arrange our passage, my lady. They are waiting near the tavern." Best not to say they were hiding under a rotting fishing boat, Gino thought.

"Signore," the captain said to Gino, "I take it these are two of your fellow travelers?"

"Yes."

"But you have two more? Why are they not with you?"

"Excuse me, Captain," the doctor said. "The lady has explained it to me, and I will tell you, but she cannot remain standing on her injured leg, sir. Please, let her have a seat."

Gino stood and offered his wooden chair, but the doctor cleared his throat and looked at the captain's upholstered leather chair. "That one would be better, sir, if you would be so kind."

The captain heaved a great sigh. "By all means, Doctor." He stood aside, arms crossed, as the doctor lowered Fiamma gently into the chair. The captain rubbed his eyes as the doctor adjusted the angle of Fiamma's leg, and pulled her cloak close around her.

The captain huffed. "Is she quite comfortable now?"

At last the doctor seemed to catch the captain's impatient tone, and turned to face him. "Yes, sir, and thank you. You see, sir, this has been a dreadful night for the lady."

"She's not alone in that," the captain murmured, leaning against the wall of his crowded cabin.

"Just a week ago she received the news that her betrothed had died of the pestilence."

Fiamma lifted the edge of her cloak to dab her eyes, and looked imploringly at Gino.

"Her father brought her to Amalfi to enter a nunnery, a decision she made in her grief. But the convent refused them because of the pestilence, and they arrived inside the gates just as they closed, and had no time to arrange other lodging." The doctor paused to cast a pitying—or perhaps adoring—eye on Fiamma.

"They made their way through the town, but at a certain point encountered a vicious dog that had escaped its owner, and it chased them through the streets. The three men tried to draw the dog away, hurling stones at it, while the women escaped, so they became separated. In the course of their escape, Lady Fiamma fell and injured her leg. I am concerned that the bone may be broken, and she will need care for some time. I feel we must take them with us, Captain, because she needs a doctor's care."

Gino managed to keep a smile off his face by looking at Betta, standing wearily by the door, and the captain, who took in the story with a skeptical frown. He rubbed his forehead, and the stubble on his chin, and then addressed the doctor.

"Since you have been but recently hired by the seneschal, you are not in a position to make this decision, doctor. I'm afraid we will have to ask him for approval."

"Of course. I don't mean to presume, Captain."

"Before we make sail, I will speak to him, and if he agrees, we will take your patient and her entourage to Naples."

The doctor swallowed hard, and glanced at Fiamma. "In the morning, Captain?"

Fiamma cried out in alarm, and began to weep as she reached for the captain's hand. "Please, Captain, my father is waiting somewhere out in the darkness. I can't bear to think of him spending the whole night not knowing where we are."

"Very well, then, send word to him with the astrologer. Take lodging above the tavern. If the seneschal agrees to take you aboard, the doctor can inform you in the morning. That time is fast approaching, and I intend to sleep an hour or two before it arrives."

Fiamma slid from the chair onto her knees before the captain, and gripped his hand. "Please, sir! We cannot! You must take us in!"

Betta rushed to her side, and the doctor tried to lift her back into the chair. Poldi pushed past them to open the door, telling Gino to take them back to the tavern.

"Stop!" The captain's command stilled the chaos. "Poldi, accompany the ladies outside. I want a private word with the Signore and the doctor."

As the captain's cabin door closed, Gino, the captain, and the doctor eyed one another. Then the captain squeezed his eyes shut and shook his head hard as he stifled a yawn. He wore his greasy hair, graying at the temples, pulled back into a ponytail.

The doctor and the captain began to speak at the same time, but at a sharp look from the captain, the younger man nodded in deference.

"This man came aboard seeking passage for five people to Praiano, and I refused him. Now, doctor, you come seeking passage for an injured woman and her four companions—apparently the same five people. Is that true?"

Both men nodded.

"Only a short time before you both arrived, I had another visitor."

Perspiration ran down Gino's back. The night air had cooled. It must be well after midnight, Gino guessed. Stale bedding and sweat reeked in the small cabin. Since the captain had asked no question, Gino said nothing. The doctor shifted in his chair.

The captain returned to the chair Fiamma had vacated. "It appears that you were both aware of that visit. Perhaps you know the reason for it."

Gino kept his eyes on the captain, but thought he caught a movement from the doctor, a glance at Gino.

"Doctor? Do you?"

"I believe the owner of the dog chased them, Captain, but the lady did not say so directly. She clearly did not wish to encounter him, so we waited until he and his men left the beach before we came to the wharf."

"And you?" The captain turned to Gino.

Where would this lead? Gino wondered how much of Fiamma's story he should go along with. Any difference would probably bring more suspicion on them, and force them back into the city. But he didn't know the full extent of Fiamma's fantasy.

"I believe it was the dog's owner, sir. Perhaps we injured the animal when we tried to protect ourselves. I know a couple of the stones we threw struck home, and it quit chasing us before we reached the beach." That probably wasn't saying too much.

"And you do not know the man?"

"Should I? I have never been to this city before."

The captain turned to the doctor with the same question. The doctor shook his head with a shrug.

The captain looked darkly from one to the other. "When he boarded my ship, after dark, with a search party, I already lay in my bunk, but I rose and met with him. Do you know why? I'll tell you. He is a powerful man in Amalfi and controls a great deal of business involving the port and shipping. A man with power over a man like me." The captain pulled a small jug from a cupboard under his bunk and poured himself a shot in the cup that served as a lid for the jug. He very deliberately offered none to Gino or the doctor. "As it happens, doctor, that man is searching for a group of five people who left his house this evening. Three men and two women, possibly wanting passage to Praiano." He swirled the cup and swilled its contents.

The doctor cleared his throat softly, then wriggled in his chair under the captain's sharp eye.

"Well?" the captain demanded.

"The lady did offer payment for their passage, Captain. She said her father could pay you well."

"Yet I see no sign of her father or his fat purse."

Gino feared that the captain was approaching the end of his tolerance for the whole affair. He retrieved the coin from its leather pouch, along with a second gold piece, and laid both on the table. "I offer that sign, Captain, from her father's purse, and beg you to reconsider. How far is Praiano? Just a short sail, and you could send us to shore in your small boat and earn a fine price, before your seneschal wakes up in the morning." He pushed the gold pieces toward the captain.

The captain's breath quickened, and his gleaming eyes locked on the coins. He licked his lips and rubbed his grizzled cheek. One hand moved slightly toward the coins, then stopped, fingers drumming softly on the oily wood.

"We would be happy with a spot on the deck to lie down, Captain. Don Carlo doesn't know we are here, and you need never—" Gino choked on his error, and the captain snorted softly.

"The man you don't know? That Don Carlo?"

Gino cursed under his breath, and realized he had spoken in English when both men frowned. "You mentioned him earlier."

"But I did not name him, Signore. I did not name him."

"The offer stands. Five of us to Praiano tonight for these gold coins. He does not know we are here, and why should he ever know?"

As the captain reached again for the coins, the doctor took Gino's arm. "Wait, you know the man? But Lady Fiamma said—"

"He is her father's enemy. If he finds any of us, it could ruin her life. A tragic prospect, don't you think, Doctor?"

The doctor leaned back to stare at the ceiling for a few moments. Gino wondered what story Fiamma had concocted to bewitch this man. The attraction between them brought Sara to his mind, her waterfall of gleaming black hair, her clever wordplay and the dimpled grin that always followed. The pleasure, the real delight, of her company, and the unspoken caution that held her back from a commitment. How long had it been? Nearly a month since she waved goodbye to him from his apartment window. She had probably moved on, accepted his disappearance as final. His throat tightened.

He hoped she was taking care of Houdini. And that she thought of him once in a while.

The doctor rose to his feet and leaned toward the captain, his hands on the table. "Captain, don't allow her to be destroyed by that powerful man. Please take them. I will accept the responsibility. I think my lord the seneschal will agree."

The captain still wavered. His fingers twitched a few inches from the coins on the table as he looked up at Gino. When their eyes met, Gino reached into the pouch and drew out one more coin, pushing it against the other two, and then a little closer to the captain.

With that, his hand closed on the coins. "*Va bene*. Go get the girl's father, and we will sail early. Doctor, be ready to explain things to the seneschal when he wakes. I will tell him we changed plans on your word." He stood and stretched, switched the coins to his left hand and raked his right hand through his hair. "Now leave me to get some sleep."

Gino paused. "Let Poldi come with me. I might need help bringing the other two back." And I want some insurance against this captain double-crossing me with Carlo, he thought. The more he and his crew can be implicated, the less likely he is to back out.

The captain stepped out and barked, "Poldi!" and soon he stood before them, receiving his orders to accompany Gino and retrieve Ottavio and Orso.

The doctor rushed to Fiamma's side, where she leaned against a coiled rope, and murmured the results of their conference. As he clambered onto the wharf, Gino saw the gleam of her teeth in the moonlight when she smiled, stroking the doctor's arm.

Clouds scudded past the moon as Gino led Poldi across the shingle to the overturned boat. As they lifted the side, Ottavio gasped and cowered while Orso brandished a stave of rotting wood for their defense.

"I'm back," Gino said, and Ottavio groaned with relief.

"Gino, thank God it's you." Ottavio unfolded himself and stepped out, shaking his cramped feet.

Orso dropped the stick and flexed his legs and arms as he stood.

"Come on, we'll help you," Gino said, draping one of Ottavio's arms over his shoulder, and gesturing for Poldi to take the other. Their breathing seemed loud in the silence of early morning, and when Ottavio started to ask a question, Gino whispered, "Wait. We'll talk when we are aboard the ship."

Ottavio hobbled along and cried out softly when he saw Fiamma and Betta huddled together on the deck of the ship. He eyed the doctor with mild suspicion as Fiamma introduced him.

"Father, I present, Doctor Niccolo. By good fortune we met at the tavern where Betta's friend hid us. He has tended my injuries."

Ottavio thanked the doctor with stiff formality. "And how is it you are traveling to Praiano, Doctor?"

"In truth, Signore, I am traveling to Naples in the employ of the seneschal to his majesty, the Prince of Taranto, who will soon return from Avignon with our blessed Queen. We have been delayed by illness, but sail tomorrow. We have prevailed upon our captain to put you ashore at Praiano on the way."

"Illness?" Ottavio drew back. "Pestilence?"

"No, signore. None aboard have any sign of it."

Ottavio crossed himself. "The seneschal is most kind to agree to this further delay."

Doctor Niccolo cleared his throat. "In truth," he said, glancing at Gino, "Your astrologer and I have convinced the captain to depart a little earlier than he planned. I will speak with the seneschal in the morning. The delay will be insignificant."

"My astrologer?" Ottavio glanced around the group until his eyes lit on Gino. He paused, and Gino's heart nearly stopped, waiting to hear what Ottavio might say. Finally, Ottavio's head bobbed slightly on his skinny neck. "He is a very unusual man, isn't he? Signore Gino, is this where we sleep out this night?" Ottavio waved toward to deck, rocking gently at their feet.

"Yes, it will have to do. We may sleep a couple of hours before the sailors are out here. Then we'll have to be out of their way. Sit next to Fiamma, Signore Ottavio, and wrap up well in your cloak." Gino shifted their positions so the doctor moved away from Fiamma. She shot Gino a hard look, but the doctor graciously withdrew.

"I will go below and rest near the seneschal. I want to be near him when he wakes."

Poldi found his own spot on the deck, near half a dozen other sailors already sound asleep. Betta snored undisturbed beside Fiamma. Gino leaned on the mast, too exhausted to sleep. They were still in Amalfi, with no guarantee that Carlo would not surprise them before they got away.

How many hours would it be until they got under way, and until they reached Praiano? And how close would they sail to Li Galli? Could this be the chance he'd been hoping for?

The questions swirled through Gino's mind, before coming around to the bigger question. Would a swim near Li Galli take him back the way he'd come?

Because if he couldn't get back, how could he survive in this strange world?

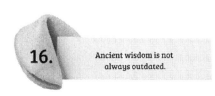

16.

Ancient wisdom is not
always outdated.

SARA'S HANDS SHOOK as she tried to find the place on the page Britt had been reading. Then she put her finger on it.

"'We met in Amalfi.'"

She glanced up. "That's very close to where he disappeared. 'The seneschal's illness forced our ship to delay there, and on the night before we were to depart for Naples, I was called to tend the injuries of a young lady. She and her companions traveled with an astrologer (for so they called him) they called Eugenio of Calabria. The party arranged passage on the seneschal's ship, but I thought it unwise to shelter them below deck with the seneschal and his family. Instead, they suffered the indignity of sleeping on the deck with the sailors. We heard no complaint from them for this, and I returned to my place near the seneschal, whose health I watched carefully.'"

Sara scanned ahead. "Okay, here's some more.

"'When sleep eluded me, I returned to the deck to see that the young lady rested well with her injured leg, and there I found the astrologer at the rail gazing at the stars. I asked him what portents he saw in the stars for our travels, and he laughed softly, and then, to my great surprise, began to weep. He quickly mastered his emotion, and turned to face me. I am no astrologer, he said. The stars tell me no more than that the sky is clear and we should see fine sailing tomorrow. If not an astrologer, I said, who and what are you?

"'My name is Eugenio the Calabrian, but I come from a land far away, a land neither you nor your captain nor even your queen has ever heard of, nor ever will. I am no astrologer, and do not believe that any knowledge is found in the stars. But I have pretended to study the stars, and have been paid well for the pretense, and many people followed my false wisdom, until I came to this time and place. (There he stopped, and looked around at the moonlit ship and town as if he had never seen them before.) This time and place, he repeated, and I wonder if this is some kind of punishment for wasting my life pretending to be what I am not.'"

Tears streamed down Sara's cheeks, and she handed the book to Britt. "Keep reading."

Britt picked up the story. "'How can you say there is no truth in it, I asked him, when you have made it your life's work? He looked at me, and his face spoke of a deep misery in his soul. My life's work? No, he said. I don't know what my life's work is. I've been too busy pretending I had some wisdom from the stars. I would give back all the money ever paid to me if I could go home now, go back and find what I should be doing, and do it well.'

"'Surely you can find a way home if you found your way here, I said, and he started to laugh bitterly, a most unhappy laugh. And he said, perhaps this ship can help me. If you sail past Sirenuse and drop me in the sea, I will be on my way home. That is where I last saw my own world.'"

Britt and Sara exchanged a long look before Britt continued reading.

"'Was this the raving of a madman? I looked to the stars and wished with all my heart that I could read some portent there. He seemed a thoughtful friend to his companions, and a man of intelligence, but to dismiss the wisdom of the heavens, to speak of being dropped into the sea—what was I to think? Perhaps the sirens were calling to him, but in the darkness around us I heard nothing of their song.

"'If you live near Sirenuse, you are not so far from home, I said, hoping this might comfort him. He seemed more agitated, and said, I don't know if it will work, but I don't know what else to do. I asked the name of his village or city, and he said a strange name, a place I knew nothing of. And then he said, it is far from Sirenuse, it is on the other side of the world. His words confused me, but I did not want to upset him further, so I tried to be comforting, and said if you were able to come here, you will surely be able to go back.

"'He grew quiet, and then asked me to sit down, so we sat together on the deck. He leaned over to me, as if to speak privately, and said that going to the place he lived was not the biggest problem, but that I would not believe the truth if he told me. I said please, Signore Eugenio, tell me and I will help you however I may. And he told me the strangest tale I ever heard, and I believe it to be true, though it is completely unbelievable.

"He asked me, What is the year, the date today? And I said, today is the fifth day of July in the year 1348. His mouth hung open, and he said, my God, my God. Tell me what is wrong, I said, and he replied, I arrived in Praiano one month ago, but I am not yet born.'"

"Oh. My. God." Sara took the book and reread the last paragraph, then stared at Britt, shaking her head. "Gino actually met this guy. Just like Elizabeth said."

"You really think it's him?"

Sara crumpled a damp Kleenex into her fist and nodded. "If he arrived one month earlier—that would be the day he disappeared, June sixth."

Britt turned the book over and looked at the cover. "It sounds as crazy to me as it did to this astrologer or doctor, whoever he is. But, like you said earlier, about the evidence, and your visions… well, it does sound like Gino."

✷ ✷ ✷

The doctor stared at Gino, wonder and pity mixed in his expression. "But, Signore, of course you have already been born. Here you are."

It could not be explained, Gino decided. He simply shook his head and looked over the rail to the northwest. "How near to Sirenuse will we sail, do you know?"

"Ships give the islands wide berth."

"Why?"

"The dangers have been known to sailors through the ages. The sirens still call men, and swirl the waters to draw in their ships. The Saracens have lived there, attacking our coast, but now I think the islands are guarded by the men of Praiano, so no enemy can make a foothold there."

"I would like to see them."

"The perils do not frighten you?"

Gino laughed. "The world is full of dangers, Doctor. The islands do not frighten me. I want to explore their mystery."

The doctor regarded him with respect. "You have courage, Signore."

Gino stared at the sea for a long moment. The moon had set, leaving a deeper blackness around them. He turned to the doctor. "Will you help me?"

"If I am able. What help do you need?"

"After the others, my friends, are delivered to Praiano, let me stay aboard until we pass the islands."

"So you will come to Naples with us? I don't know…"

"No, I will go to the islands, if the ship can just pass near them."

In the dim starlight, Gino detected a frown on the doctor's face. "I am a strong swimmer, and I will make my way there."

The doctor gaped, and took Gino by the arm. "You can't mean it, Signore. It is madness!"

"I swam there once before," Gino said. It seemed so long ago, that leap into the sea from Marco's boat. The clear tone drifting over the water, the glimmering light on the sea floor. "I survived, as you can see. And I saw no sirens." He didn't mention the clear, sweet tone he'd heard.

"But you know our situation. We cannot delay while you swim in the sea. The seneschal will never allow it."

"Do not wait for me. I won't return to the ship. I'll make my way home from Sirenuse." Or not at all, Gino thought.

"But what will your friends think?"

"We can tell them I am going to Naples with you. They know I intended to leave Praiano."

"To visit the sirens? They encourage you in that quest?"

"They know I am not an astrologer, and they have no further

use for me. I intended to part from them in Amalfi, and perhaps find my way to Salerno."

The doctor paused and Gino could barely see the glint of his eye in the deep darkness. "Lady Fiamma spoke of you fondly."

"She will understand my departure better than anyone."

The doctor considered that for a minute or so. "Has she refused your suit?"

That thought brought a smile to Gino's face. "No, I did not pursue her. She kept me company these past few weeks, so knows me better than the others."

"And her betrothed? Did you meet him?"

Gino quickly looked away, shaking his head. "No." Why had Fiamma invented that story? He didn't want to lie any more, but she would need to straighten out this problem. "She is in a vulnerable position, doctor. I'm afraid that her father's circumstances may force her into a convent. From my brief friendship with her, I don't think that life would suit her."

"No, no," the doctor murmured.

The doctor turned his back to the rail and peered toward Fiamma, sleeping against her father's shoulder a few steps away. Gino turned too, leaned against the rail, and stretched his neck and shoulders.

The doctor spoke softly. "What sort of woman is she, Signore?"

"Lady Fiamma? She is full of life, eager to learn. Unafraid."

"Like you? You seem to admire her."

"In some ways, I do."

"Yet you do not pursue her."

Gino turned back to the rail, thinking again of Sara. "My heart is drawn to another woman. If I can find my way home. Doctor, please, tell me you will help me get to the islands."

The doctor frowned. "I cannot help you end your life, or we would both forfeit our souls."

"My life is in another time and place. The first step is Sirenuse. I don't intend to end my life there. The islands may be my only hope of reclaiming it."

The doctor gazed for a long time into the starlit night before he leaned toward Gino. "I don't understand you, sir, but I do believe you. I will do what I can."

Then the doctor went below to check his sleeping patient. As the dark sky over Amalfi slowly faded to gray, and the stars dimmed, Gino thought through his plan. If the ship dropped him close enough to the islands, he hoped he could get back. Back to a new life, probably. What kind of comeback would he have, without his horoscopes? What kind of comeback with Sara? Would it be simpler to start again, in a new place, like someone in witness protection? He tried to imagine himself explaining his disappearance and return to his friends and family, even Sara. But if his astrology writing put her off, she may want nothing to do with him when she heard this story.

Even if he returned to a completely different life, the first step was getting to Li Galli, and that called for energy he didn't have. The tension and sleepless nights caught up with him, and he slid to the deck, leaned against a crate, and slept.

✵ ✵ ✵

Sara reread the last few lines. "Look, Britt. Now we know when he is there—1348. And the fifth day of July."

"So?"

"He's going back to Li Galli the next day. July 6." Didn't Britt get it? She still wore a puzzled frown. Sara laid the book face down on the coffee table and took hold of Britt's shoulders. "July 6 is only a week from now! He is trying to get back in a week."

Britt's eyes widened, and she glanced at the book and back to Sara. "Right. That is, if this Dr. Niccolo guy really helps him, and the seneschal guy doesn't throw them all off the ship, and the guy with the dogs doesn't come back for them."

Sara's smile evaporated. Obstacles littered the path. Then a light dawned. "The book will tell us," she said, reaching for it. She flipped it over and ran a finger down the page they had been reading, and paused for a moment of wonder at Gino's statement – I am not yet born.

Britt went to the kitchen cupboard and returned with a trash bag. She started tossing in the white cartons from their Chinese food, and the empty soy sauce packets.

"Leave that, Britt. Sit down and listen."

Britt gave the trash bag a toss toward the kitchen and sat cross-legged on the couch next to Sara. "Okay, read on."

Sara had been scanning ahead. "The astrologer agrees to help Gino get to the island, but he's reluctant about it. Okay, here: 'He told me that Lady Fiamma had become his closest friend, but he had not pursued marriage to her. A fire of jealousy burned in me as he spoke of their friendship, for she had both spoken of him and looked upon him with great fondness. Lady Fiamma lit a flame within me, but I had neither the right nor the freedom to pursue her, having no money, and my living in the service of the seneschal was hardly secure.

"'And why should Signore Eugenio confide in me any matter of his heart? He surely had no reason, but he had spoken so openly, without guile, of his other concerns, and of another woman, that I had no real reason to doubt him. Surely my envy swayed my thinking on the matter.'"

Sara sighed and took a big breath before plunging ahead.

"'The sky began to lighten. I knew I must sleep at least a little, and wanted to be near the seneschal, so I excused myself to go below.'" Sara skimmed along. "Okay, the doctor wakes up and realizes they are already sailing. He wants to explain the extra passengers to his boss. And when he does, the boss, that seneschal, is pretty mad, and they go up on the deck. Then there's this…

"'Lady Fiamma stood at the rail near the prow, her auburn hair flowing around her shoulders in the breeze, flanked by her father and the two servants. The captain called a command, and the sailors adjusted the sails, directing us to the next point of land.

"'There it is, Father, Fiamma said, rising to her toes, and her father said yes, it is Praiano. She turned to embrace her old serving woman, and as she did, she saw me and the seneschal watching them.

"'She leaned toward her father with a quick word, and then took his arm as he turned to greet us. Her limp diminished after the night's sleep, she bent her knee and bowed in courtesy to the seneschal, spreading her skirts wide, and thanked him for his indulgence while her father stammered his greeting, bobbing his head.

"'Only then did I see Eugenio at midship, looking west toward the specks of islands in the glittering sea.'"

Sara began to skim again.

"The seneschal is still mad, but wants to get rid of them at Praiano. The doctor is trying to smooth things over, worried about keeping his job. Then he goes back to check on Fiamma's injured leg. 'I looked up to remark on her speedy healing, but when our eyes met, I flushed deeply and could not speak. She took my hand and I wanted the moment to last forever, to be left alone with her, but her father's laughter broke the spell and she leaned near me, saying help me up.

"'I pulled her to her feet and she stayed very near me as we walked the few steps to her father's side. I felt Eugenio's eyes on me, from some secret vantage point around the deck, seeing even my intimate thoughts toward her. Though such knowledge seemed unlikely, all I knew about him was unlikely. Fiamma's father asked after her recovery.'"

Sara paused, reading silently for a minute.

"They're still talking about putting the girl in a convent, but now she wants to go to a convent in Naples instead of Amalfi, and Gino asks what convent it is in Naples, and maybe it would be a better idea for her to go there. The seneschal goes down to his cabin when all this is going on. Here he's talking about Gino again. 'Signore Ottavio found her less persuasive than I, until the Calabrian leaned near him and whispered something I could not hear. They exchanged a few words. He paused, looked doubtfully at his daughter, and then ordered her to wait where she stood. The two men drew me aside and asked to speak to the seneschal.

"'I balked inwardly, knowing his displeasure at having these additional passengers without his approval. But the thought that Fiamma might be brought to Naples, even as a nun, moved me to seek my overlord in his quarters below. I found him at the bottom of the stairway, urging his wife to take some fresh air on the deck. Perhaps the stale air below brought him up as much as my request.

"'Signore Ottavio bowed and nodded, obsequious before the seneschal, and barely able to voice his request. In the end, Signore Eugenio made plain that Ottavio wanted to send his daughter to Santa Chiara, and would be grateful if the seneschal agreed to take her, and her maid, and as additional protective escort for the women in Naples, the Calabrian himself offered to accompany them.'"

"Wait a minute, now there's a footnote," Britt said. "Damage to the manuscript leaves several pages illegible at this point." She flipped to the next page and scanned a few lines. "That's all it says about Gino and the boat. The next part is in Naples, in the winter, it sounds like."

Sara took a look for herself, and then flopped back against the couch cushions. "He's going to Naples now? So he won't get back to the islands next week. I mean, the sixth of July." She sighed deeply and closed her eyes. She imagined Gino on the ship, planning to escort a nun to Naples. Her emotions roiled inside her like tainted food, but she forced her fears away. A chuckle bubbled up from deep inside, and grew into a belly laugh.

Britt smiled uncertainly. "What is it?"

"Gino escorting a nun? I mean, really, can you imagine it?"

Britt laughed half-heartedly. "This Fiamma doesn't really seem like nun material to me."

Sara wiped her eyes, and a wariness settled on her. "Gino escorting a beautiful redhead—that seems more likely. And this doctor says she's very fond of him. I get the impression they are close."

"But she's flirting like crazy with the doctor, when Gino is right there. He doesn't seem jealous. He already told the doctor he wants to jump ship at the islands."

"He's trying to get home."

"That's right—home to another woman he loves." Britt leaned close and put her arm around Sara's shoulders. "Back to you."

"He never told me he loves me. It might be–"

"Of course it's you!" Britt rolled her eyes. "But you haven't exactly encouraged him!"

Sara thought back to the weeks before Gino left for Italy. Britt was right, of course. But she hadn't trusted him enough to talk about her family, and her clairvoyance. Now that she'd told Britt, and Elizabeth, telling Gino didn't seem so risky. If she ever got the chance to tell him.

"But will he do it? Will he come back?" She leaned into her friend's warm hug. "Oh, Britt, what should I do?"

Britt said nothing for a few moments, then gradually relaxed her hug. "You still didn't tell me about your dad. Why show up now?"

Sara glanced at the clock as midnight approached, then pushed aside the thought of work in the morning. Grady would understand. She leaned back against the arm of the couch, thinking of how much she'd not told Britt about her family. "He came because my mom told him to, and that's almost as shocking as the fact that he came to visit me at all. You know what a rough relationship we've had."

"I had the impression your mom caused most of the problems. But she didn't come, huh?" Britt raised her eyebrows.

Sara drank the last of the melted ice from her glass. "No. Just Dad. My mom, she's…she is mentally ill." Sara felt Britt go still as she listened. "She's worse now than when I was younger, and she rarely leaves their house. The problem between us, well—she believed that I was mentally ill. She made me see psychiatrists for years. For a long time, I didn't realize that she was the one with mental health issues. But she made my life pretty miserable. Impossible, really."

"So, what did your dad say?"

"That Mom has been worrying about me and telling him I needed help. It started when Gino disappeared." Sara watched Britt to see if she realized the implication.

Britt met her eyes with a deep frown. "Wait, you told them?"

"No. Nobody told her. They didn't even know I knew Gino. And she started telling him I had this problem before I even got the call saying that Gino disappeared."

"Whoa! How can that happen?"

Sara looked Britt in the eye for a moment, then looked at the floor. "The same way I knew about it before they called me from Italy." She shrugged, unable to avoid saying the word. "She's clairvoyant. Just like me. And I just found out today."

Britt gave her head a little shake. "Your dad told you?"

"Not exactly. But when he told me how long she's been worried about this, I knew it was before Gino even disappeared. That's the only way she could have known, and Dad confirmed it. Here's the weirdest thing. She made him promise to give me a message. 'Tell her to keep looking. Tell her not to give up.' He didn't even know what I was looking for, but now that I've told him what happened, he thinks it's Gino."

"Whoa, that's wild." Britt paused and shook her head again. "What was it like to see your dad, after all this time?"

"Scary at first but also sad. I mean, he's just been trying to take care of her, and I couldn't fit into that picture back then, five years ago. I thought I never would again, but now I think maybe I should try. I realized I don't want to lose them completely."

17. You are the best person
to change your life.

SARA CALLED GRADY AT NINE the next morning, and felt relieved to hear his voice as her vision of him in a morgue flitted across her mind. She said she'd had a bad night, but would come in by one and work late to make up the morning off. When she arrived, the lights were off, and she let herself in, surprised to see no sign of him. The additional three hours of sleep, and then a hot shower, had cleared her mind. She debated telling Grady what she now suspected about Gino when they broke for dinner. Would he believe it?

The answering machine light blinked, showing three messages, and she pulled a note pad from her top desk drawer. As she reached for the button, the phone rang, and the caller I.D. showed Grady's cell number.

"Hey, boss."

The slow, gravelly voice that answered her barely sounded like Grady, and Sara froze as she listened. "Glad you're there, darlin'. I need a favor."

"What's wrong, Grady? Where are you?"

"I need you to take a taxi up here to the Harborview E.R. and check me outa this place. The doc here won't let me go by myself." Grady coughed, and then groaned softly.

The hairs prickled on Sara's scalp and her heart hammered as she remembered Grady's image in the morgue. "Are you okay? What happened?"

"I'll tell you all about it on the way home."

Sara grabbed her purse, locked up, and ran two blocks to the nearest hotel with a cab stand. The cabby had her at Harborview in seven minutes, and she held out a twenty and asked him to wait.

Grady sat in a wheelchair, signing the last of the hospital paperwork for a nurse. "Looks like your ride is here," the nurse said. Sara made a beeline toward him.

He looked up and the movement made him wince, reaching for his neck. He had a bruise on his left cheek, and three or four small cuts on his forehead, so much like the vision she had of him in the morgue that she gasped.

"Magarry! What happened to you? Did you wreck your car?"

His soft chuckle made him wince again. "The car's a wreck all right. I want to walk out of here," he said to the nurse, but after one attempt to stand, he eased back down, resigned. "All right. Push me."

Sara trotted ahead of them, and flagged the taxi up into the loading zone, wondering how she would get Grady into his house. "Are you going to need a wheelchair to use at home for a few days? How bad are you hurt, Grady?"

He said nothing as the nurse helped him maneuver into the back seat. Sara slid into the front seat and turned to look at him. "Your house, right?"

A knock on the cab window startled Sara, and she turned to see the nurse. "You forgot your bag, Mr. Magarry." Sara opened the door and took the white plastic bag labeled *Patient Clothing*. She frowned at the stiff bulk of it and peered inside. What she saw made her head snap around to the back seat. She gaped at Magarry.

"I was about to say, you saved my hide, darlin'." He gave the cabby his address in West Seattle. "And pull through the Burger King on Fourth South. That'll have to do for the dinner tonight." He glanced at Sara without turning his head, and added softly, "And I owe you a hell of a lot more than that today."

Sara turned to look out the front window, with the plastic bag weighing heavy on her lap. He didn't want to talk about it any more in the taxi, she could tell. But he'd worn his bulletproof vest today—his armor, he called it—and she knew he hated using it.

An hour later, he rested on his couch within reach of the French fries. Sara bit into her burger as she listened.

"I got hold of the paramedic right quick, and he remembered the guy in Padgett's car. But he thought the guy had been in the car when it was hit. Said the guy spoke to Padgett in Russian, and when he got out and went to the other car, the paramedic thought he went to check on them, get insurance information, that kind of thing."

"Great, Magarry, but what happened to *you*?"

He fiddled with a French fry, and it took Sara a second to realize he did it to cover for his shaking hands.

"Where's that bag with the armor in it? Pull the chest plate out." He eased a fry to his mouth while she got the bag and took out the bullet-proof vest, holding it up between them.

"I went duck hunting this morning. But the ducks turned on me. If I hadn't worn that today, you'd have been picking me up at the morgue."

Sara shuddered. "Oh, Magarry." She turned it to look at the front. The fabric was torn on the left side. Sara gasped. "The Russians? You mean they shot you?"

"They did." Magarry groaned as he shifted on the couch. "They'd have killed me, too, if I hadn't worn that thing, and I wouldn't have worn it if you hadn't hounded me about being careful. Like I said, you saved my life."

The three bites of hamburger in her stomach hardened to concrete, and the bite in her mouth turned to sawdust. She thought she would choke, and ran to the kitchen, spit into the sink, and started to cry, big sobs that she couldn't hold down. She crossed her arms on the counter and rested her head until the big gulps subsided, and Magarry's voice came through.

"I meant that to be *good* news, darlin'." He paused. "Sara?"

She couldn't help laughing a little, and looked for a tissue but settled for the paper towels, and went back to the living room. "It's good news, Magarry. The best. What happened to the guy who shot you?"

"He drove off, but the cops who came to the hospital to talk to me said he's been picked up already. The bad news is, I lost us the job. Along with the attempted murder of me, they're opening up the Padgett case as a homicide. The insurance company will have us stand down."

"In this shape, you could use a couple of days off, Magarry." Sara glanced at the ER discharge papers on the end table, and took a deep breath. "In fact, I wanted to ask for some time off myself for a few days."

"You still helping out with that fortune-teller business?" His voice was low and kind, and Sara felt a surge of gratitude.

"Yes, it's about Gino. I know I just took yesterday off, but things have taken a turn." She hoped this wouldn't cost her the job, but with Britt, her dad, and Elizabeth all convinced of her clairvoyance, maybe Grady would be too.

Magarry swiveled his eyes toward her. "Did they find him?"

"No. They aren't even looking any more. But I think maybe I can find him."

Magarry turned his head a fraction of an inch in her direction, wincing. "Do you now?"

"Look, can I go fill this Vicodin prescription for you? Then I'll tell you my whole crazy story while you are falling asleep."

She returned from the pharmacy in half an hour, and by five o'clock, Magarry had heard it all—Sara's visions, the psychic, her dad's revelation, the book. She spared him the vision she'd had of his body in the morgue, but it never left her mind. She'd pulled her chair to the end of the couch by his feet, so he didn't have to turn his head to see her, and he listened quietly through it all.

When her story trailed off, he spoke up. "That's one helluva case, darlin'. Too bad I won't be able to help you solve it."

"I'm sorry I've been so distracted from work."

Magarry raised one hand, barely bending his elbow, and waved away her apology. "Take two weeks, Sara, and call me if you need more time. If you get this knot untangled, I want to hear about it. I won't be good for much for a few days anyway, so we'll just close the shop and have a little vacation. I'll have Fay call the clients. And that's two weeks paid vacation for you. You want it paid in advance?"

Sara laughed. "Magarry, are you sure *you're* not a mind-reader? That would be perfect."

"Get Fay on the phone for me, and I'll set it up. You can go in and pick up a check, and put a message on the phone and a sign on the door saying we're closed until the fifteenth of July."

Sara picked up the fast-food wrappers. "Can I get you anything?"

"If you set one of them happy pills and a glass of water right here where I can reach it, I'll be fine. But I'm curious, what are you planning to do?"

"Well, most of my information has come from my visions and the book. Britt and I found all we could in the book last night, so we thought… Well, I've never done it before, but we thought we'd try to bring on another vision on purpose, to try to get more information."

Magarry chuckled softly. "Pretty unorthodox means. Have you ever thought of becoming a private investigator?"

"Very funny, Magarry. But you're the one who always says 'leave no stone unturned'. Britt is going to bring a strobe light over and I'll let you know what happens."

✳ ✳ ✳

"Are you ready?" Britt sat on the sofa, her finger poised near the ON switch of the strobe light she'd rented at Party Central. The drapes and blinds were all closed tight.

Sara sat in her wing-back chair facing the coffee table where the strobe light sat, and wiped her sweaty palms on her jeans. For almost fifteen years she had fought off her visions, and here she was trying to bring one on. *I've already consulted a psychic and read a medieval astrologer*, she thought. *Is this so much crazier?* But how else could she learn more about Gino, to help him get back? Maybe she was wrong about it being a curse. Maybe clairvoyance was a gift after all. She'd actually been able to help Magarry—much to her own surprise. Could she find a way to help Gino too?

She gripped the arms of the chair. "Okay. Yes, turn it on."

Her cottage became a lightning storm and she heard Houdini yowl as he ran for the bedroom. Blinking rapidly, she could barely pick out the familiar landscape, her TV, the couch, even Britt's blonde head, in the blinding flashes. The old panic that came over her in thunderstorms rose up around her now. She closed her eyes but the light penetrated her eyelids. She let go of the chair and covered her eyes, but the light had done its work.

Her mind filled with a watery mist, a murky blue-green everywhere she looked. From somewhere a clear tone sounded, but she couldn't make out the source or even the direction. Turning every which way, she faced the same watery scene, and the sweet ringing rose in volume. Sara felt she had to find the source of that voice, and as she struggled through the mist, it suddenly cleared, and a moonlit sea glimmered all around her. Ten yards away, mossy grey stone rose up from the sea, and in the water, bumping against the stone in the rippling wavelets, drifted a lifeless body with curly black hair and a tattooed shoulder.

Britt shook her, then gripped her in a bear hug, and called her name. "You're okay, Sara! Stop screaming now. Stop! You're scaring me."

The strobe was off, and Britt fumbled for the reading lamp. The soft steady glow of the low setting revealed Britt's terrified face. Sara still gasped for breath, her heart pounding.

For a few minutes, Britt held her tight, until her breathing calmed. "Here, do you want a Kleenex?"

Sara pressed it against her eyes, and then blew her nose. She stared at her trembling hands holding the wad of tissue for a couple of minutes.

Finally, Britt broke in on her reverie. "What did you see?"

Sara met her eyes. "He drowned," she said, her voice cracking. "In the sea next to one of those islands."

"Oh, Sara." Britt frowned, and handed her another tissue. "Is there any way to know when it was? Back then, or in the future, I mean?"

Emotion surged, overwhelmed Sara. "How should I know? I saw him floating in the water." Her voice rose, strained. "I saw his tattoo! I couldn't help him, couldn't reach him," she said, pounding the arms of the chair.

"Okay, I'm sorry," Britt said, reaching for Sara's hand. "But we read that he went to Naples. I thought he decided not to jump off the ship."

The uncertainty in Britt's voice made Sara stop to ponder what they had read, and the vision she had seen. "He must have done it anyway, and maybe left the doctor to take care of that girl,

Fiamma. I know what I saw—those islands, the same place he disappeared."

Britt sat back on the sofa, lost in thought. Then she leaned forward and touched Sara's arm. "I'm sorry. Maybe we shouldn't have tried this."

Sara's mind still swam with the image of Gino's body floating in the sea, but she pushed it away. "I wanted to, Britt. It's not your fault. I just wish I could stop it, change it."

Britt pulled her feet up under herself. "It's so frustrating—to see something like that. It hasn't happened yet, but you can't do anything about it."

Sara caught her breath. "What did you say?"

"You can't do anything about it?"

Sara's heart threatened to explode. "But maybe I can, Britt."

Britt shook her head, mystified.

"It hasn't happened yet. It's only the end of June. If the timing in this book is right, he hasn't left Amalfi yet." Sara sat up straighter in her chair, heart pounding now with excitement. Britt listened warily from the sofa.

"We know he intended to go back to the islands on July sixth. That's what he told the doctor, before he said he would accompany Fiamma to Naples, right?"

Britt nodded.

"They expected to be going by the islands after stopping at Praiano early in the day, so they might pass the islands later in the morning, and go on to reach Naples before the end of the day, right?"

"Right." Britt drew out the word, making her uncertainty clear.

"We don't know if he goes on to Naples or leaves Fiamma on her own, or with the doctor. But we do know Gino really wants to come back. So let's say he jumps off the ship."

Britt nodded again.

"Now we do this," she said, waving a hand toward the strobe on the coffee table, "and I see him sometime later—at least sixteen or eighteen hours later, but maybe days."

Britt frowned. "Wait, why do you say it's that much later?"

"Because it was night time. In my vision, I mean. With moonlight on the water, and the only other lights came from the windows of a house up on the island."

"Lights in the window? You mean like candles?"

Sara thought for a few seconds. "No, brighter than that. Like a window with the lights on. Maybe a yard light."

Britt grabbed her arm. "A *yard* light? Did they have yard lights back then?"

Their eyes locked. Sara swallowed, then spoke slowly. "No, I don't think so. It looked like an electric light. It would have to be now!" Sara leapt from her chair and paced to the front door and back. "That has to be now! And if he comes back to now, maybe… if I was there…" She took a step back and looked at Britt for a long moment and thought about Magarry and his bulletproof vest. "Maybe I *can* change what I saw."

18. If you don't take a chance, you'll never know what might have happened.

GINO COULD NOT BELIEVE HIS EARS. Did Ottavio really think Fiamma had a future as a nun? With all that had transpired in Amalfi, Gino hoped thoughts of the convent had been forgotten, but apparently not.

"Signore Ottavio," Gino said, after the doctor went to find the seneschal, "Do you think the convent in Naples will accept Fiamma?"

Ottavio heaved a sigh. "I don't know. Who knows if the pestilence awaits her there? And perhaps they require a gift to assure her welcome."

"You could send a gift with her."

Ottavio shrugged and heaved a hopeless sigh. "What gift?"

"The purse still has a few coins in it. She can—we can take one with us to Naples." Gino heard the seneschal's voice behind him, and he leaned close to Ottavio and whispered, "Maybe another coin will buy our passage."

The doctor's eagerness balanced the seneschal's reluctance, Gino thought as they greeted Ottavio.

"My lord, a request," Ottavio began with a quaver in his voice. "My daughter is destined for the church, and she hopes to enter the royal convent, Santa Chiara in Naples. If she could stay aboard this ship, my lord, and go to Naples today…" His voice trailed off at the stormy look on the seneschal's face.

Gino waited only a few seconds before stepping in. "My lord, perhaps your queen will look favorably on your act of charity, if so many have died in Naples. The royal convent has no doubt lost many, and a novice from a good family might be very welcome."

The seneschal narrowed his eyes in contemplation, and after a brief silence, Gino added, "Of course it need not be entirely an act of charity, my lord. Signore Ottavio is prepared to compensate you for the service you would do him." He opened his hand enough so the glint of gold caught the sun.

The seneschal's brows rose, and he looked with more respect at Ottavio. "Perhaps it would not be too great an inconvenience, since we sail for Naples anyway."

Ottavio stood silent, still incapable of contributing any useful remark, so Gino continued. "My dear friend," he said, indicating Ottavio, "is troubled to be parting with his youngest daughter, of course." Gino turned to Ottavio. "And it's time for your farewell to her."

The doctor could barely contain his delight. Gino saw him exchange a glance with Fiamma, both of them covering their smiles as Ottavio approached and took her in a tentative embrace.

The captain barked that the boat was ready, and Gino caught the seneschal's eye. "Are we agreed, my lord?" He held the coin near the seneschal's hand, but the man waved him away.

"Yes, yes, we are agreed. We'll conclude this later. Get the others into the boats now. No more delays!" The seneschal crossed the deck to his wife, waiting by the far rail.

Orso clambered down the rope ladder into the skiff and soon Ottavio returned to the rail. Gino touched his arm.

"Signore Ottavio, here is the purse. I have a coin for the seneschal and one for the convent. You should keep the rest."

Ottavio looked with distaste at the leather pouch of money stolen from his brother. "Gino," he said, pushing the pouch away, "You have proved yourself a great friend, and you may need coin for your own food and lodging in Naples after you see my daughter settled in her new life."

"Signore!" the boatman called up, waving Ottavio toward the rope ladder.

Gino took Ottavio's hand and placed the pouch in his palm, closing his fingers around it. "No. I'll be fine, Signore Ottavio. Betta has restored some of your fortunes. Make the most of them—dowries for your daughters, repairs to your palazzo. Maybe you will marry again."

The captain called a harsh command, and Gino saw the seneschal glaring at them. Gino steadied Ottavio as his feet found their places on the rope ladder. He descended until could just see over the rail, and then paused. "Gino, I can't leave you with nothing." He held the pouch over Gino's palm and shook until a few small coins fell into it.

"Go now, Signore," Gino said hoarsely as a lump rose in his throat.

When would Ottavio learn of the betrayal Gino intended to perpetrate within the next couple of hours?

✳ ✳ ✳

As the ship slipped through the glittering water, Gino turned from the cliffs of Praiano, and watched the islands. He faced a long swim, and shrugged the tension out of his shoulders. He reckoned they were nearing the closest point, if the ship kept to her course.

Glancing around the deck, he caught the eye of the doctor gripping the rail near the prow, about thirty feet forward of Gino's position. He glanced toward the islands and back to Gino, then shook his head.

Gino turned away, refusing to be dissuaded from his plan. A southerly breeze carried the ship along quickly, and Gino hoped he could dive clear of any obstacles, and the dinghy trailing behind. The sails billowed taut and white in the sun, speeding them toward the Cape of Sorrento and the Bay of Naples.

Fiamma and Betta sat on the deck near where they had slept. They conspired together, heads bent, and Gino imagined them talking of Naples and the unknown awaiting them there. The sun shone bright and hot on them, and a breeze pulled at wisps of Fiamma's hair.

This is the last I'll see of them, Gino thought with a pang. They'll make their own way in Naples. He looked at the silver coin in his palm, and made a quick decision. "Doctor," he called, striding across the deck.

"Thank God," the doctor said, gripping Gino's shoulders as they met at midship. "You have abandoned your mad plan."

"No, I have made a better plan," Gino said. "Better for you and for Lady Fiamma, I hope."

The doctor turned an adoring glance her way at the mention of her name. "Listen," Gino said, and opened his palm between them. Three pieces of silver glittered there alongside a larger piece of gold. "You can make better use of this than I can."

"No, Signore!"

"Yes. Your interest in her welfare is obvious." The doctor flushed. "The gold is her dowry, intended to smooth her way to Santa Chiara. But I fear she will not fare well in that life. Do as you think best for her. I turn her guardianship over to you."

The doctor gaped, opened his mouth and closed it again.

"The silver is yours for the service you do me, and Fiamma, and Signore Ottavio. Perhaps it will help you fulfill your own dreams. And by doing this, you allow me to pursue mine." Gino glanced at the approaching islands. "Go now. Distract her so she doesn't see me." Holding the rail, Gino backed away from the doctor and moved toward the stern, until the doctor closed his fist around the coins and pressed it to his heart, then lurched toward Fiamma as the ship rolled over a wave.

Taking the hem of his tunic, Gino pressed the one remaining silver coin between the stitches and into the hem, then tied the fabric in a knot. Steeling himself, he turned back to face the sea.

A house gleamed golden in the sun on the largest of the islands, and he made that his focus, a point to aim for as he swam. With one more quick look around, he put his right foot on the rail, hoisted himself to a standing position, and dove. Just before he hit the water, he heard Fiamma's scream. And when he surfaced and shook the water from his ears, she gripped the rail, calling his name. Betta and the doctor stood by her side.

He sought out the gleam of the house on the island, its walls reflecting the mid-day sun, and began a steady crawl in that direction, hoping his strength would take him the distance. When he paused to get his bearings, the low tone of a flute reached him across the glittering surface of the sea.

✳ ✳ ✳

After debating the best approach, Sara told Marco and Lia that she needed to see for herself where Gino disappeared to help her get over the loss, and ask them to go with her. They would understand—they struggled with the same loss themselves. Then if, God forbid, she was wrong about the whole thing, no one else would know about the visions.

On July 6, she and Lia huddled on the narrow prow of Marco's boat as they motored north past Amalfi and around the next point of land, where Praiano clung to the hillside. All along the coast, towers stood guard, many of them derelict, some converted to private homes or tourist housing. *Torre Saraceni*, they were called, designed as a warning system in case of Saracen attacks. When the tower in Praiano came into view, Sara slowly stood up, staring.

Lia watched her anxiously, and stood next to her. "Are you okay?"

Sara whispered a soft "yes" and nodded, then swung around to the north and shaded her eyes. There, there were the islands, rising from the water ahead. Hope nearly burst in her chest, but she had to keep up the appearance of the grieving friend just a little longer.

"Could I use the binoculars?"

Lia pulled the strap over her head and handed them to Sara.

As Sara brought the islands into view, she felt Lia's hand of comfort on her shoulder.

Sara had talked with Marco—with Lia translating, of course—about sailing to Praiano and visiting Li Galli with her that afternoon. He finally agreed, with no enthusiasm. Afterwards, they had rooms booked in Praiano, and would head back to Sicily the next day.

Near the peak of summer tourism, sails dotted the sea. Speedboats trailed white ruffles, and a breeze relieved the heat of a brilliant sun. Sara watched boats cruising around Li Galli, and dozens of people at play.

Lia linked arms with her, and when Marco circled the boat wide around the islands, Sara said, "Would you ask him to go where

Gino went into the water?" When Lia paused, Sara reached for the bouquet of flowers tucked behind her. "I want to leave them there."

Lia crept along the narrow rail and spoke quietly with Marco at the back of the boat. After a few minutes he changed course. Ignoring the speedboats and party boats, he steered to the west side of the islands and dropped the engine to idle. "Sara," he called, his voice husky, and waved her over to the back of the boat. They stood together in the small space.

"He's going to tell you what happened," Lia said. "I'll translate."

Sara tried to imagine how hard this must be for Marco. His ramrod stance at the tiller could not hide the pain. "Thank you. Grazie." She nodded to them both, then gripped the chrome rail and faced the islands.

Marco spoke a few words in a tight, strained voice, and Lia's mellow, accented English followed. "We approached the islands from the south, like we just did today, and Gino said he wanted to go into the center."

Rolling in the wakes of the pleasure boaters, they approached Li Galli slowly, producing no wake of their own. "I didn't want to sail in there, the legends and currents, you know. But we came closer. About to here."

Marco cut the engine. "Gino threw off his shirt, kicked out of his sandals." He paused, pursing his lips to stop a quiver. Lia took his hand, and laid her head on his shoulder. After a minute, he went on and she translated. "I didn't want him to swim. The sun was almost gone, but he wanted to see the island up close. He swam to that one." Marco pointed to the nearest island, about a hundred yards away now.

Sara lifted the binoculars and brought the rough walls into focus. "That's where you last saw him," she said. "That's where I want to put the flowers."

She heard Lia translate, and knew from the tone of the ensuing conversation that Marco did not want to go any closer. But she had to keep them there, somehow. Today was the day, according to the astrologer's book, that he leapt from the ship and swam to the islands, trying to get back—back to her, Britt had said. She hoped that part was true.

Sara's mind darted here and there, much like the motor boats and Jet Skis around them. Would he really come back? And if so, where and how? Maybe they would miss seeing him in this expanse of water.

The sailboat purred a little louder, and they drew up about twenty feet off the jagged rock wall. Marco cut the engine.

"This is La Rotonda, the dome," Lia said, and Marco added something. Lia turned back to her with tears in her eyes. "He says Gino called them Sara's islands."

Sara couldn't swallow the lump in her throat. Had she meant that much to him, in spite of her brushing him off? She'd been so afraid of getting close, but now being closer to Gino was her heart's desire. And after all that had happened with Magarry, she wanted desperately to change her last vision of Gino too – not the body floating lifeless but the man back from another time.

She grabbed her bouquet and moved forward by herself, wiping her eyes, then sitting on the narrow prow. She scanned the inside of the circle of islands through the binoculars. The inhospitable walls flung back every wave that licked them. From her pocket, she pulled her phone and started the international geocaching app. Regardless of what happened, she wanted to remember this place, and she could record the exact coordinates, take some photos. She looked at the nearest rock wall thrust up from the sea. Not a welcoming spot for a homecoming, she thought. If Gino came home.

She snapped a couple of pictures, then switched back to the binoculars. The early afternoon sun glared on the water. She focused on the surface, looking for anything that might be a person swimming or floating.

After a few minutes, Sara realized that Lia and Marco were talking, almost arguing, back by the tiller. They probably wanted to leave. She picked up the bouquet and pulled the ribbon off it. Maybe she could buy some more time if she dragged this out. She pulled a sunflower from the bunch and tossed it into the wavelets, then breathed in the cinnamon scent of a white carnation while the sunflower drifted away. One by one, sunflowers, burgundy dahlias, and carnations floated around the boat.

A speeding Jet Ski circled near them, engine roaring. Waves

from the wake pushed the flowers against the wall of La Rotonda. Sara peered over the edge of the bow, which hung over the line where the water turned from deep blue to turquoise. A gleam deep in the water caught her eye, like a red light glowing among the rocks and sand far below them.

"Someone is playing a flute," Lia called from the stern as the Jet Ski disappeared between islands. "Do you hear it?"

A mournful couple of notes drifted across the water, and Sara shaded her eyes, scanning the big island, Gallo Lungo, where a few houses perched on the clifftops.

Lia made her way to the bow and picked up the binoculars lying next to the last couple of flowers from Sara's bouquet. She stood and scanned the islands. "Marco, do you hear it? Go a little closer."

The engine jumped to life, and the boat lurched forward as Marco pushed the tiller. Lia screamed. Sara turned to see her off balance and grabbing air as she cleared the bow and splashed into the sea.

"Lia!" Marco yelled. He cut the engine and began shouting at Sara in rapid-fire Italian as he hurried along the narrow walkway to the bow. He spotted Lia sputtering and gasping just a couple of yards from the boat, and lay on the deck reaching a hand out to her.

Sara grabbed a rope coiled at the bottom of the mast, and hung one end down to Lia, and she and Marco hauled her up. Only when she sat shivering on the deck, dripping rivulets of water from her hair and clothes, did Sara hear the panic in her voice as she talked to Marco, and realize Lia was crying.

They hadn't come planning to swim, but Sara found a towel in the cabin. Lia seemed a little calmer with the towel wrapped around her. She had the hiccups.

"Lia, what's wrong?" Sara sat beside her.

"I—something bumped me in the water. A big fish or something." She shuddered and hugged the towel tighter. "It felt like it tried to grab me."

"Really?" Sara knelt by the rail, looking into the water. "Where?" The ripples looked like they always had.

"I'm sure it swam away by now." Lia toweled her hair, and her dark curls sprang back to life. "I can still hear that flute—or are my ears just ringing? Do you hear it?"

Sara looked up. The boat drifted toward the center of the circle of islands. Marco stood, his gaze fixed on something dead ahead about sixty feet.

"Lia, what is that?" Sara pointed.

Lia straightened up from shaking water out of her ears and peered toward what looked like driftwood. She reached for the binoculars, but Marco grabbed them first. With his eyes fixed on something, he took a staggering step.

"Gesu Maria!" he breathed.

Sara and Lia asked the same question in two languages: "What is it?

"*Dio mio*!" Marco dropped the binoculars and practically ran to the stern. "Deee-o meee-o!" Then a torrent of Italian, and Lia began to cry.

"*Non e possibile*. No, Marco." She fumbled for the binoculars as Marco started the sailboat's engine.

"What is it?" Sara demanded, shaking Lia's arm.

Lia shoved the binoculars at her. "You look first. He say—he says it is Gino."

Sara's hands shook so much she could barely bring the spot into focus. Now about fifty feet away, what had looked like driftwood now splashed. Black curls rose above the surface, and she thought she glimpsed a tattoo on his shoulder.

As the sailboat eased forward, a Jet Ski roared up behind them. Sara turned to see them headed straight for Gino, and the driver laughing and looking over his shoulder. Without a conscious thought, Sara yanked the phone from her pocket and flung it toward the oblivious driver as he sped past Marco's boat, as she screamed, "Stop!"

As the phone arced through the air, she gripped the chrome rail. "Please stop," she whispered.

The phone struck the driver's arm. Just a couple of yards from Gino, he jerked to the right. A wall of water washed over Gino. The driver cut power and stood up as the machine slowed, shaking a fist and yelling curses in Italian. Marco continued toward Gino, ignoring the tirade.

Sara saw Lia and Marco talking, maybe even to her, but the sound all softened to a hazy white noise. "Gino! He was right!

Gino! You came back!" Sara couldn't tell if she whispered or yelled. She had seen a vision of the future, another death, and she had changed it.

Marco cut the engine and the boat slowed to a near stop with Gino just off the stern. Sara and Lia scuttled along the side toward him. Marco grasped Gino's arm and pulled him aboard.

Gino coughed up some seawater before he spoke. "Grazie." He threw his arms around Marco, who pounded his back, and then gripped his shoulders and held him at arm's length for a good look. Lia slipped into the cabin for a blanket and laid it over his shoulders and gave him a squeeze.

"You waited a long time for me. I thought you'd—Sara!"

His confused expression faded as she wrapped her arms around him and held him tight. "You came back."

He slowly released her, his eyes questioning. "I'm getting you all wet."

"I don't really care," she said, and embraced him again, then kissed his salty cheek. "I was so worried about you." She rested her head on his shoulder. Gino enclosed her in a very tentative hug, and she realized how strong her feelings had grown since he left. Did he feel the same, or had she misunderstood what the astrologer's book said? She let go and stepped back, sitting on the narrow bench seat.

Marco and Lia hovered around him. Their questions in Italian meant nothing to Sara. She could see him struggling to explain—not struggling with the language, but with an explanation of his experience. She wished she could understand his answers.

Lia broke in using English. "What's this you're wearing?"

The bedraggled green tunic dripped seawater. The sleeves were gone, and a frayed hole revealed his pale belly. Gino just shook his head.

Lia rattled off something to Marco, whose mouth hung open. His eyes never left Gino.

"Si, si." Marco waved toward the cabin.

"Marco has extra clothes in the cabin." Lia nudged Gino in that direction. "You need to dry out. Look at your wrinkled skin, like you've been in the water for hours. Or weeks!" They all shifted in the crowded stern of the sailboat so Gino could open the door.

Gino stepped down the two steps. As he closed the door, Marco's knees buckled and he sat hard on the bench beside the tiller. Lia knelt next to him, crying and laughing together.

Then Gino pulled Sara into the tiny cabin behind him.

19. The truth is all you truly have.

AS SOON AS THE DOOR CLOSED, Gino took her in his arms again. He held her tight, trembling, and then said with genuine confusion, "What are you doing here?" Without giving her time to answer, he embraced her again. She breathed whispered repetitions of his name like a mantra, and stroked his back. After a long minute, he leaned away from her. "Really, Sara, what are you doing here?"

"Finding you."

He shook his head with a brief laugh. "You couldn't have found me."

"But I did." She pulled close to him again and whispered in his ear. "I know where you were, Gino. From the astrologer's book."

He tensed, feeling doubtful and cautious, and pushed her back so he could look her in the eye. "You don't believe all that."

"You knew him as a doctor, and I think he helped you get back."

At that his breath caught, and a tingling sense of shock filled him. "He did help me." He looked at her curiously, thinking of the doctor standing at the rail, afraid for Gino's life. "And when I came to the surface today, I thought that Jet Ski would run over me. That's the first thing I thought—I escaped from the past just to be killed by a water toy." He saw her face cloud up with some memory of her own. "What is it?"

"You're right. That thing would have run over you."

"Would have? If what?"

"I threw my cell phone at him. Did you see him veer off?"

Gino looked away, thinking back through those few moments. "Yes, but then Marco's boat pulled up, and everything went a little crazy."

"They're in shock, I think. They don't know where you've been," she said, with the slightest tilt of her head toward his cousins on the other side of the door. She laid one hand on his chest, not pushing away, but a tender barrier, a caution.

"What do they think?"

"Oh, Gino, everyone thought—still thinks—you're dead. They stopped searching weeks ago."

The weight of her words struck him. He had imagined their frantic search for him continuing, but not that they really believed him dead. "My parents—" he began, and she took a ragged breath and dropped her head to his shoulder.

"Your dad came to Seattle, and I helped him clean out your apartment." She paused. "They are planning a memorial service for you in a few days."

Gino groaned. "Oh my God. I have to call them…but what will I tell them? They'd never believe what happened to me. I can barely believe it myself."

"I didn't know if…" She faltered momentarily. "…if you'd get back from there. If the astrologer was right."

He stroked her forehead gently and pushed her hair behind one ear. Then he leaned close and whispered, "The astrologer? Have you taken up with another astrologer while I've been gone?"

He finally got a grin out of her, and the fleeting appearance of her dimple took the breath out of him again.

"I told you, he was the doctor you knew. Remember the book I gave you? The one by the medieval astrologer? When Marco sent your stuff back, it looked like you had started reading it, and I read some of it too. At first I just wanted to hold onto something you had touched."

None of that made much sense, but footsteps sounded on the

deck, and the boat shifted. "The sail's up." Gino ran his fingers through her hair. "What cryptic message did the medieval guy have that convinced you I was still alive?"

"Nothing cryptic at all." The boat rocked a few times, crossing the wake of another boat, and Gino took her arm as she got her balance. "Where are Marco's clothes? We have rooms in Praiano tonight. Turn around, I'll dry your back."

"Nothing cryptic? Just an ordinary astrological reading for someone who wouldn't be born for six hundred years or so?"

"Not even that. He wrote about you in that book because he was your friend. The doctor."

Gino had the tunic halfway over his head when he felt another rush of shock. "What?! You mean that astrologer and the doctor are the same person?" he said as he yanked it off and turned to face her.

Sara put a hand up and turned away from his nakedness. She picked up a towel and handed it back to him. "That's what I've been trying to tell you. The doctor from Salerno, on the ship with you going to Naples—he's the same guy who wrote that book. He became an astrologer."

"And in that book he said Gino Calabrese from Seattle jumped off the ship at Praiano so he could get back to his life in the future?" Gino dried off and wrapped the towel around his waist. When he touched Sara's shoulder, she turned to face him.

"He called you Eugenio the Calabrian, but he said enough that we recognized you."

"We?"

Sara pawed through the cupboard and came up with a pair of jeans, but no underwear. Gino shrugged and pulled them on. "Who's 'we'?"

"Britt is the only other one who knows. Well, there's one other person." She looked up sheepishly. "A psychic in Bellingham. And I had to tell Magarry."

Gino leaned against the door, brows raised, and appraised her. "You went to a psychic? You are just full of surprises."

Sara ran her fingers over his tattoo. "Not the same girl you left behind. Actually, a lot has changed."

Gino's scalp went prickly. What had driven Sara, the pragmatic, straightforward realist, to consult a psychic? He'd thought for weeks about how she might be responding to his disappearance, but consulting a psychic? That had never crossed his mind.

"Better hang this to dry," Sara said, reaching beyond him for the tunic on the floor.

"I'll get it." Gino snatched it before she reached it. He ignored her look of surprise, and pulled the tee shirt from her hand. "Would you go see where we're headed? I'll be up in a minute."

He watched her go, and closed the door gently behind her, then considered the lock for a moment. He pulled Marco's T-shirt over his head. Then he held the tunic up in front of him and felt along the hemline.

There. He rubbed the knotted corner between his fingers and picked at the stitching until it came loose. A silver coin dropped to the floor. He turned it over in his hand, taking in the cross, a king's image, and a worn Latin inscription. Shoving the coin in his jeans pocket, he hung the tunic on a hook, and opened the door to the hot afternoon sun.

His eyes adjusted to the light, and the cliffs of Praiano rose before him. Ahead on the right a crumbling tower capped the headland, and Marco steered into the cove below it. Gino couldn't take his eyes off the tower, remembering the way it had looked as he sailed away after leaving Ottavio and Orso at Praiano—nearly new, and with repairs from the earthquake almost completed. To him, it seemed just a few hours ago.

Lia stared at him, and Marco glanced his way again and again. Gino even caught Marco crossing himself, with such a look of confusion Gino wondered if he should be sailing the boat.

Marco dropped anchor and launched the dinghy. He rowed ashore with Lia. While Gino and Sara waited, he scanned the town above. Whitewashed houses, cars zipping by the spaces between them, the noise of the speedboats on the water at his back, and big band music from a restaurant patio above them on the left. The noises overwhelmed him, as the silence had a month earlier.

Sara shifted beside him. "Were you in that tower?"

He glanced up at it. "Yes, just for a night."

She grinned. "It must all look very different now."

"Oh, yeah," he said softly. What could she know about it? Of course things change in six or seven centuries.

Sara had splurged, run up her credit card, booking a whitewashed splendor of a hotel with connecting rooms, and two double beds in each. Paying for it herself helped to silence the objections of Lia and Marco. She'd told them she wanted to treat them, for making her visit to Praiano possible. She couldn't share the hope rising in her heart like bread dough in a warm oven.

Now she marveled that she'd been able to find him at all, to rescue him from the tragedy in her vision. They sat outside a little pizzeria, having finished three pizzas and a bottle of wine. Sara toyed with her half-full glass as their conversation devolved into awkward silences following questions Gino avoided answering. Marco stared at him, and Lia kept shaking her head and saying, "My God."

How hard this must be for him! Sara wanted to talk with him alone. Maybe she could reassure him, or help him figure out how to return to Seattle, sort out his life. He'd have to find a new job, though she didn't know what that would be. His horoscope column had closed down with a brief obituary, so it would be very awkward to resurrect it.

During the short walk back to the hotel, Gino searched the surrounding buildings, streets, churches, disoriented and inattentive to conversation. He took her hand a couple of times, but let it slip away as he looked around.

The joyful celebration of his return, this first night, was not unfolding as she had imagined.

They approached the entrance to their hotel. The heat and her anxiety conspired to create a line of perspiration that trickled down Sara's back. Marco held the door open, but after Lia went through, Gino balked.

"I need some clothes. There's a shop open a couple of doors down." His hand went to the back pocket of the jeans, where his wallet would have been. He realized Sara had seen the gesture and swore softly.

She took his arm lightly. "I've got one of the keys. I'll go and help him pick out something." Marco shrugged and followed Lia in.

"You don't have to—"

"Glad to help, Gino. Your credit cards aren't worth much since you were presumed drowned. You can use mine and we'll even up later."

Gino's pace slowed as he chewed on some thought. "Do I even have any money? I mean my bank accounts?"

"Yes, it takes a while to clear up that kind of thing when someone…you know, disappears. I'm pretty sure your parents haven't closed them yet." Her voice trailed off as they entered the nearest shop. The shopkeeper, a man in his forties who was combing his hair in front of a mirror by a rack of sunglasses, appraised them with a glance and greeted them in English, then let them browse on their own.

"Oh, God. What am I going to tell my parents?" Gino pawed absently through a stack of shirts, and then held up a pair of jeans, checked the length, and tossed them over his arm. "I hate to have you pay for this stuff."

"It's okay, Gino. Get what you need. Really, you can pay me back." She certainly hoped he could pay her back. She mentally ticked off the charges to her credit card for this trip. Even with her paid vacation time, the expenses were adding up.

He took a T-shirt from one of the racks. "What about this?"

"Great," she said, barely seeing it. "Anything else?"

He craned his neck to scan the rest of the shop. "Think they have any underwear in this place?"

"I think I saw some at the back."

The shopkeeper looked from one to the other and smirked as Gino dropped the clothes on the counter and Sara pulled out her credit card. Gino surprised her when he stared down the man without cracking a smile.

Sara took his arm as they left the shop, and noticed Gino again scouring the houses. What was this like for him? "Are you looking for Fiamma's house?"

His head snapped around and he stared at her. "What did that astrologer's book say about her?" He looked wary.

"He said you and Fiamma were fond of each other, and her father wanted you to take her to Naples to become a nun." She paused, trying to organize her random thoughts. "He said you told him you weren't an astrologer, even though that's what people called you."

Gino's brow furrowed as they approached the hotel. "What did he say that convinced you to come here?"

"You're the one who convinced me. You told him you were going to try to get home if you could get to the islands, if he would help you jump off close by. And he had already said what day it was. You asked him the date."

"It's still hard to believe it worked." He pulled open the hotel door. "What room are we in?"

Sara looked down quickly, hoping he hadn't read the surprise on her face. Did he assume they'd be sharing a room? She hadn't talked with Lia about a contingency plan if Gino showed up alive. She fumbled in her pocket and read the tag on the key. "Fourteen." He seemed lost in his thoughts, anxious and distracted.

They passed the noisy buzz of the ground-floor bar, and climbed a flight of stairs. The interior walls were the same brilliant white as the outside of the hotel, brightened by oversized paintings of bougainvillea, scarlet geraniums, and Asiatic lilies. Sara unlocked the door, and Gino followed her in.

Like a sanctuary, the cool clean room calmed her. Gino tossed his shopping bag on a chair and looked around, taking in the two beds, the sleek modern bath.

The setting sun threw golden beams far into the room, drawing them toward the French doors and the balcony. He went to the rail. Latin dance music drifted up from a waterfront club. Gino's gaze leveled on the islands and stayed there.

The ringing hotel phone jarred her. It was Lia.

"I thought I heard you next door. Is everything okay?"

"We're fine. Why are you whispering?"

"Marco fell asleep. Should I…I'll just sleep in here on the other bed, Sara."

Sara glanced at Gino on the balcony, and then to the door that connected the two rooms. She apparently felt more awkward than anyone else did about the sleeping arrangements. There were two beds in each room, so nothing had to be assumed. "That might work best, Lia. Thanks. I think Gino wants to talk for a while, but he's tired, too."

"We'll talk tomorrow. *Ciao*."

Sara breathed a deep sigh, a sure sign of anxiety. Gino still sat on the balcony, on one of the lounge chairs, pondering the islands.

She slipped out through the French doors, startling him. The sunset was just a golden crack between sea and sky, and the faint breeze felt good. She sat on the other lounge chair and slipped her shoes off. Conversation just seemed awkward, so she closed her eyes, relaxing into the striped cushion.

A couple of minutes passed, and she heard Gino stir, and his sandals—Marco's spares from the boat—plopped softly onto the floor. His hand touched hers, and he gripped her gently and entwined his fingers through hers.

Stars began to dot the darkening sky.

"Sara," he said softly, "why did you come here?"

Tension gripped her again. Was he really saying she shouldn't have, or that he wished she hadn't? "I couldn't believe you were gone. I actually *didn't* believe it, but everyone else believed you'd drowned."

He let go of her hand and propped himself on one elbow facing her. "You said earlier, on the boat, you knew where I was."

Her heart lurched. "I…I read the astrologer's book." She shifted onto her side to face him. He'd lost weight, she realized.

Gino frowned. "But he didn't know about the tower, and you did. That couldn't have been in his book."

The thought of opening herself up nearly paralyzed her, the risk of being the crazy person in his eyes. But the truth was all she had. "I saw you in that tower, in a vision."

He started to laugh—he clearly thought she was joking—but his expression turned to wonder when he realized she told the truth. His eyes narrowed. "What do you mean?"

Where to start? "Remember when you were at those Greek ruins—Paestum? And you called me because I had left a couple of messages?" He nodded. "The day before that there was a thunderstorm in Seattle, and I saw a vision of you, wet and cold, being led somewhere by six or eight rough looking men, and you didn't want to go with them. they had knives, and pulled you along in the dark."

Gino remembered that night, washing up on the shore, and Ottavio's men taking him to the tower. "So the thunderstorm gave you this nightmare?"

"Not a nightmare, Gino. I was awake, unlocking my front door after I fed Houdini that day." She knew he'd be skeptical, and tried to push the frustration out of her voice. "I've had visions of things in the future since my childhood, and talking about them never turned out well, so I just quit saying anything. I haven't told anyone in probably ten years, but the visions didn't stop. Lightning sometimes triggers them—or other flashing lights."

After a long pause, he said, "Is it always weird stuff like this? Time warps or whatever happened to me?"

"No. It's always something that will happen in the next few hours or days. And it always happens the way I see it." Her heart pounded and her throat choked off her voice but she forced herself to speak. "Well, not always, not lately. Not with you." She flicked away tears, and reached for a tissue, but realized they were in her purse inside the room. What if someone heard them from another balcony?

She stood so fast the teak lounge chair clattered on the tiles. "Let's go inside."

He followed her through the French doors, taking her by one arm so she turned toward him. "What do you mean, not with me?"

She sat on the edge of the nearest bed, blew her nose, and tried to swallow the lump in her throat. "I mean, things didn't happen like I saw them in the last vision because…because I couldn't just let that happen."

Gino slid his arms around her and she turned toward him, burying her face in his neck. He held her, and his warmth and nearness calmed her. He tilted his head and skimmed his hand across her cheek, lifting her chin to look into her eyes. "You okay? What did you see in this vision?"

"I just didn't know if I could do anything that would change it." She reached up and cupped her hand along the side of his face. "I saw you drowned—and probably run over by that Jet Ski," she whispered, "but we got there before it happened. Because the astrologer's book told us what you were going to do."

Then she leaned in and let her tears of relief soak into his new T-shirt.

20. Sometimes you get an answer to a question you didn't ask.

GINO'S THOUGHTS WHIRLED and pulled at him like the current that had sucked him through centuries of time. The thought that had sustained him for weeks, the thought of being reunited with Sara, had come true. But he hadn't imagined it this way. *Sara, clairvoyant?* All this time he'd been making up fake futures for people, and she could really see into the future? *No wonder she held me off.*

As Sara sobbed in his arms, he still had a lot of questions. Had she really saved his life? She made it sound like he had dodged a bullet, and when he remembered the Jet Ski coming straight at him, he thought she was probably right. What could he tell his parents, or for that matter, anyone else he knew, to explain his month-long absence?

And Fiamma. He had promised her father he'd take care of her, deliver her to the convent, but instead he gave the job to the doctor. What happened to them all—Fiamma, Ottavio, old Betta, the doctor? With the fog of exhaustion rolling over him, he couldn't think of a reasonable answer to any of those questions. That might haunt him the rest of his life.

Sara nestled beside him, stroking his arm. A few strands of her black hair clung to her face, damp from tears. She slumped like a week-old helium balloon, probably as tired as he felt. He squeezed her, pushed a strand of loose hair behind her ear, and kissed her temple. "I predict a sound sleep for you, Madame Sirena," he whispered.

She looked up at him with a tired smile. "You too?"

"I'm going to shower first." He rubbed a hand across his stubbled chin, thinking he probably needed a haircut, too.

"I brought something for you." Sara went to the dresser and pulled out a flowered toiletry bag. Gino remembered the pattern from the smaller make-up bag she carried in her purse. She rummaged in it and with a note of triumph said, "Here it is!" She handed him a disposable razor and a toothbrush, still in their store packaging.

Her thoughtfulness touched him, but more than that. "You were pretty confident you'd find me, weren't you?"

She smiled in reply and put the flowered bag on the bathroom counter. "You can use my toothpaste, and if you don't mind the baby powder smell, my deodorant too."

"Thanks." He stepped through the bathroom door.

"I brought your passport back with me too. Just in case."

"Wow." He reached out and touched her face, brushed back her tumbledown hair. "You thought of everything."

Something uneasy still marred her expression. Because of the sleeping arrangements? He'd heard the phone call from Lia earlier—in fact, he could hear both sides of it, because the patio door to Lia's room had been open too. His family all assumed he and Sara were a couple, and he had never said anything to deny it.

"Gino," Sara said, pulling away ever so slightly, "Marco is planning to sail back tomorrow, but Lia and I booked the train. I couldn't think of any good way to tell them I thought we'd find you. But do you want to stay in Praiano a little longer? I saw you looking around earlier like you were trying to find something."

"If you're all leaving—"

"They might change their plans, now that you're here. Before we all have that conversation tomorrow, I wanted to know what *you* want to do. Maybe you have some kind of…" She paused and shrugged, still wondering about Fiamma. Did he regret leaving her behind? "Some unfinished business here."

"What do you mean?"

"I don't know, Gino. You're the time traveler. Maybe you need some kind of closure."

He stared at her, surprised at the uncharacteristic edge in her voice. His own frustrations rose up to meet hers.

"You think I need closure because I wonder what happened to the people I spent the last a month with? The girl I promised to take care of, but then left with somebody else?" Sara flinched and Gino realized he was waving his arms. "Sure, I'd like closure, but all that happened six or seven hundred years ago, so how the hell am I supposed to find out?"

He closed the bathroom door and turned the shower on, stripping out of his clothes and standing in the steam for a minute. Then he stepped into the hot running water. A month of grime and sweat started running down the drain. The flash of anger went with it. He'd make it up to Sara after the shower. But for the next fifteen minutes, the glorious pleasure of hot running water owned him.

Showered and shaved, with his teeth brushed and hair clean, some of Gino's energy returned. He'd forgotten to bring his new clothes into the bathroom, so he stuck his head out the door. "Sara? Can you hand me that bag?"

No answer. Maybe she'd fallen asleep. One lamp pooled light between the two beds, and the shade had been lowered over the French doors. "Sara? Sara?"

She was gone. He groaned, thinking back to their harsh exchange.

Gino wrapped the damp towel around his waist and retrieved the shopping bag. As he turned back toward the bathroom, the pool of light shone on a book resting on one of the pillows. The astrologer's book, her gift to him. Tucked into the cover like a bookmark he found a short note.

"Gino, This book held the answers that helped me find you. Maybe it will answer some of your questions too. S."

Guilt assailed him. She had come over here to find him, to save his life, she claimed. He'd been dreaming for weeks of returning to her. But he hadn't bargained for all the uncertainty, all the unanswered questions for both of them. Had he chased her away? Where could she have gone?

He carried the book into the bathroom and opened it on the counter as he ripped open the underwear package. With just a glance at the academic introduction, he flipped to the table of contents, looking for something that might sound familiar. A chapter called 'In the service of the royal family' caught his eye. Turning there, he skimmed half a dozen pages, finding references to the queen and a rebellion against her, the death of her child, another rebellion. Nothing to do with him.

In frustration, he turned back to the table of contents, weighting the pages with a wrapped bar of soap and Sara's hairbrush. "The astrology of Plato and Aristotle." "The traditions of Byzantium." "Astral wisdom of the Abu Ma'Shar." When did the doctor study all this? Some of the titles he recognized from his dabbling in astrology, and others made no sense at all to Gino.

He finished dressing, took the book to the room's one upholstered chair, and switched on the reading lamp. How had Sara learned anything about him from this book? As he thumbed the pages, the book hung open about two-thirds of the way through. There, with a little pencil underline, he read his name: "Eugenio of Calabria." Gino Calabrese.

In half an hour, he read through the doctor's account of their meeting and journey to Praiano. His scalp prickled reading about the events he had experienced only twelve or fourteen hours earlier, yet recorded by the doctor hundreds of years ago. When the passage ended abruptly, noting damage in the original manuscript, Gino swore softly, flipping through the next pages to see if Sara had marked the book anywhere else. He found none. What had happened to Fiamma?

He glanced through the following chapter but found more about Queen Joanna's problems and the activities of the royal household the following fall and winter. He scanned through it, but nothing significant leapt out at him. The next chapter was no better.

Putting his thumb on the page edges, he flipped through, looking for chapter titles, but they were all vague and meaningless to him. He was about to toss the book on the table when he saw a star penciled in at the edge of one page. The star marked the entry for Calabria in the book's index, and a list of several page numbers.

Gino turned the page, searching the 'F' entries. Fiamma had several. Some were on the pages he already read, but he quickly found the next entry: "In early spring I received word from Santa Chiara that Lady Fiamma's father had fallen victim to a winter fever."

Ottavio came to his mind, fearful but determined to do right by his daughters. He hadn't survived a year. How had the three girls coped with his loss? He read on.

> The abbess inquired whether I could accompany Lady Fiamma to Praiano for a final visit with her family. She assumed I was a friend of the family because I had escorted Fiamma to Santa Chiara many months earlier.

Gino skimmed through the doctor's arrangements until Amalfi was mentioned.

> She begged me not to take her to Amalfi. I found no other ship available, and I tried to encourage her, saying we could hire horses in Amalfi, and reach Praiano late today if all went well. Her distress remained, and as we walked toward the harbor she began to weep.

Gino remembered Amalfi with much the same sentiment. Surely the doctor wouldn't force her to go back, would he?

> There is only danger for me in Amalfi, she insisted. Then she poured out the story of her wicked uncle, a man who had raped her mother and threatened to ruin her family, the same man who had chased her into my life.

> We found passage to Sorrento instead, a brief journey, and hired mounts there…

Gino skimmed over their travels—the doctor delighted to be with her again, and Fiamma more mature after her months in the convent. Her somber reunion with her sisters and the Bishop of Ravello, their father's friend, who was helping them with arrangements for suitable marriages. Then another mention brought Gino up short.

> When the Bishop mentioned the name of their uncle in Amalfi, Fiamma paced around the room, and then called for some refreshments, and asked the bishop to hear her confession in the family chapel. I remained with her sisters, the elder quite somber, and the second a bitter girl, and we spoke of their life in Praiano, and their father's illness. They showed no suspicion or concern for Fiamma's interruption of their conversation. Her need for a private conversation with the bishop seemed a natural need for her new life.

> Later she confirmed to me that she warned the bishop of her uncle's ill intent, and he agreed to serve as guardian to her sisters himself.

Gino reread those two paragraphs, glad to know Fiamma and her sisters had the help of two men they could trust. The doctor had not met the sisters before, nor the uncle, but he and the bishop clearly believed Fiamma's concerns about him. The doctor described a little more of their visit and then their return to Naples.

> We sat beneath an olive tree and ate a little while our horses cropped the grass. She wanted to rest, and lay her head on her folded cloak and slept as I continued to watch the sea. A bit of her red hair showed at the edge of her wimple, and my heart gladdened that it had not been cut, though it surely would be when she took her vows.

> That thought nearly broke me, for I had come to see that her life in the convent had strengthened her, and tamed her a little, but had not broken her spirit, that flame of life that blazed so brightly when we first met. Her name, Fiamma, still suited her, but she seemed more a burning coal, her youthful eagerness tempered by training and wisdom.

Should I declare my love for her, rekindled in these days together? Perhaps she now sensed a calling to religious life. She did not speak against it. So I determined to hold my peace.

Gino whispered, "No!" to the page, wanting the doctor to share his feelings with Fiamma, to give her a choice in her future if nothing else. Then he thought of Sara, coming all the way to Italy in hopes of saving his life. Didn't she deserve to know his honest feelings too?

At 11:45 p.m., Gino stood up and laid the book on the dresser, marking his place with Sara's note. He thought maybe she'd just gone for a walk, but hoped she wasn't still walking around this late. He stepped out on the balcony where the perfumed evening air enveloped him in warmth. A chattering group of girls walked along a street below the hotel. The soaring aria from an opera drifted across the dark undulating landscape. He wanted to be listening with Sara, soaking in this warm scented air with her.

He shot through the room and down the hall, and found the night clerk behind the front desk reading a tabloid.

"Did Sara Shore go out?"

The man's eyes asked what took him so long to get down here. He shook his head almost imperceptibly, and then pointed—again with his eyes—to the bar across the lobby.

"Grazie," Gino said, and headed there, glad that it had quieted down from when they arrived. One group of eight surrounded a big table, laughing as a guy in a suit poured wine. In the farthest corner, Sara sat alone nursing a glass of red wine as she looked out on a garden with little spotlights highlighting large potted palms.

"Hey," he said softly. "Mind if I join you?"

"Sure." She didn't look up.

He slid into the seat across from her, and she nodded toward the garden. "Isn't it beautiful?"

"Mm hmm." Before the silence grew too awkward, he said, "Thanks for leaving the book."

She met his gaze. "Did you find your friends?"

"Yes. Not everything, but I think there's more in the book about them. It looks like things are turning out well."

The waiter approached the table. "Another glass of wine, miss?" he asked in English. She shook her head, and he turned to Gino. "And you?"

He caught a little nod from Sara. "Yes, please. A bottle of Montepulciano d'Abruzzo."

Sara's eyes widened. "A bottle?"

"It's a great red. I hoped you could help me with it." A hint of smile made an inroad in her weary face, and he breathed easier. "Sara, I'm sorry I blew up at you, especially after all you've done. If you don't want to try the wine, we could take the bottle with us—have it another time."

She looked at him with a tight smile, and nodded. "We're all a little tense. It's okay." As the waiter approached with the bottle and two glasses, she said, "Make mine half a glass."

They watched in silence as the waiter poured their wine. As he walked away, Gino lifted his glass and tipped it slightly toward a clock on the wall. "Look, it's after midnight. The first day of my new life begins. *Salute!*"

Sara swirled her glass of wine, and clinked it gently against his, knuckles grazing. "To your new life."

The wine went down well, and Gino relaxed. "Last time I saw you, you were waving Houdini's paw at me when I took off to the airport." He smiled at the memory, and leaned closer to her. "I know you're not a regular reader, but do you know what's happened with my column?"

She looked surprised. "Yes—your column ended a couple of weeks ago with a notice about your disappearance. More of an obituary, actually."

His chest felt suddenly hollow, and he swallowed more wine.

"Everyone thinks you drowned." She reached for his hand this time. "Sorry, Gino. But it really will be a new life for you, a new beginning."

Now Gino stared dejectedly out at the garden. "I guess I'm back to square one." His so-called astrology career ended with his disappearance. He wasn't sure he wanted it back but what would he do instead? He'd never thought much beyond bringing down the money and having a good time.

"I've been wondering what you would do for work now, too." She released his hand and toyed with the stem of her wine glass. "Maybe you can do what you said in the book."

He frowned, trying to remember, then said, "What was that?"

"On the ship, you told that doctor you wanted to go back and start again and do it well this time. That's how he put it, anyway." Her words held a hint of challenge, and her eyes as well. He remembered speaking those words. But could he meet the challenge, now that it lay before him?

Life was so much easier, Gino thought, just having a good time, skating by. Easier than having this conversation. Dancing at a waterfront disco, swimming in the hotel pool, flirting over drinks—he excelled at those things. He didn't have much practice at real relationships, he realized, because when that point came along, he always split.

This time, he didn't want to split. He wanted to stay with Sara, or at least see if there was a possibility of staying with her. He took a deep breath.

"At UW, as a student, I did a little translation work. And some Italian tutoring."

Her eyes flicked to his. "Did you like that?"

He glanced out the window again, thinking back. "Yeah, I did. I was pretty good at it. Had a job offer from a language school once, but about then my column was picked up for syndication." He looked up at her. "They've probably filled the opening by now."

Her velvety laugh melted his insides. She brought her hand toward his, but paused and just tapped the tabletop. "Couldn't you do that kind of work on your own? Kind of like freelancing with your column? Print up some cards, put a sign on the bulletin board in the Italian Department at the U, and you're in business."

"You make it sound pretty easy."

"Easier than what you've been doing for the last month, I bet."

It suddenly felt like too much for him, the exhaustion, the wine, and the beautiful girl just out of reach. Had she simply come to Italy to save his life, or for something more? He swallowed hard and pushed aside his empty glass. "Sara, can we take the rest of this upstairs? It's been a really long day."

"Sure." She drained her glass and stood up.

"How did you get time off to come over here, anyway?" He took the bottle in one hand and held his other arm out for her as she stood. She said nothing until they were out of the bar, headed across the lobby.

"My boss got shot."

"What?! Is he okay?"

"He will be, but he decided to close the office for a few days, and gave me the time off."

"What happened to him? I mean I didn't think you guys worked on dangerous stuff."

"We don't, usually. This one surprised him."

"But he's going to be okay?"

She paused as Gino opened the door to their room. When it shut behind him, he looked up at her, waiting for an answer. "Yes." She locked eyes with him and whispered, "I saved his life too."

Gino pulled her into his arms and she melted against him. "You're getting good at this life-saving business," he said softly.

"Oh, Gino," she said, and lifted her head from his shoulder to look him in the eye. "I'm so glad you're safe. But I don't want to make a career of this." She leaned into him again but he put one hand on her cheek and tilted his head. He wanted to see the truth in her eyes.

"Didn't some fortune-teller predict you might have a new career a few weeks ago?"

She grinned. "You know that guy was a phony!" But she still seemed troubled and he wasn't sure why.

"How did you save Magarry's life?"

Sara took a deep breath and eased away from him. "Pour me just a little more wine, and I'll tell you all about it." She found the water glasses on the bathroom counter and handed them to him. "I'll be right back." She closed the door.

When she came back, Gino had piled all the pillows on one bed and lounged against them. He patted the space beside him, and nodded toward the bedside table, where her water glass held a couple of inches of wine. "Come and tell me about your boss."

Sara slipped out of her shoes and paused. He was fully clothed, but she wondered if they'd both sleep here. She sat beside him and took a sip of wine, then leaned into the crook of his arm and began the story of Grady Magarry's duck hunting expedition.

She was talking about closing the office when she realized that Gino was out, sound asleep against the pillows. The air conditioning hummed, but the room would be too hot without it, so Sara eased to her feet and pulled a blanket from the other bed. Gently she covered Gino, and then slipped in beside him. She fell asleep absorbing his smell, his strong presence beside her, his warm breath in her hair.

✳ ✳ ✳

Sara woke with a start, the room bright with daylight, to voices rising and falling in the next room. Her hand slid into the empty space where Gino had been, and then recognized his voice and the cadences of English rather than Italian coming through the wall. Who was he talking to in English?

She pushed the blanket away and sat up on the edge of the bed, raking through her tangled hair with her fingers. The clock read 9:18. Could she take a shower and get into some clean clothes before Gino came back? She listened intently, and at that moment Gino raised his voice. She clearly heard, "Yes, Mama!"

Relief flowed through her like a rush of warm water, and Sara realized how worried she had been about all the complications of Gino coming back, and how hard it would be for everyone, especially his parents. Now, at least they knew. Sara leapt into action, rummaging through her open suitcase for capris and a sleeveless cotton blouse. She showered in record time, blew her hair mostly dry and dabbed on a little makeup. She slipped into her sandals, and pulled the sheers back from the balcony doors. Sky and sea were brilliant contrasting shades of blue, and the warmth of the day invited her out.

From the balcony, she could clearly hear Gino talking to Lia and Marco in the next room. She guessed it was a replay in Italian of the conversation with his parents.

There were still a lot of questions for Gino to work out. Would he even come back to Seattle? He had to make a new start anyway, so this would be a great time for him to relocate. He didn't even have an apartment there anymore. And would she ever understand all he had been through? Would it be a wall between them, like the wall she had made of her own past? Or would he feel beholden to her for saving his life, creating a different kind of strain on their relationship?

Out in the bay, sailboats slid through the water at a slight tilt, one drawing her eye toward Li Galli. Sara thought through the strange string of events that had brought her there. Her dad's visit had especially unnerved her, and yet encouraged her to trust her visions, to be her true self. She needed to let him know she'd kept looking, and found her friend.

The call was short, but when she finished the room next door was silent. She approached the connecting door to listen, and noticed a folded paper with her name on it in Gino's neat block lettering pushed under it. "Come down to the bar for a cappuccino when you're ready. I want to walk through Praiano with you. G. (I have the book.)"

She tossed sunglasses and a tube of sunscreen into her handbag, then pulled a small box from her toiletry bag and removed the cameo locket, Gino's gift to her. With it clasped securely around her neck, she locked the door behind her and found Gino in the bar, at the same table they sat at last night. He downed the last of an espresso, and stood to greet her with a kiss on the cheek.

"Cappuccino? Pastry?"

Sara nodded yes. "Is there something with almond, like the cake your mother sent you?"

"I'll ask."

She sat down while Gino went to the bar to order. He bantered in Italian with the barista, and Sara wondered if the Italians detected an American accent in his speech.

The pastry quieted her growling stomach, but after two bites she said, "Your mother's cake is better."

Gino smiled and picked up the astrologer's book from the windowsill. Sara noticed strips of a paper napkin hanging out as bookmarks in six or eight places.

"You must have been up early, doing all that reading."

Gino nodded. "You want to go on a walking tour of Praiano with me? Marco and Lia went to check on the boat."

"Sure." Sara savored the last of her cappuccino, still a little hungry. "If we can pick up a gelato along the way."

The brilliant sunshine and rising heat energized her. Gino led her along a street that followed the contours of the hillside. The steep terrain allowed them to look over the rooftops toward the sea on their left, while on their right, doorways led into houses built against the hillside. Gino paused every hundred yards or so to look more closely at the town below them and the view of Li Galli, while Sara gawked at the tiny cars, whitewashed houses, and now and then a steeply terraced garden. For twenty minutes, he guided her toward the water, sometimes along the streets, and sometimes down stairways that connected one street to another. She paused now and then, unable to contain a sigh at the sight of brilliant flowers against gray-green foliage, or tiny three-wheeled pick-up trucks in the narrow parking lane. Gino gave her a crooked grin each time, and she realized he was trying to get his bearings, and it wasn't easy. His gaze kept returning to the tower at the bottom of the hill. Whenever a building blocked his view of it, he picked up his pace until he could see it again.

Sara felt like she'd tumble down the cliff into the water if she took a few steps off the narrow lane. Gino paused and then retraced their steps for thirty yards or so. Finally, he stopped in front of a hotel. "I need to get directions."

As he disappeared into the lobby, Sara thought of her phone with the international GPS, lost in the water at Li Galli. She'd paid for the Italian maps on it, but now she wondered if it could really navigate these tiny lanes. Instead, she had Gino. The thought stunned her. She relied on her GPS for a sense of knowing her precise place on planet Earth, but was that just a technological substitute for knowing where she belonged in life? And could Gino, maybe, be where she belonged?

She heard him through the doorway, Italian flowing from his tongue like it flowed through his veins. A smile spread through her and made its way to her face. When Gino reappeared, calling 'grazie' and 'ciao' as he closed the door, he looked up at her and stopped.

"What?"

"You look happy."

"I am happy." She grinned and reached for his hand. "And thank you for the locket. It's perfect." She touched it lightly. "Did you find the way?"

"Yes. We're almost there." He found a narrow drive sloping down to the cliff edge, and soon the tower came into view. A small green three-wheeled truck parked at a wide spot, and from there a concrete walk and stairs led part way down the rocky cliff to the tower.

"Can we…" Sara stopped when a woman came up the path carrying a basket of laundry. Gino greeted her and launched into a friendly banter, nodding first toward the tower, and then to Sara. The woman smiled slyly at Sara and winked, then waved Gino on down the path.

"What did you tell her?"

Gino put his arm around her as they approached the tower. "This is a vacation rental now. I told her I had stayed here before, and I wanted to show it to you. The guests checked out early and she's cleaning."

"That's all you said? What were the smile and wink about?"

"I tried to be persuasive."

"No doubt. You seem to be pretty good at it."

They stopped in front of the door, and Gino gazed around at fresh stucco, the windows, the rocky path leading to the edge of the cliff. Tension hardened his face to a frowning mask, and Sara wondered what phantoms of memory he struggled with. She recalled her first visions, of Gino in a stone room.

A minute passed before she said, "Do you want to go in?"

He pushed the door open and looked in at whitewashed walls and designer furniture. He took a deep breath. "No. Let's walk around to the other side." He closed the door and took Sara's arm.

In the noonday sun, they found a bench in a sliver of shade against the north wall of the tower. The relief from the heat and glare was welcome, and Gino's arm around her even more so. They sat in comfortable silence as Gino gazed at the islands and then searched the town above them.

"It must look very different now," she said.

"The palazzo, Ottavio's house, is gone—or so changed I can't see it. But it doesn't matter." He pulled the book from his pocket. "I know most of what happened—you know, after I left. I can read the rest later."

Sara wondered if the book would tell him enough. "You mean what happened to Fiamma?"

"Yeah. She married the doctor, and he became an astrologer. Sounds like they had a pretty good life, as far as I can tell. He really cared about her."

Sara's throat tightened and her eyes began to sting. She whispered so her voice wouldn't crack. "Well, that's good."

Gino pulled her close and when she leaned against his shoulder, he kissed the top of her head and held her tight. "I told my parents I'd fly back tomorrow. There's a flight from Naples in the morning." He hesitated, then said. "I'd like you to fly back with me. Can you change your ticket to stop in St. Louis?"

"I think so. Did you tell them I was coming?"

"I told them I hoped you would."

"Really?"

Gino tipped her chin up to look her in the eye. "Really." He kissed her forehead. "I have to start a new life. I know there will be a lot of adjustments to make—but I'd like you to be part of it. And I'm not talking about Madame Sirena any more. I mean you, Sara."

She relaxed against him and took a deep breath of the warm, salty air. "I have some changes to make, too. I need to reconnect with my parents—and that will be a new start for me. I'd like you to be part of that too, Gino. I'd like that a lot."

The End

Acknowledgments

The Islands Call has percolated in my mind and on my computer for a few years. I appreciate the encouragement of my family and my writing community, which reaches from small town Washington state, where I live, across the country and world via groups like the Historical Novel Society and many Facebook groups of readers and writers. Special thanks to four beta readers, Carol Lichten, Chris Ayre, Jeannie McPhail, and Tinney Heath for their thoughtful comments, which helped me reach this finished novel.

Do you like true stories?
I hope you'll try The Drive in '65!

In May of 1965 two sisters, Winnie and Phyllis, packed up a van with their mother and their five kids and hit the road from Anchorage, Alaska, headed for adventure and discovery. They wanted to show their Alaskan-born kids the rest of their country.

I was thirteen years old that summer, and our journey went far beyond sightseeing. The escalating war in Vietnam dominated the news. We gained shocking insights on civil rights issues as we drove through the south. New music resonated from our tinny transistor radio – music we now call classic rock.

Fourteen weeks and 22,000 miles later our Wayward Bus rolled back into Anchorage, our lives forever changed by the drive in '65.

I published this story using my maiden name, Sandra Lynne Reed, but you'll find it on my website, www.SandyFrykholm.com, and it is available in paperback or e-book from many book outlets. Your local bookstore can order it for you.

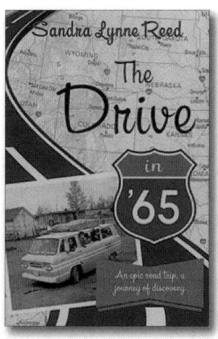

Made in the USA
Columbia, SC
17 February 2023

12409224R00131